MERMAID MATES

MERMAID MATES

THE MERMAN'S SPARK, BOOK ONE

by

GINNA MORAN

ISBN: 978-1-942073-99-4 (softcover)

For Inquiries Contact:
Sunny Palms Press
9663 Santa Monica Blvd Suite 1158
Beverly Hills, CA 90210, USA
www.sunnypalmspress.com
www.GinnaMoran.com

For the romantics in the world

1

OUT TO SEA

LAUGHTER ECHOES THROUGH THE AIR, coming from the dock where Captain Briggs greets our guests to welcome them aboard the Ocean Jewel. Usually, I love voyaging up the California coastline toward where my parents live in San Francisco, but I nearly backed out at the last second because the full moon rises tomorrow.

The call of the ocean, irresistible and undeniable, forces me to transform into a merman every full moon. If it weren't for the magical sea stone ring on my finger, I'd never have legs, so heading out to sea once a month isn't so bad.

If the money for a week-long gig wasn't so good, it

would've been easy enough to request time off. But, I know I can manage. I've set sail during a full moon numerous times before. Luckily, I can ignore the call of the sea long enough to sneak out of the cabin and overboard late enough to where no one misses me, and I can arrive early enough to start my day with the other crewmembers.

"This is so amazing!" a girl with bronze hair yells, climbing onto the deck to greet her friends. Three other girls and two guys my age peer around.

"Where's Ava-babe?" one of the guys asks.

The bronze haired girl flicks her hand toward the dock. "Give her a minute, Matty."

He pushes his sunglasses onto his head and moves toward the ramp to look at the dock. "Damn, Giselle. You should've dragged her on."

Giselle shrugs. "She'll come aboard. I know it."

"Fifty bucks says she changes her mind and leaves," the other guy says.

A girl with beachy waves slaps the guy on the arm. "Seriously, Logan?"

Matty extends his hand to his friend. "I'll take that bet. Fifty says she comes on board. Twenty says she stays."

"Deal. Making it too easy, dude."

Turning my attention away from them, I stroll down the ramp to help Keith load the rest of the luggage. I'd think this group was planning to stay aboard for a month with all the luggage they're bringing aboard.

I glance down the dock, searching for the girl the two guys were taking bets on. A blond girl shuffles in our direction with only a small duffle bag hanging from the tips of her fingers. She slows, searching the marina and then peers out toward the horizon. A sea breeze catches tresses of her hair, blowing the blond strands away from her face and neck.

My breath catches.

I never believed what Dad used to tell me about finding a mate growing up until now. He was adamant that the moment I laid eyes on the one person who would complete my life, I'd know. I'd feel it deep in my being, burning brightly within the same spark that carries my merman essence.

This girl, staring at the ocean like it'll rise to swallow her whole, stirs something inside me I've never felt in my life. I hesitate, gazing between the Ocean Jewel and the long dock between us. The last thing I want to do is accidentally mess up the one chance I get to make a good impression. What do I even say to her? Why am I so nervous? I never get nervous around anyone.

She slows even more, and I know if I don't do something she'll turn right back to shore and abandon the ocean for land. My heart picks up pace, thrashing against my ribcage. I'm pretty sure it'll break through my chest at any moment to follow her if I don't move my legs. If she leaves, I'll never get to find out if my dad was right. So I jog forward.

The girl shifts her gaze to me, and she gives me a once over, taking me in for a moment. I close the distance between us, offering what I hope is a nice smile and not the one my insides try to force on my face from my nerves wanting to get the best of me. Her eyes, the same crystalline blue as the sky, squint as she returns my smile with a nervous smirk. The bright sun overhead creates streaks of gold through her hair and across her face, and I notice a few tiny freckles on the bridge of her nose.

"First time out to sea, huh?" I ask, taking the bag from her to hook over my arm. *Be cool. Be cool. Don't be creepy.*

It's rare to meet someone who has never been out to sea coming from Azure Waters because I'm pretty sure it's mandatory that all the mansions along the beach automatically come with a boat and a marina slip. And if she's part of the King's guest list, one of the wealthiest couples I've had the pleasure to work for, then I don't doubt she lives here.

"That obvious? I haven't even been in the water since I was a kid," she says, linking her fingers together.

I gaze at her, watching her bottom lip puff out slightly. Confusion washes over me, listening to her words. I can't deny the strange urge to get to know her burning through me, but I never dreamed a potential mate would dislike the ocean. It goes against my nature. The ocean gave me life, makes me who I am, no matter if I choose to live in the sea or on the land. But this girl? I don't have to ask to know the ocean might have wronged her in some way.

I don't know how to respond without overwhelming her with a ton of my silent questions, so I offer her my arm to guide her forward instead. Maybe this is the ocean giving me a sign that my love of the land and desire to remain on the surface was the right decision despite what the majority of merpeople think. No one could ever understand why my parents chose to raise me on the land. Of course, those merpeople never ate a hot meal, laid on a king-sized bed, watched TV, or have taken a steaming shower. And dessert. You can't find anything sweet with all the salt in the ocean. Living on land is awesome.

"I wasn't even going to come, but my best friend basically threatened me—mostly with a good time," she adds, licking her lips, filling the silence I'm leaving between us.

Pulling myself from my thoughts, I grin, summoning everything within me to keep my gaze on the dock in front of us no matter how much I want to study her endless eyes, more beautiful than even the best kept secret tropical waters throughout the world.

"I can promise she's right. The Ocean Jewel speaks true to her name. I even have fun, and I'm on the job." I continue to smile, hoping I don't sound as dumb as I think I do—a real poster boy for the Ocean Jewel.

We reach the ramp to the deck to board, and she slows, tugging me to match her pace. She peers around again, searching for something I can't see in the water. The wind lifts her hair again, and I catch the scent of coconut and something sweeter that clings to her. Chocolate? Maybe. It makes me inhale a small breath through my teeth. Everything about her burrows into me, and I say a silent prayer to the ocean. I hope my words were enough to get her to stay so I can impress her.

I had no idea I had been waiting my whole life for this moment. It was something I knew would eventually happen, but I never expected it to happen like this, with a beautiful girl who doesn't even know all the magic and adventure I could offer her. But I can't say any of those things. It'd make me sound crazy, anyway. And creepy. I've watched enough TV shows to know that I can't just tell a girl I've said a few words to that she might be my soul mate.

She turns away from me to look down the dock. My chest tightens, knowing she's going to leave, and there won't be anything I can do about it. I'd have to stand here and watch her go because it's the human thing to do. I can't chase after her or beg her to stay all because she makes my heart beat wildly.

She takes a step away, and I do the only thing I can think of. I slide in front of her and smile again. "Why don't you board before you make the decision to bail? We won't leave port for another twenty minutes or so. You can change your mind if you hate it. And if it makes you feel any better, I'm an excellent ocean swimmer and diver. We've never had a single person fall overboard, either." I inwardly cringe. Even mentioning the possibility of falling overboard isn't what anyone, even people who enjoy the ocean, likes to hear.

"And I'm supposed to trust you? I don't even know your name." She crosses her arms over her chest, hugging herself more than scolding me.

Yes. Please, trust me. I'm a merman. I know these things. I don't speak my thoughts out loud. Instead, I hold out my hand, following the human customs I've grown used to, though she just looks at it. "Carter Stevens, deckhand, steward, activities coordinator, cook—basically, I'm at your service..." It takes everything in me to keep a straight face. I can't believe I put it like that. But I would be at her service if she asked.

She meets my gaze, her lips pursed, and reluctantly shakes my hand. "Ava Adair." *Ava.* I repeat her name in my mind, though I recall one of her friends mentioning it. But that was different. Hearing it come from her, soft, breathless, I wish she'd say my name like that.

When our fingers meet, a wave of warmth washes from her fingers to mine, sliding up my arm to make its way to the merman spark in my chest. It feels like it's burning hotter than ever, making every cell within me buzz. I wish I didn't have to let go.

So I don't. I pull her forward and onto the ramp. It shakes under our feet, and Ava gives me the cutest fake death glare, making me smile even wider. I'd be okay if she spent the rest of the trip glaring at me like that, half in amusement and half in something else—something good.

She heaves a breathless laugh as I tug her up the stairs the short distance onto the yacht. Without letting go of my arm, she strolls by my side across the main deck, peering around at the magnificence of the Ocean Jewel. I've grown used to it over the last year since Dad got me a job on Captain Briggs' crew so I could finally start to create the life on land I've always dreamed of. And now, my life has gotten even better, just seeing Ava watch me in my peripheral vision.

I wave my hand out. "This is the saloon, my favorite area of the vessel."

Ava nods without saying anything, peering around at the luxurious room. All the metal and glass shines within the light woods. An eighty inch TV rests in an entertainment center that divides the room into two sitting areas, one with white leather sectionals and the other with tables and chairs. Mostly, guests hang out here at night, though not always. Each stateroom has its own TV, too.

Leading her to the elevator, I don't give her much of a chance to look around. I can't give her too much time to think about running off the yacht, so I take her to where her friends pick out their staterooms on the upper deck.

Ava takes in the panoramic view of the horizon through the portholes in the lounge area. Voices hum from the hall leading to the staterooms. Ava's friend with bronze hair, Giselle, swings her arms over her head when she catches sight of us. She gives me the same once over Ava did, and I press my lips together to stop from smiling. Ava and Giselle lock gazes, speaking silently to each other about me. Since merpeople communicate underwater telepathically, I've grown accustomed to knowing when I'm left out of the conversation, but what I wouldn't give to know exactly what Ava was thinking about me.

"I already picked out our room," Giselle says, tugging Ava toward the five staterooms set apart from the owner's suite stationed near the bow of the yacht, where the Kings will stay.

I quietly follow behind Ava, carrying her bag, studying her as she peeks into every room, waving to her friends along the way. I nod and smile politely, but don't pay much attention to anything apart from how Ava's blond hair sways with the same rhythm of her hips. Her room is the last one in the hall with two beds. Ava perches on one of the beds and watches me set her bag down. I offer her another smile. I can't help it. My mouth's taken on a mind of its own.

I force my legs to take me back to the doorway, and I place my hand on the frame, leaning slightly so she won't notice how nervous I've become. Because she's getting comfortable, which means she's staying. I can already tell. I'll get to spend an entire week with Ava and hopefully get to know her.

"This is your last chance to get off," I say, peeking into

the hall behind me.

Giselle swings her gaze to Ava. "You're not going any-where."

Ava leans back, tilting her head up while smiling. "You're right. I'm not."

Thank the Ocean. Swallowing to keep my voice even, I say, "Enjoy your stay aboard the Ocean Jewel, Ava."

Giselle waves me goodbye, and I step into the hallway, grinning when I hear Giselle call me cute. Making my way back toward the lounge area, I spot the first mate waiting out-side the elevator.

"Everyone getting settled?" Hank asks, looking past me.

Before I have a chance to respond, familiar laughter sounds from behind me, drawing my attention away from Hank. Ava and Giselle head in our direction, and I smile again. Damn does Ava make me grin. With the smile she re-turns, a deep part of me believes that maybe my heart was right. She wouldn't have followed me if she wasn't interested. I think.

"Welcome. It's a pleasure to have you aboard the Ocean Jewel. How do you like it?" Hank asks, greeting Ava and Giselle with a smile.

Ava slowly turns her attention from me to the first mate. "It's lovely, thanks. We were actually going to just ask Carter to give us a tour."

I open my mouth to respond when Hank says, "I'd be

happy to show you two and the rest of your friends around. I'm Hank, by the way."

I inwardly groan at Hank, missing the fact that Ava doesn't want an official tour of the boat, but I can't and won't say anything. I'm pretty sure Ava wishes he'd get the hint, too, because her smile falters.

"That would be great, thank you," Ava says, her voice soft.

Giselle sighs, her shoulders slouching, making me smile. She's definitely not as polite as Ava. Hank misses her reaction, though. He's too busy glancing at his watch.

"Perfect, I'll be waiting in the saloon for when you're ready. We'll leave port shortly thereafter." Nodding to me once, Hank leaves us, heading toward the stairs, the elevator strictly for guests unless invited otherwise.

As much as I want to follow Ava and join her for the tour of the yacht I know like I grew up on it, I can't. Work calls. Keith's probably groaning about getting everything ready for the water activities later.

I smile at Ava again, my cheeks starting to hurt from doing it so much. "You two have fun. You'll get a better tour with the first mate, anyway. But I'd be happy to take you out on the water when we anchor after lunch."

Giselle beams a smile. "Definitely!"

Ava frowns with a shrug, turning her gaze to the ground. I'm an idiot. She barely wanted to come on the yacht and already expressed that she hasn't been in the water. I'll have to think of some other way to get to know her. It's weird, having to think of something that doesn't involve the ocean. But for Ava's company, I'll think of something.

Voices echo from behind Ava, and I glimpse her friends leaving their rooms. Giselle links her arm through Ava's, tugging her away. "Come on, Aves. Let's get the stupid tour over with."

Ava shifts her sky blue eyes to mine, a small pout puckering her bottom lip. "I guess I'll see you around."

I smile without responding and watch her go. If only I could follow.

To try to keep my mind off Ava, I've thrown myself into work. I've spent the last hour helping Rita chop vegetables in the kitchen, failing miserably at not thinking about Ava. I spent ten minutes wondering what kind of foods she likes. I'm pretty sure I was never this curious about anyone's eating habits before or how I suddenly have the urge to hunt, my merman instincts sneaking out thinking of ways to impress her. *What is wrong with me?*

Bringing Ava a fish straight from the sea with my bare hands will more likely result in her never speaking to me again. I'll have to call Dad at the next port for advice, though he might not be able to help me since he and Mom were born in the sea.

Strolling to the dining terrace, I head behind the bar to prep water glasses for lunch. Voices trickle through the air as the guests enter for their first meal. The scent of salmon and garlic wafts through the air from the buffet table, and I keep busy arranging glasses under the counter to not seem like I've been waiting for Ava to appear.

Her melodic laugh swirls through the air, sending my heart racing, and I stand up, straightening my back. So much for keeping it cool. Ava follows her friends in, and her gaze travels across the room and locks on mine.

My mouth grins before I have a chance to control it, and I can't stop my eyes from trailing from her sky eyes to her slightly sheer dress, covering her bikini. She must be heading to the pool or spa on the sundeck after lunch while her friends take the jet skis out. I'll have to bribe Keith to take over so I can have a moment with her.

I swallow, my eyes unwavering and unable to shift away from Ava. She looks incredible, strolling in my direction, her hips swaying, her short dress moving on her thighs. My heart falters when she doesn't come straight to the bar like I had hoped. She follows the others into the buffet line, letting Trish fill her plate. *Salmon, baby spinach, garlic pasta, and a roll.* She likes fish. This is good news. I couldn't imagine what I'd do if she didn't. If she was scared of the ocean and disliked sea food? I don't even know how I'd handle something like that. I'd yell at the ocean for thinking it was funny.

Ava sets her plate down on the table next to Giselle and across from the Kings' daughter without sitting. She smiles at her friends and heads in my direction, slightly bouncing with her steps, making me smile even more. My cheeks will never recover from Ava. I'm sure of it.

"What can I get you, miss?" I ask her, more formal than I'd like to be, but with the Kings sitting at the table in listening distance, I mustn't push my boundaries in front of them.

She leans her elbows on the counter, closing as much distance as she can between us. "Lemonade, and it's Ava."

It's like she can read my mind. Nodding, I rub a lemon wedge over a glass and dip it into a tray of sugar, not missing how she checks me out, looking at my arms instead of my eyes. "Okay, *Ava*." I love saying her name out loud. "Anything else?"

"A Coke for Giselle."

I hand Ava the second glass, wishing she'd get drinks for all her friends so I can talk to her longer, but she doesn't. "Enjoy your meal."

Instead of leaving, she hesitates, just standing in front of the bar holding the two glasses as she tries to think of something more to say. I open my mouth to say something to fill the silence, but her friend Matty slides up next to her and asks if I can sneak rum in his Coke.

I don't. Instead, I apologize and turn my gaze back to Ava. All of her friends look in my direction, laughing while talking.

"Oh, my God, you guys!" Giselle throws her hands up, shouting. "Shut up about it. Ava's got it under control."

They're talking about me again, and I can't help silently thanking the ocean. Bonds are the most important thing under the sea, and I know that idea mirrors the same ideals on land, so knowing Ava's friends aren't trying to convince her to stop looking at me is a good sign.

Blush sweeps across Ava's face, and she throws a dinner roll at Matty for something I couldn't hear him say. If I could move closer, I would. But Keith motions for me to join him to get things ready at the garage.

Laughter trickles through the air, catching on the sea breeze above me. Keith pats my back, "Hey, dude. What's up? You're quiet today."

I shrug, pressing the button to lower the jet skis onto the launch platform. "Got a headache." The lie comes easy enough, though it's partially true. Thoughts of Ava ruin my concentration.

"These kids know what they're doing, so I can stand watch after we help them launch if you want," he says, stretching his arms over his head.

I nod, trying to suppress the urge to smile. "That'd be great. I'll owe you one."

"Nah, dude. I like this shit."

The guests arrive with Giselle leading the way. Matty and

Logan formally introduce themselves to Keith and me, and Matty points at the Kings' daughter and introduces Sapphire as his girlfriend. The other two girls introduce themselves as Daisy and Chloe.

Giselle grins at me. "This is going to sound weird, but can you go check on Ava for me in a bit?"

I nod. "She won't come out?"

Everyone looks at each other, but they don't rush to tell me anything about Ava.

Matty shrugs. "Maybe you could convince her."

After helping everyone onto the jet skis, I heed to Ava's friends' advice to find Ava. Their encouragement was exactly what my confidence needed. From their grins and whispers, I'm now sure I have a chance with Ava, and that the ocean wasn't setting me up to be let down for choosing the land over it.

I find Ava leaning on the railing on the sundeck near the pool, watching her friends zoom around the open water on the jet skis. She grips the railing, turning her knuckles white, obviously uneasy while watching her friends. It takes everything in me not to ask what happened to her that made her fear the water so much, but I don't want to pry or make her feel uncomfortable that I've noticed.

"I can take you for a ride if you want when they're finished," I say.

She jumps at the sound of my voice. "Shouldn't you be

down there watching them?" she asks, ignoring my offer.

I frown, regretting asking. "I asked Keith to take over. They're fi—" I snap my mouth closed, watching Giselle and Chloe wipe out and hit the water. "Ouch."

She spins back to peer at her friends and whispers, "Oh, God. Come on, Giselle. Get back on."

I know she didn't intend for me to hear her words, but I can't stop myself from responding to hopefully make her feel better. "They're fine, Ava. If they were in danger, Keith would get them."

The glower she gives me, narrowing her eyes and twisting her lips, makes me cringe. "But how do you know they're not?"

I shrug off her intense reaction and touch her shoulder, feeling her body tremble under my fingers. "Hey, whoa. It's okay. Look." I point at Giselle and Chloe mounting the jet ski.

Tears sparkle in Ava's eyes, glittering in the sun shining from overhead. My chest tightens, something dark stirring within me because there's nothing I know I can do or say to make Ava smile in this moment. I can't help staring at her, all words lost to me. Flush burns over her skin and she blinks her glassy eyes.

"Excuse me. I need to lie down." She nudges past me, releasing a shuddering breath.

"Ava, wait up," I call without following her. She looks

mortified, and I think anything I do or say will make it worse.

She doesn't stop and turns to run down the stairs like the thought that I might follow her into the elevator freaks her out.

Turning to the ocean, I ask, "What did you do to her?"

Ava disappears, and I let her go. It's the only thing I can do.

2

IT'S A DATE

"HEY, CARTER MAN. Where's Ava?" Logan asks, strolling onto the dining terrace where I helped Rita set up the buffet dinner. Daisy and Chloe follow behind him, whispering to each other. They greet me with smiles.

I concentrate on hiding the rejection consuming me since I messed things up on the sundeck. "In her cabin," I respond, taking my place behind the buffet to serve them.

Logan points to everything, humming under his breath. "She cost me some serious money."

Daisy slaps his arm. "Seriously, Lo?"

He laughs and doesn't comment. Probably better for him with the way his girlfriend glares daggers at him. I help Chloe load two plates and offer to carry the extra one. She bounces as she walks next to me, her deep tan making it obvious she hangs out in the water as much as I do.

"The jet skis were cool, right?" I ask her to fill the silence.

She nods, smirking. "Love them. Love everything about the water. You surf?"

"When I make it back to shore, I do."

"Awesome, you should come with us at one of the ports. I plan to chase swells with my brother the rest of the summer when we get back."

"Sounds like my kind of summer."

We enter the sundeck from the elevator, and the bright setting sun casts an orange glow over everything. My heart picks up speed before my eyes can even catch up to find Ava perched on the end of a lounge chair next to Giselle. Our eyes meet, and I can't stop from smiling.

She looks away.

"Oh, hey Ava. I'd have brought you a plate had I known you were up here." Crossing to where Ava sits next to Giselle, Daisy sets her dinner on one of the small tables. "We decided to eat up here to get the best view of the sunset."

I open my mouth to offer to get her something, but Ava cuts me off by saying, "It's okay. I'll go ahead and grab something myself."

She strolls past me so closely that the skirt of her dress brushes my hand. As much as I want to spin to chase her, I hesitate a moment to make sure the others don't need anything else. Luckily for me, she's not rushing to escape, so I catch up to her before she enters the elevator or takes the stairs.

Reaching out, I touch her shoulder. She spins, her eyes narrowed at me, and I take an automatic step back and cross my arms over my chest. Ava's presence calls to my merman essence so much that I almost forgot how some humans are protective of their personal space, and Ava's guard keeps me out just like earlier.

I smile despite wanting to frown, pressing my lips together. Something changes in her expression and her face softens. She releases a small breath. "I apologize for earlier. I'm a little on edge being here. You don't need to worry or check on me, though. I'm fine."

She doesn't sound fine. The quiver in her voice messes with my heart, and it fights with me to do something when my head says not to. Something haunts her beautiful blue eyes, and all I want to do is hug her.

"Really, I am," she adds, sounding like she's trying to convince herself more than me.

Words lock in my throat. Usually talking to people is easy. Merpeople are social by nature. But something about Ava tells me that she would prefer it if I didn't try to drag out small talk. Like she's okay with the silence falling between us. And it's not a bad silence. Her company alone is enough.

She glances away from me and to her friends behind us. I call for the elevator for the sole reason that she looks like she needs to keep moving before she gets lost in whatever is on her mind. She steps onto the elevator and makes room for me, silently inviting me on instead of forcing me to take the stairs. The scent of her coconut hair drifts over me, and I hold my breath not to let it get to me. Being so close to her while she purposely tries not to look at me drives me crazy.

The elevator door opens, and she looks ready to dash off, and all I want is for her to stay for a second. To look at me. To give me one more chance.

"Ava," I say, my nerves getting the best of me to where my voice barely sounds above a whisper.

She freezes in place, her pouty mouth slightly open as she sucks in a tiny breath. Her tense shoulders relax, and she turns her attention to me. I grin, both excitement and relief washing over me.

She smiles, releasing a musical, breathless giggle. "You probably think I'm ridiculous."

Ridiculous is the last word I'd use to describe the girl who sends my heart beating in overdrive only hours after we met. A million thoughts rush through my mind. Now that I have her attention, I have to get things right.

"No, I think you're intriguing is all, but that's not what I was going to say." I rub my hand over the back of my neck. Dad never prepared me for how scary this moment would be, putting myself out there, hoping that a girl like Ava would give me the time of day.

She tilts her head. "What is it then?"

I inhale a small breath to control my nerves. I had never planned on finding someone who could be my future mate on the Ocean Jewel, but here Ava is, standing in front of me looking so perfect, and I'm not so sure that I can impress her. Human dating is hard. I force myself to speak anyway. "I know this is your vacation, and you and your friends are here for a good time, but I was wondering if maybe later tonight you'd hang out with me."

Ava smirks. "You make it sound like hanging out with you won't be fun. Is this a line you use on every girl who catches your attention on one of these trips?"

I'm doomed. I should've thought about what I would say instead of spending the day thinking about how the sunlight made her hair golden or how musical her laughter was. Now, she thinks I use dumb pickup lines on every girl who comes aboard.

"I—what? No." I should give up now. The ocean probably really is playing a joke on me, putting me in the path of a girl who is afraid of the sea. I shift uncomfortably under the weight of her stare.

Reaching out, she glides her fingers along the muscles in

my forearm, surprising me. She smirks, and I realize she wasn't accusing me of anything. I managed to miss the fact that she was teasing me.

I meet her gaze. "So, do you want to?"

She rubs her lips together, thinking over my words. Her silence confuses me, and now I'm not sure what's going on or how she feels. All I know is that I want her so badly to agree to hang out with me, so I can show her I can be more than the awkward, nervous guy I am now.

"I'd like that," she says, finally agreeing after what feels like the longest moment of my existence.

I grin, my tense nerves relaxing. "Cool." I'm afraid if I say anything more, I might mess it up, so I follow her to the dining terrace in silence. I have to stop while I'm finally ahead.

As Ava attempts to grab a plate, I take my position behind the buffet table and dish out crab legs, mashed potatoes, and mixed veggies for her. I'm pretty sure if Mr. and Mrs. King weren't sharing a candlelit dinner at the table behind Ava, she'd insist on serving herself.

"Will you grab a few water bottles and a can of Coke to take up?" Ava asks, taking her plate from me instead of letting me carry it. I'd carry everything for her if she let me, but she clearly likes to do things for herself, which I like, too.

Ava strolls next to me on the way back to the sundeck, brushing her arm against mine. I don't know what changed in her, but she's letting her guard down with me, and I can't help but say a silent thanks to the ocean. I should've never doubted the ocean or how it fated me to meet Ava. It's sometimes hard to remember the magic that lies within its depths when I'm here on the surface.

Ava's friends meet us with smiling faces and unspoken words meant just for Ava. Heat crawls across my neck when Giselle takes the Coke from my hands and wags her eyebrows at me, like she knows what's going on in my mind—thoughts I could never breathe a word of. Keeping my merman secret from Ava will be hard enough. There are consequences regardless of my interest in her. But the consequences are the last thing on my mind. I'm not messing this up anymore. I'm going to take things slow and see what happens between us.

Leaning over, I whisper, "I'll come find you tonight." Because I want to get to know her without her friends laughing and scrutinizing my every move. Ava makes me nervous enough as it is. She'd be more forgiving if I say something weird. I can feel it.

Ava smiles at me and watches me stride away. I look over my shoulder at her a few times, wishing the sun would set already. Entering the stairwell, I rest my back on the wall and smile. Now that Ava agreed to hang out, I need to figure out how to impress her. Watching a movie in the saloon sounds lame, considering her friends might be there, and a night swim in the pool might be too much.

"Did I just hear what I think I did?" Chloe's voice trickles from the sundeck, drawing my attention from my thoughts. I know I should head back to my cabin to shower and change, but I can't stop myself from eavesdropping.

"You did," Ava responds. The excitement in her voice makes me smile.

"Oh, my God. It's a miracle." This comes from Daisy. She laughs and says, "Ava has a date." Hearing her friend talk about Ava like maybe she doesn't date much makes me even more confident now. Because in all honesty, I have no idea what I'm getting myself into. Merpeople courtships fall on the serious side of things. Couples tend to know the moment they start interacting. But Ava's human. She's different.

"It's not a date. We're just hanging out."

I blink, listening to Ava's words. Maybe I misjudged things, or maybe she's just saying it not to make a big deal with her friends.

A masculine laugh sounds through the air. "It's definitely a date," Logan says.

"You're going to make her nervous. Can't we all just celebrate that Ava came along and now she's going on a date with a really hot guy?" I smirk to myself, hearing Giselle's words. I want the whole world to celebrate that I didn't mess it up this time.

"You guys. Stop. It's not a big deal," Ava says. She might not think it's a big deal, but it's huge.

"Hey, it is," Logan says. I think I'm starting to like her

friends. "I lost fifty bucks the moment you stepped on board and another twenty when you stayed." Thank the ocean for that.

"Seriously?" a feminine voice says. I can't tell who it is over the sound of my heart pounding in my ears.

"It's fine," Ava says. I can imagine her crinkling her nose. "Matty deserves the seventy bucks for having faith in me."

"Harsh, Ava-babe. I have plenty of faith in you. I'm willing to bet Carter will kiss you by the end of the night." I chuckle to myself at the new bet. I'll be happy to let him win if Ava allows it.

Giselle groans. "Not helping your case, Lo."

The elevator dings and a new masculine voice says, "I'll take that bet."

Forcing myself to move before someone catches me, I head away from Ava and her friends. I know exactly what I'm going to do when I pick up Ava to hang out—I'm going to show her that this is definitely a date, and hopefully the first of many more.

The bright, nearly full moon taunts me from overhead as I click on the flameless candles I borrowed from the kitchen. Trish, the yacht's chef, outdid herself allowing me to take one of every dessert she had baked for the next few days. Rita suggested the silver tray, and I never thought I'd be so thankful for my crewmates. They really do make this the best job I've ever had.

Strolling the pathway toward the saloon, I twist my hoodie between my hands, suppressing my nerves. My merman essence flares with the call of the ocean, reminding me how important this moment with Ava is. It also reminds me how inhuman I am. She's expecting to hang out, and I can't stop my mind from wandering, imagining exactly how I'll win her love with the whole ocean between us. Secrets, especially my kind of secret, don't go over well when someone suspects one of hiding something. It's the main reason many merpeople stick to the sea—though there aren't plenty of merpeople. Just over a thousand, and only a handful human born.

"Ava, your hottie's waiting!" Sapphire yells.

Ava narrows her eyes at her friends as they continue to shout their hellos to me, raising glasses of the champagne they stole from the owner's suite in my direction. Blush sweeps across her face, her smiling eyes reflecting the silver moon, turning her sky eyes into a stormy gray.

She shivers, trailing her gaze over me at the same time I drink her in, wearing a sundress that flows around her thighs. I hand her my hoodie, and she shrugs it on. Smiling, I watch her press the collar to her nose as she breathes in. She tilts her head up and peers at the sky, the night breeze blowing strands of her moon drenched hair.

Touching my hand to her back, I guide her down the pathway toward the stern. Her eyes light up at the sight of my dessert tray. She trains her gaze on me, smiling. I notice she doesn't look at the black to her ocean around us, giving me her full attention.

I force my mouth to work before I get lost in her intensity and forget how to use my voice, something I don't need underwater. "I know this might not be as fun as—"

She reaches up and presses her index finger to my lips, her touch softer than I imagined. "It's perfect, Carter. If you haven't noticed, I'm the outsider in my group of friends. They're used to me bailing on them."

I *have* noticed, and the question has flown through my mind a dozen times today. But even if she treats herself like an outsider, I don't think her friends see it that way. I don't say my thoughts out loud though. I'd much prefer to hear why she thinks it. "Why is that?"

She lifts and drops her shoulders. "We have different interests is all. Kinda like me and you."

She says it like it's the truth. Like she's certain she knows me. But it doesn't bother me. Actually, it makes me smile because I'll prove her wrong. The ocean wouldn't drop us in each other's paths if there was no chance for us.

I raise an eyebrow, still grinning. "You say that like you know me." It's all I want—for her to get to know me.

"You love the ocean. I don't."

That's where she's wrong. If I loved the ocean as much as I loved the land, I'd never leave it. I'd never get a job or worry about human social norms. I'd have headed out to sea the moment I turned eighteen.

Shifting toward her, closing the space between us, I say, "That's where you're wrong. I love the land more."

Ava tilts her head to gaze at me, her blond hair cascading forward to veil her shoulders. Her lips pucker into a pout I imagine kissing. "You're not joking."

"No."

"But you work on a yacht." She makes a point, but it still doesn't change the fact that I've only entered the ocean as a merman on the full moon for the last six months, sticking to my human form.

"It pays well, and I have a place to live," I say. Which is true. I've been saving up to hopefully one day start up my own watersports store like my parents. It's what keeps them on land, and I'd like to have that same motivation to continue to breathe air instead of the sea.

A sudden swell lifts the yacht, and Ava tenses, releasing an audible yelp and then laughs nervously. She grips the sides of her chair and doesn't respond to me right away. Reaching out, I lace my fingers through hers to silently assure that I have her, and there's no way I'll let the ocean interrupt my date.

She inhales a long, shaky breath, composing herself. Her fingers stop trembling in mine. I hope it's me who's helping. "So, you don't have a place near Azure Waters?"

"Only when we dock there."

It takes everything in me not to lean forward to kiss the pout that suddenly takes over her kissable mouth. Warmth heats my chest, my merman essence burning at the thought that Ava likes me enough to be disappointed I don't live in Azure Waters.

"Oh."

Even though her cute pout stirs all sorts of strange things in me, I want nothing more than to change her expression. I smile and say, "I'm not gone as often as it would seem. We charter a lot of weekend getaways and day long excursions up and down the coast, but anything more than a week or two only happens two or three times a year. Plus, I have most nights off."

She holds my stare. "That's a pretty adventurous life, Carter. You probably think I'm so boring. I mostly split my time between home and Giselle's and Sapphire's houses. I do volunteer at the Surf and Swim Museum downtown two weekends of the month."

She might not find her life adventurous, but I find everything about Ava exciting. Her love of her friends shines through, reminding me how close merpeople are with their pods—immediate family. "Sounds fun," I say, because I can't tell her exactly what's on my mind.

"Liar. Just so you know, there's not a lot to do that doesn't involve the ocean in our town."

Her fear of the ocean gets to me more than it should. Not

because of her, but because I can't help wonder why. Instead of flat out asking her, I nod, thinking about all the amazing things we can do together on land that doesn't involve the ocean.

Rubbing my thumb over hers, I squeeze her hand. "You know, I'm a great swim instructor." If it were her lack of swimming skills, I'd carry her through all the seas until she was comfortable enough to do so on her own, but the expression she gives me, all serious and almost annoyed, tells me my assumptions are off base.

"I know how to swim," she says.

"I can protect you from all the ocean animals, too." Which is true. Merpeople have no natural predators in the sea.

She rolls her eyes. "It's not that either."

I was hoping her fear stemmed from something simple, something we could work through—I could work with. But I'm afraid my instincts about the ocean doing something unforgivable to Ava were right.

I flick my gaze to the ocean and back to her. "Something happened to you."

She responds with silence, which confirms my suspicions, and it's obvious she doesn't want to talk about it, so I won't pry. I'd rather change the subject and talk about all the great things about the land from her beautiful eyes.

"I'm sorry," I say, feeling the need to apologize for the ocean.

She starts to say something, but a loud holler cuts through the air, interrupting us. Ava's friends stumble into view from the pathway, laughing and calling Ava's name. Ava rushes from her seat to Giselle who nearly falls flat on her face when one of her flip-flops slips off. I rush from my seat and help Sapphire into the chair at the table.

Matty wobbles, clearly drunk off his ass from the champagne they stole from the Kings' suite. I can imagine him falling overboard now with how fidgety he is, laughing and using the railing for support.

He shrugs me off and turns to Ava. "Ava-babe!" he yells from two feet away, his voice making me cringe. "How's your date? You guys kiss yet?"

I hover next to him and Ava, ready to intervene. He wraps Ava in a hug, rocking her back and forth, making me nervous as hell because of his sloppy movements. It takes everything in me not to force him to sit down, which I could do if it came down to it.

Another swell rises under the boat, and Ava screams. I close the space to Ava and hook my fingers to her hips to steady her on her feet. She releases a sweet breath against my neck and meets my eyes like she's so relieved I'm here.

"Hey, Aves. Come here! Look into the water," Matty says.

If I wasn't holding onto Ava, I'd cross the space between us. Not only is he annoying the crap out of me, his words dig into me. But I don't know how Ava would react if I got in the middle. The last thing I want is for her to get mad at me for yelling at her friend.

I don't have to, though.

"Don't be a jerk, Matty," Giselle quips from the table, glaring.

Ava shifts in my arms to look between Giselle and Matty. His idiotic self stands on a rung, overlooking the dark water lit with a streak of silvery moon.

I don't get the chance to drag him back because Ava inches forward, taking control of the situation with her friends. "Matty, get over here before you fall over."

Matty laughs, spinning his arms in circles to joke with her. She screams rushing forward, too upset and afraid for her friend's life to realize he's messing with her. I step forward, my fingers curled into fists, ready to react in a way that I'm sure Ava might not forgive me for.

Matty swivels, his arms flailing out. "Hey, cool it. I was only mes—"

I yell out Ava's name, the edges of my vision darkening. Matty punches her right in the back, sending her stumbling into the railing. I'm too slow. Her dress slips right through my fingers, and she falls overboard.

The ocean rises up to catch her as all her friends scream. She disappears under, and my whole world, every single idea I had about my future, every hope of getting Ava to fall in love with me, vanishes with her. The ocean steals the beautiful girl who loves the land just as much as me, and there's only one thing I can do.

I jump after her.

3

THE SPARK

DARK WATER ENGULFS me, sucking me under after Ava. She disappears in the churning night sea far too fast for me to reach her without transforming into my most powerful form. Quickly stripping off my board shorts, I undress and drink in a deep breath of the ocean, the saltwater pushing away the sweetness of the desserts I had shared with Ava.

My body adjusts to the cool temperature of the water and my vision changes, lighting the ocean aglow, making the subtle moonlight above appear almost like the sun. And the soft beams of light shine on Ava hovering in the water.

My heart races, the edges of my vision shadowing at the

sight of my beautiful possible mate lifeless in the sea. How the ocean could bring her to me only to rip her away seems cruel. Why taunt this beautiful soul for years, threaten her, and now this? I can't bear it. I won't let her be taken from me.

Swimming forward, cutting through the sea faster than the yacht could ever travel, I close the distance to Ava, scooping her into my arms. The moonlight glows across her skin, bubbles still clinging to her, and I push her blond hair from her face. Her azure eyes glitter before me, wide, full of panic. But they're not empty. She's not gone from me forever, but she'll never make it back to the surface in time.

I do the only thing I can.

Brushing my lips to hers, I kiss her, stealing away her last breath as a human only to return it to her from my very essence. Heat crawls up my chest and to my mouth, slipping from me like my heart floats from my chest to Ava's. But it's not painful or terrifying feeling a piece of my being rip away. The act fills me up with an indescribable emotion that overflows in me to spill into Ava.

Please, don't take her from me, I pray silently, sending the thoughts into the sea. "Ava, please. You can do it. Follow the light."

Ava's skin erupts in a flash of light, her heart flickering in a warm glow pounding slowly at first before picking up to match the speed of my racing heart. Her floating hair haloes around us, and I meet her for one more kiss, feeling my life and essence course through her veins. She thrashes in my arms, and I jet us to the surface, breaking through.

She coughs and spits out the ocean water from her lungs, shivering in the cold sea around us. My mind races with thoughts that aren't my own, Ava's mind catching up with her body. I hold her tighter, feeling the smooth skin of her legs brushing my tail. She's too disoriented even to realize I'm not in my human form, but I must tell her what I've done.

To save her life, I stole away her human world. And we can't stay here. The full moon rises tomorrow night and will transform her into a mermaid. I'll have to take her out to sea to one of the colonies for her to adjust.

Tears burn in my eyes as my actions, my inability to let her go, to let the ocean steal her from me, sink into my bones. She'll never forgive me for what I've done, stealing her choice from her about being a mermaid. And I gave up my one chance to change a human on a girl I've known for a day.

What have I done?

Ava gasps, clinging to me, pressing her body to mine even more. Her heartbeat pounds against mine, pushing my thoughts away.

"Ava, you're okay. You're alive. Just keep breathing. Stay with me," I say, peering around the night ocean. A light flash-es over the water from the Ocean Jewel as they search for us. If I'm going to take Ava away, I have to do it now.

But she turns her attention to me, meeting my stare. The

moonlight sparkles off the beads of seawater clinging to her skin—and she's even more beautiful than I remember moments ago. Her pouty lips puff out another breath, and I lose myself in her azure gaze lit by the silver moon.

"I—I died," she whispers, choking back a sob before coughing again. "But now I'm alive."

She knows. She knows something's different, that something within her changed. And I can't swim us away. I can't bring myself to ruin her life all because I selfishly couldn't let the sea take my mate from me.

I laugh nervously, squeezing her tighter against me. Another swell pushes us higher toward the nearly full moon and back down again. "You're very much alive," I say. "But I have to tell you something."

If only the words didn't stay locked in my throat. If only the glowing light of the yacht in the distance didn't grow brighter as they draw near. I need time. I need a moment to let everything catch up.

I don't get the chance.

The hum of the dinghy closes in on us, one of my crew mates shining a light over the surface. Voices yell out, calling our names, and I realize I'm still in my merman form. Ava relaxes in my arms, her head lolling as she fights to stay conscious. Her body already starts the change which will complete tomorrow under the full moon when the call of the ocean will force her to take her very first breath of the sea. Her pearlescent skin shines against mine, and she blinks, moaning.

"Ava," I say, her name sounding like a soft plea on my lips. "Ava, listen."

She groans, resting her head on my shoulder for a moment.

"Ava, please. Look at me," I beg, adjusting her, so she has to meet my gaze.

She opens her eyes, peering at me with a new serious expression. Her gaze trails from my eyes and to my forearms where my caudal fins jet from my skin. I swallow, afraid she'll scream and thrash away from me, but she closes her eyes again, and I duck under and transform back into my human self, sliding my board shorts back on from where I wrapped them on my arm.

Releasing a small breath, now looking at me again, Ava shakes her head, pushing away the confusion lining her hypnotic eyes. I hug her tighter, so I don't have to face her. So I don't spill my heart out in a moment where I can't give her the answers she'll need.

"I'm truly sorry for this," I whisper into her salty hair.

She doesn't respond.

"I didn't have a choice," I add. "I couldn't let you die." Like my apology will make up for destroying her life. Because I'm not sure what'll happen now. She's a mermaid. My essence beats in her chest, and I hate how much I don't regret it. I can feel her confusion, her fear, every emotion washing through her coming to me. I don't know how I'll survive when she realizes what I've done. I don't think I can handle the hate that could follow or how she might never be able to love me because of it.

My beautiful accidental mate still has a chance, and I'd save her all over again.

I just need to tell her. "Ava?" I ask her, watching her eyes blink a few dozen times. "Ava, please. Listen to me."

It's no use. She can't keep focus. The ocean's taken a toll on her.

And Keith calls my name, throwing me a lifesaver to grab on to pull us to the dinghy. Ava passes out in my arms, and all I can do is hold her.

It's going to be okay, I think to myself. *She's alive. It's all that matters.*

I can't bring myself to leave Ava's side. Sasha, the Ocean Jewel's onboard medic, gave me a strange look when I sat on the cot across from Ava, but since neither Ava nor Mrs. King said anything, she allows me to stay while she examines Ava.

"I'm fine," Ava says, her voice still slightly hoarse. "Can I please just go back to my room?"

Mrs. King wrings her hands together, standing in the doorway to give us all a little space. She glances between Sasha and Ava.

Sasha sets her stethoscope on her metal tray. "You're very

lucky, Ms. Adair. Your temperature is slightly lower than it should be, but I think with some rest and some warm liquids, you should feel fine in a few hours."

I release a breath, but I never doubted Ava wasn't going to be physically okay after I gave her my merman essence. Her heart flickers in the exact rhythm as mine almost like I've split my heart to give her a part of it—maybe I did. I wasn't prepared to couple with Ava without the traditional merpeople ceremony. My parents will be so disappointed.

"So, we don't have to cut the trip short?" Ava asks, turning her gaze to mine.

Her cheeks flush when I offer her an awkward smile. I'm surprised by her words, though. She was terrified of the ocean, and I was certain her falling overboard would have cemented that fear into her, and she'd have wanted to return to shore, where I'd have to break the news to her, but now I'll have to do it here. And soon.

Sasha lifts and drops her shoulders. "That's up to Mrs. King."

I half wish Mrs. King would ask us to turn the boat around. Ava's first mermaid transformation from the Ocean Jewel will test my luck. She won't be able to resist the pull of the ocean as long as I can. It might very well cause us to have to abandon land altogether if we're caught missing overnight.

Mrs. King grimaces, worry wrinkling the corners of her eyes. "Are you sure you feel all right, Avie?" The sweet nickname she gives Ava proves how close the woman is to Ava, and I wonder about Ava's life on land and how much I want to know about it. To see it for myself. It's a world I can't imagine. I've always lived a simple life. "Your health is more important than this vacation. Maybe I should call your mom—"

Ava raises her hand out. "No! You'll freak her out for nothing. I'm not hurt or anything. She doesn't need to know. Please, Ruby. You remember how she was after—"

Sadness washes from Ava to me, her feelings radiating from her soul through our accidental bond—one she doesn't even realize I now have with her. It takes everything in me not to stand and hug her, to try to steal the sadness, so she doesn't have to feel it anymore. Because my deep-seated need to give her everything she could ever want, to make her smile, to feel everything beautiful about her soul is all I can think about. Like loving her is my sole purpose. Protecting her, too.

The need is so intense I feel like I'm going crazy. I sound crazy. Dad never warned me of all this. But how could he have? There weren't any prospects for my eternal mate until now.

And now I have the sudden urge to swim.

But I can't.

"I suppose you're right. I want you to come back here and check in with Sasha in the morning, okay?" Mrs. King says, pulling me away from my thoughts. She turns and smiles at me. "You were very brave for jumping in to save Ava, young man. You don't know how grateful we are, and after speaking to my husband and Captain Briggs, we'd like to reward you."

Guilt rushes through me. The last thing I want is to be rewarded for ruining Ava's human life. "I don't need a reward, ma'am. I'm just thankful I was there to help."

"As are we, and that's why the captain agreed to grant you time off for the remainder of the trip, and we're providing you with a bonus," Mrs. King says, smiling. I'm torn between wanting to accept—because I should, since I'll need anything I can get to help Ava transition, but I still have a job, one I desperately need to take care of Ava.

I shake my head, my good senses winning. "That's very generous, ma'am—"

"Ruby. Call me Ruby," Mrs. King says, cutting me off.

"Ruby," I say, her name feeling strange coming from my mouth. "But I can't take you up on the offer. It's not fair for the others who'd have to pick up my slack."

Sasha huffs like she can't believe I'm rejecting Mrs. King's reward. "Carter, we'll survive. Captain Briggs wouldn't have agreed if he didn't think we could handle it. I'm sure the others will agree with me." And they will. Because the other crew mates have been like my family away from home. They're all I've spent my time with for months.

"Then it's settled," Mrs. King says, patting my shoulder. "And tomorrow, we'll see you at breakfast."

I push the tiny bit of fear gripping me away. This is Ava's

world. Her life and all the people she loves. I need to figure out my place in all this. Because I really want to. There's nothing more I want than to immerse myself in her whole world and show her mine.

Ava slides off the cot and follows Mrs. King out of the sick bay, where they'll take the stairs to the elevator that'll head to the staterooms. Sasha gives me a quick check-up, chatting about how lucky Ava was that I was a phenomenal swimmer.

"It'll be a date she'll never forget," the medic says, chuckling when she's through.

If only she knew.

"I hope she gives me a chance at a second one," I respond, though all I want to do is find Ava to check on her again myself.

But I don't right away. I force myself to shower and change out of my damp clothes first. After the voices and excitement on the upper deck dies down, I make my way to the staterooms. I have no idea if Ava's even awake, but I can't wait until morning to see her. The longer I wait, the less time she has to prepare herself for the transformation. I wish this could've happened after the full moon to give her as much time as she could get, but the ocean can't be reasoned with. And I can't deny how grateful I am that it let me save Ava.

I quietly stand outside her door for a minute, gathering my nerve. Tapping my knuckles on the wood, I listen to Ava move around inside the room. I don't have to see her to know it's her. I can feel her presence nearing mine, making my heart race because it's like my piece returns to me in the form of a beautiful mermaid created for me.

Ava swings the door open, her full lips slightly parting as she stares at me. I raise my finger to my mouth before she says anything and reach for her hand to pull her from her cabin. She follows next to me, and I watch her watch me in my peripheral vision, dozens of thoughts on her mind, thoughts I'll hear the moment the full moon rises and drags us out to sea.

Ava only wears a tank top and pajama shorts, so I grab a throw blanket from the leather sectional in the saloon and wrap it around her shoulders. I lead her up to the sundeck and to the last lounge chair with the best view of the night-darkened sea. Without having to ask her, I know she sees it with new vision. Until she completes her transformation, she won't be able to resist her mermaid essence, and it'll give her everything she needs to survive the seas.

She shares the lounge chair with me, pressing her knees into mine. She studies my face like she's seeing me again for the first time, just taking in my features. I never want her to look away either. My heart pounds under her intensity, and I yearn for her to close the space even more between us.

Reaching up, she glides her finger along my cheek, mapping my jawline while sinking into her own thoughts. A small spark lights the blue of her eyes, igniting with a beautiful smile.

"You look awfully sad for being my hero," she says, still holding my face in her hand.

I cup her hand, pressing her fingers deeper into my skin, just wanting to feel her closeness. "I'm not a hero, Ava."

"You saved my life," she whispers, the light and her smile fading away.

It hurts that I can't reciprocate her happiness. Not now. Not when I'm about to rip hers away from her.

"Do you remember anything?" I ask. It'd be so much easier if she did, and I didn't have to destroy her life as she knows it.

A dozen thoughts cloud her crystal eyes as she thinks about the events of the night. Her gaze darts back and forth, and she peers at the ocean, the lightness in her face darkening like the black depths of the deepest part of the sea.

She shivers. "I died. I know it. But you—you saved me."

"Yes." Torment courses through me, confirming her thoughts out loud. "But do you remember how?"

She closes her eyes, inhaling a long breath, searching herself for answers I'm afraid to give. I'm afraid of how she'll look at me once she knows what I've done and how I stole the choice she would have had to make in the future had I earned her love. Love I might never get now. There's a reason merpeople are only given one chance to transform a human. We give part of our very essences, and that's that. If Ava doesn't share the same need born in me, I'll be forever trapped unrequited in my feelings.

But still, I know I wouldn't have let her die. I couldn't give up the possibility of a future with the one person who I knew could complete me, and now does, even if she doesn't realize it.

"This is going to sound crazy, but I touched an underwater flame. The spark..." Ava's voice trails off. The spark she saw, it was me in the water. It was my essence begging for her to bond with me. She wobbles for a moment, losing herself in her thoughts, her eyes opening and darting from me to the open sea. "Everything looks weird, Carter. Something's wrong with me. Maybe you should take me back to Sasha."

But nothing is wrong with her. She doesn't need Sasha. She needs me. She needs to see everything for herself, and there's only one way I know how. Closing the space between us, I brush my lips to hers, opening up my mind for her, letting her into my being as I recall the memories myself.

Her hands lock onto my shoulders, her surprise melting away as she devours my kiss, mashing her mouth to mine in a way that makes me want to scoop her up to jump overboard with her so she can know me for who I am. A mixture of lust and love pour through me, making me release a low moan against her lips, which she steals away with another kiss full of yearning—desire for answers revealed in my kiss, desire for me.

I'd kiss her all night if I didn't need to explain myself to her. To apologize.

Ava gasps and pulls herself away as I show her the final moment of her human life when I took her last breath and gave her mine. Her hand flies to her mouth, and she touches her lips, her eyes wide and full of something indecipherable within the jumble of emotions she sends to me through our bond.

"Ava, I'm so sorry," I say.

She continues to stare at me, her brows puckering as they lower over her eyes like she can't believe I'm apologizing. I showed her everything she needs to know to realize what I've done, yet she doesn't scream at me. She doesn't react at all.

"I'm so sorry," I repeat, brushing stray tresses of her blond hair from her face and behind her ear.

"Stop apologizing for saving me. Everything is fine. I'm fine." She shifts her leg between mine, bowing toward me.

I frown. She doesn't understand or believe what happened. And why would she? No one knows about the existence of merpeople. We're only in fairytales.

"Ava, what did you see when I kissed you just now?" I ask.

She licks her lips, fidgeting under my stare. "You're a merman." Her expression changes from confusion to awe, her eyes igniting again with a light I crave to see in them forever. "And you breathed life back into me—the spark, it still lingers in my heart. I can feel it with every beat."

She feels me. She feels the bond. It's all I could've hoped for, but still, I can't be certain of where this will lead us.

Lying back in the chair, she processes what's happening to her while staring up at the nearly full moon. The silence between us weighs heavy, but not in a world-ending way. I could wrap myself in the silence, just feeling Ava's presence and be okay. I want her to be okay, too. More than anything.

"I'm like you now," she whispers to the glittering sky above us. "That's why you're apologizing. You didn't save me. You changed me."

I cringe at her words. She's right. I didn't save her life because I wasn't fast enough in my human form. I failed her before I even had a chance to prove my worth, and now she realizes it. She covers her face with her hands, inhaling a breath. Yet, she doesn't lash out at me like I expect.

"You'll transform under the full moon," I whisper.

She only nods and meets my gaze again. "But it's not forever, right?"

I can't bear to tell her that it is. That even though I have legs now, it doesn't change that I'm a merman and she's a mermaid, and the sea now gives her a new life apart from the human world she was born in.

I take a breath and pull out the necklace I've been wearing around my neck since the moment I moved out of my parents' apartment. The necklace that carries the ring that matches the one on my finger that allows me to walk on land every day except for the night of the full moon. It was a gift given to me by my parents created by King Attilonious, the merman who made a life on land for those who choose it possible. A life on land he could easily take from me for breaking tradition and transforming Ava without taking the proper steps.

But I can't think about that now.

"This is an enchanted stone infused with the ocean," I say, allowing Ava to hold it in her fingers.

The light of the moon sparkles in the blue stone, and Ava says, "It's beautiful."

"It allows me to transform at will...except for the full moon."

Her calm features shift into a grimace, and she unleashes a wave of grief and despair through me. "What happens otherwise? Will I be trapped in the ocean? Oh, God. My parents—I can't put them through this. You have to fix me."

Her heart breaking steals my breath, shadowing the edges of my vision. I've never felt something so horrible and intense before, and I hate myself that I'm the reason she's drowning in the most painful emotions.

Tears drip onto her cheeks, sparkling in the moonlight. "I can't be like you, Carter. Please, fix this."

My breath pants, and I panic, unsure of what to do, of how to fix this. Because I can't change her back. I can't do anything but watch her life implode and the ocean swallow her whole.

Wrapping her in my arms, I hug her against me, trying to hold her together as she falls apart. "I can't stop the transformation, but I'm not going to force you into a life you clearly don't want, Ava." Even if I end up jeopardizing my life on land. The king will have to understand. I'll make him. I'll make everyone. But until then, I'll keep Ava away. I'll see to it she keeps her human life.

"How?" she asks, pulling away from me, tears branding moon drenched streaks on her soft skin.

I unclasp my necklace and hold out the ring to her. "With this. It was intended for the one I choose for a mate, but I want you to have it."

Her eyes widen. "I barely know you."

But damn do I want her to know me. To feel me as I feel her. "I'm not asking you to be my mate. I'm offering you a chance to continue to live your life the best you can. This is all my fault."

"Carter..." She closes her mouth, not sure how to react or what to say. This wasn't how I expected to give my ring to Ava, but I silently pray to the ocean that she takes it and allows me into her life. I hope she gives me a chance to show her everything I can offer her. I hope she gives me the chance to make her smile again.

She releases a sigh. "Are you sure you want to give that to

me? I'm thankful to even be alive. It's just—why?"

I've never been more certain of anything apart from my decision to save her life. Uncurling her fingers, I slide my sea stone ring into her palm, feeling her fingers trembling in mine. How do I even answer her question? How do I tell her I couldn't give up the amazing future I imagined us having. How I knew she could be my mate, the one who'll hold a part of me forever. My purpose in life. But I don't think she'll understand. Getting her to forgive me is the best I can hope for.

"I couldn't let you die," I finally say. "I've never met someone who loves the land more than I do. I couldn't just let the ocean have you."

She blinks tears away. "But it does have me."

I shake my head. I'll help her see. I'll make sure she knows that this isn't the end. It's only the beginning. "No, Ava. You now have the ocean."

4

ACCIDENTAL MATE

I WISH THE night wouldn't end. Ava's legs rest over mine, and we share the throw blanket, watching the sky turn from midnight to lavender. She tilts her head on my shoulder and stares at our fingers still twined together. She hasn't pulled away at all since I hugged her until she stopped crying, though sadness still sheens her eyes every time silence falls between us. So I stopped letting it. I spent the night telling her everything I possibly could and showing her things I didn't know how to explain through kisses I never want to stop giving.

She sucks in her bottom lip, meeting my gaze. "Will I ever see the colonies? Meet the king?"

I shrug. We should head to Pearlestria tonight, my home colony where I was born before my parents took me to land to raise me, but I'll do everything I can to ensure we return to the Ocean Jewel once the sea releases us. "Maybe one day, if it's something you want."

"What about you? Why aren't you there?" she asks, tickling my arm with her warm breath.

I lean back to meet her sky blue gaze. "I was raised on the surface. My parents love the land, and I do, too. Don't get me wrong. I love the ocean. I feel my most powerful underwater. But I like the adventure and excitement of people above water." Plus, there is no hot food, TV, comfortable mattresses, even anything sweet, really. It's boring. I don't say it, though. Ava might fear the ocean now, but she could eventually decide she loves it more than the land, and I'd follow her anywhere, whether it's the land or sea.

"Oh," is all she says. She turns to the lightening sky and yawns, sinking against me. "God, this is so unbelievable."

I rest my head on hers. "I'll be here with you for everything. You can ask me whatever you want. Anything. I want to do whatever I can for you."

A whisper of a smile plays on her lips, and she leans closer and kisses me. "Thanks. I'm just—" She yawns again and laughs.

"Let me walk you back to your room," I say. "You need

to get at least a few hours of sleep for tonight."

She only nods as I help her to her feet and guide her back to her stateroom. She kisses me again in the hallway in such a way that desire rushes over me, filling me up with everything Ava is in this moment. I force myself to pull away first before I get ahead of myself. This is only a kiss to Ava. She can't feel what I feel yet if she ever will at all. I've never heard of anyone changing a human into a mermaid on a whim, and I must proceed with the same caution Ava shrouds herself in.

Ava smiles at me as she closes the door, a new light shining in her eyes. The world doesn't feel like it'll sink us underwater with the look she gives me, drinking me in with her eyes once more before shutting the door completely.

Instead of heading down to the cabin I share with three others, I take the stairs back up to the sundeck to peer at the ocean, imagining diving under tonight to show Ava the world that flows through my veins. I just hope I can figure out a way to get Ava off the yacht unnoticed. If I can't, our lives on land will be over.

I drift off to sleep, dreaming of Ava and her transformation, imagining how it'll affect the both of us under the full moon. I've never seen someone's first transformation before, because human-born merpeople are rare, and I hate to admit I'm a little scared. But my fear can't compare to what I'm sure Ava will experience. Breathing water for the first time, taking the sea into your heart, goes against her nature as a human—

even if she's no longer one.

Water splashes over me, pulling me from the half-sleep state I had fallen into, and I throw my towel from my face to find Ava and Giselle standing in the pool in front of me. I can't stop the smile from crossing my face. The last thing I had expected was for her to return to me so soon, but it's like the universe can't keep us apart.

"You're swimming," I say, gazing from her damp hair to her cleavage peeking from her bikini top and back to her beautiful eyes. It's hard not to be surprised she's in the pool after knowing her fear of the ocean, but I guess a few feet of water she can stand in is nothing like the ocean we'll submerge under tonight.

"More like wading," Giselle remarks from next to Ava. Her bronze hair clings to her cheeks, and she smiles at me before looking to Ava to see what she does next.

Ava licks her lips, raising her eyebrows when I can't find the words to speak. "So, are you going to just watch us or are you coming in?"

I lean back in the chair and grin, taking her flirtatious bait. I could look at her all day if she'd let me.

But I don't get the chance. Giselle tips her head back and laughs, splashing me with water. I accept Ava's invite, tugging my shirt from my head to join them. Ava and Giselle both stare at me, smiling, and a wave of excitement rushes over me. I thought staring at Ava all day would be fun, but the way she looks at me drives me crazy in the best way possible.

She doesn't take her eyes off me as I sit on the edge of the pool and swing my legs over. She presses her lips together, turning her gaze to my legs like I'll suddenly sprout a tail, though I already told her I wouldn't as long as I wear the sea stone ring on my finger, the matching ring that now glitters from her hand.

I sink into the water up to my neck and swim in her direction, making her squeal at my speed. Even without my tail, I can swim better than the average human. I lift her off her feet by her waist and dunk her under with me. Feeling her skin against mine in the water almost makes me wish the moon would rise already.

Pushing us to the surface, Ava and Giselle both laugh, tackling me, and I let them send me back under. Hearing Ava laugh, seeing her joke and play around with her friend, cements my decision to do what it takes to keep her safe in her human life. If I can manage to live on land, I can help her manage, too.

Ava and Giselle swim to the edge of the pool and quietly whisper to each other. I know Ava's trying to figure out a plan to make sure her friends don't come looking for her after the moon rises, but I'm not even sure how it'll be possible. I can only whisper a prayer to the ocean.

Swimming a lap around the small pool that feels like a bathtub compared to the open ocean, I shake off my nerves and bring my attention back to Ava. She swims to me and slides her arms around my shoulders.

"Giselle's going to sleep in Matty and Logan's room tonight to give us some privacy," she whispers, holding my gaze.

I suck in a small breath at the flush crossing her face. I know we won't be in her room, but the idea alone sends my heart racing imagining what it would be like. She doesn't even have to say anything for me to know she's thinking about it too. Her attraction to me is enough to give me hope of something more between us. That the ocean wouldn't have allowed me to give my essence to someone who had no possibility of being my mate.

"It might just work," I finally say, realizing I haven't responded.

She sucks in her bottom lip, her eyebrows puckering with worry. "It has to. I'm really counting on it."

Ava bounces on the window seat next to me, peering around the saloon at her friends and then to the setting sun. Fiery oranges and yellows light her skin in golden hues, turning her eyes gray in the light of the coming night.

I lean into her, hoping the strength of my body can somehow get her to stop trembling with fear. Her anxiety beats at me, trying to get into my essence, but I hold strong the best I can for Ava. This isn't something I'd have gone through with alone if I hadn't already given her my life essence and devotion to save her life. There's a whole transformation ceremony and coupling ceremony, which would have provided my chosen—Ava—with the support she needs to embrace the ocean, but now I have to prove my worth and summon all the strength of the merpeople colonies into me alone for her. And I will.

Pressing my lips to her ear, I whisper, "We're going to wait as long as possible after sundown to hit the water. I can resist the transformation for a few hours, which makes it a lot easier to slip away unnoticed, but you won't be able to. Not yet. You'll also start to feel what I can only describe as an uncomfortable pull at any moment. Don't let it scare you. Your transformation will take a bit since it's your first."

She pales, shuddering a breath. "Is it going to hurt?" Guilt rises in my chest at the soft sound of her voice. I hate that I put her in this position, but I have to remind myself of the alternative. One night of fear for a life is something I doubt Ava would ever complain about, though it still doesn't make me feel any better. Because what if she hates her life? What if she grows to resent me?

"It'll be an adjustment for you. But pain? No, I don't think so." I wish I could be more confident in my words, but I don't know exactly what it'll be like for her. For me, it's just life.

Ava pales even more, her eyes darting around the room. She pulls her hand away from me to wring them together in her lap. "I'm going to be sick. I can't do this. Maybe I'll just lock myself in the bathroom."

I grasp her chin to get her to look at me, to get her to push away everything around us, so she concentrates solely on me. I'm afraid if she can't focus, she'll lose it and cause commotion I can't afford if I'm going to get us off this yacht unseen. "That's the pull of the moon you're experiencing. Resistance will make you feel like you're dying until you do. You're a mermaid now. Without the sea, you won't survive the night."

She blinks tears from her eyes, her panic digging into me. "Please, there has to be a way."

Startling in my arms, she inhales a deep breath, gripping her legs. Muscles twitch under her skin, and a flash of terror crosses her beautiful face. I jump to my feet at the signs of her inevitable transformation. It won't be much longer, and I don't want to risk having to carry her out.

Ava clutches onto me, leaning on my shoulder while squeezing all the feeling from my hand. She forces herself to smile, glancing and waving to her friends who watch us leave. If I wasn't so focused on getting Ava away, I might be embarrassed by the shouts and laughter her friends direct at us, Logan exclaiming he might actually win a bet. And I thought merpeople were brazen. I'm not sure I'll understand the bond Ava has with her friends.

Guiding her to her stateroom, I help Ava grab the waterproof bag I gave her earlier to put our belongings in. She groans, clutching her stomach, the pull of the ocean probably worse than I've ever felt. I'm pretty sure if I wasn't holding onto her, she'd give up to curl in on herself on the floor.

I've never been so grateful for an empty sundeck. It's not an ideal jumping point because of the height of the yacht, but this is the only place with a spot out of the line of sight from anyone below. The rest of my crew mates should be cleaning and prepping for tomorrow by now. If Ava could hold out, I'd have taken her to jump in from the swimming platform, but now is not a good time with Keith looking over the equipment.

Ava grips the guardrail, peering at the darkening ocean in front of us. Her fear radiates so intensely from her I can't help mistaking it as my own. But I have faith that the ocean didn't give me this chance, bringing Ava into my life, only to make us both miserable in its depths. If that were the case, it would've dragged us out to sea already. I know it.

Ava breathes through the muscle spasms rolling through her body, and I rub my hand on her back. We stand together, watching the purple sky fade to dark blue. I want to hold off as long as possible, giving us the best chance at the night shielding us.

A small swell lifts the yacht, making Ava groan. Her body trembles so badly that I can't stand to watch her holding onto the last moments of her life as she knows it any longer. She needs to jump. She needs the ocean to fill her lungs. She needs to breathe water.

"Get ready to jump, Ava," I say, pulling myself away from her to circle the deck to make sure it's all clear and we can jump without being seen.

I turn my gaze away from Ava and strip out of my clothes, holding them in front of me to wait for Ava to slide her dress into the bag so I can put mine in. She glances in my direction, her eyes widening and blush heating her cheeks as she stares at my clothes in my hands. I try not to smile at her reaction and shove my clothes in the bag. Her eyes dart everywhere else but at me. Human social norms aren't lost on her just because she's about to transform into a mermaid. I didn't even consider she'd be embarrassed to undress in front of me or react the way she is now as I stand naked in front of her, but I can't help but love how cute she looks flushed and flustered.

"You can undress. I promise I won't look," I say, turning my gaze to the ocean.

"What? I'm not getting naked here."

I feel her gaze boring into the side of my face but keep my eyes trained on the water. "You might rip your bikini."

She inhales a small breath. "I have more."

I don't argue with her. The last thing I want to do is make her more uncomfortable than she already is. Silence falls between us for a moment, and I turn my attention back to her as she loosens the ties on her bottoms a little.

Swaying on her feet, she clutches the guardrail, her hands turning white. Her skin shimmers in the darkening light as her body starts to evolve into something fitting for the sea. Her blue eyes sparkle, almost lit from within like an aquamarine diamond catching rays of sunshine. My heart races, thinking about what's about to come. Ava's incredibly beautiful now, but seeing her as a mermaid ignites an intense desire through me, poking at my very nature.

"Come on, it's time to go," I say. She looks ready to fall over, and I need her to be able to jump.

I climb the rungs of the guardrail to the small ledge on the other side and help Ava over. Her gaze darts from me to the water and back to me, and I can't stop from grinning at her failing effort not to look at me. But I want her to look at me as I am. I want to see the desire she tries to ignore sweep across her chest in a rosy blush.

She finally holds my gaze. "What if I don't jump far enough?"

"I'll make sure you do."

"What if someone sees us?"

"They won't."

"What if—"

Reaching out, I lace my fingers through hers and pull her hand to my heart, watching the light of my merman spark glitter against her pearlescent skin. She snaps her mouth shut, silencing the hundreds of questions she wants to ask. But we're running out of time.

"The moment we hit the water, we're going to dive, okay?" I ask.

She nods, keeping her gaze on the ocean.

"Are you ready?"

She gasps another breath like air refuses to go into her lungs. But it's the transformation calling her to sea. Soon, she'll feel like she's drowning breathing air until she inhales her first breath of the ocean.

"No," she whispers, her soft voice making me want to pull her into my arms to hug her.

"Ava, look at me." I summon as much strength into my voice to push away any sort of hesitation inside me. Because my nerves threaten to sink me to the ocean floor. "I won't let go of you until you're ready. If you want me to hold your hand until morning, I will."

Her brows pucker over her sparkling jewel eyes, and she relaxes her shoulders but squeezes my hand harder. "Okay, count to three. Let's get this over with."

I shift the waterproof bag on my shoulder. "One. Two. Three."

Bending my knees, I launch into the air, pulling Ava with me to make sure she gets far enough away from the yacht. She doesn't scream or anything, just closes her eyes as we break through the surface into the icy sea.

I watch her for a moment through the bubbles glittering around us, and she stares at the surface and the taunting full moon shining down on us.

The sea claims me.

5

BREATHING WATER

I DIVE AVA DEEPER BEFORE she tries to fight back to the surface. She hovers in front of me, gripping my hand, staring at my chest. My heartbeat thrums in sync with hers, the light of our sparks creating a soft glow between us.

Sucking the ocean into my lungs, I transform before Ava into my merman form. She clears in my vision as my eyes adjust, and I watch her study me. Oxygen clings to her beautiful face, her cheeks puffing out with the air she refuses to let escape her lungs. She reaches out her hand, running her fingers across my tail. My muscles twitch under her gentle touch, and

I let her explore my body until panic lights her eyes. She clings onto her human nature as her mermaid form fights to break free.

Ava kicks her legs, trying to pull away to swim back to the surface far above us, and I hold her tighter to keep her with me. I promised I wouldn't let her go, and now she's panicking because she won't give in to the sea.

I let go of her hand only to cup her face between mine so she'll focus on me long enough to let me help her. If only she could hear my thoughts, I could tell her to calm down and breathe as she normally would as a human. Because she can't drown now.

"Just breathe," I mouth to her, holding her close enough to read my lips in the water.

Still, she resists.

"Breathe," I repeat.

She squeezes her eyes shut and inhales a long breath of the ocean, letting her lungs fill with the sea. Her body relaxes, a smile of wonder and relief crossing her face. Her transformation takes hold of her. She meets my gaze with her aquamarine, sparkling eyes, and the spark in her chest blooms to travel down her torso. I keep my eyes trained on hers, allowing her to use my shoulder to support herself as she unties her bikini bottoms. I snatch them from the sea before they can drift away.

Grimacing, Ava arches forward. Her muscles spasm under

her skin, and I peek at the short dorsal fins growing from her arms. The light from her spark illuminates the scales sprouting from her smooth legs.

"That's it, Ava. You're almost done," I think to her, feeling her mind open to me. Her racing thoughts flicker through my mind as fast as our hearts beat. She wishes she could see herself in her mermaid form, hypnotized by the shimmer of her breathtaking tail.

Her caudal fin expands out wider than mine, fanning the sea, though she doesn't move. I take her hands and pull back to take in her incomparable beauty—the way her blue eyes remind me of the sky above, how her skin glimmers like a pearl, how amazing everything is about her, her soft voice in my mind, the smooth touch of her fingers. I can't believe she carries my spark in her chest, that she will be my future mate if she lets me. I pray silently to the ocean that she does.

Her blond hair floats around her, veiling the water between us. She smiles, trailing her gaze to my chest. I grin back at her, just drinking her in, imprinting how beautiful she is as a mermaid. She leans closer like she wants to close the space between us, so I do it for her. Small bubbles sparkle on her face, and she rubs her full lips together.

"You're beautiful, Ava," I think to her while drawing her even closer.

I can't stop myself from leaning forward to brush my lips to hers. I test her reaction, just grazing her mouth with feather softness. I send her an image of herself as a mermaid as I see her before me now, giving in to her need to see what she looks like. Pressing into me, she rubs her tail against mine, igniting desire through me. She deepens our kiss, sliding her tongue into my mouth. She tastes like salt and something sweet, driving me wild. I brush my fingers through her hair, wishing we could hover together all night. I might if she'd let me. I'll devour every kiss and still crave a thousand more.

"Whoa," she thinks to me, startling herself away at the sound of her voice through our telepathic link.

I consider closing the space between us again, but the sudden urge to swim, to show her everything around us, to see her eyes light with wonder takes hold of me. I motion for her to swim with me, and she flicks her tail, jetting us both sideways, reminding me of my merbabe cousin after he was born.

I laugh out loud, shooting bubbles to the surface. I can't help how cute and flustered she looks as she attempts to control her new, powerful form. I wrap my hands around her waist and tip her forward so she lies parallel to the surface. The last thing I ever expected was to give swimming lessons to a mermaid, but I'm happy to have the opportunity.

Ava peers below her at the kelp forest reaching for the surface around us. A school of yellowtails swims under us, and I refrain from letting go of Ava to hunt one to offer it to her. My merman instincts battle with the human norms I know Ava's accustomed to. The ocean life hypnotizes her, and she smiles like I'd shock her if I dare harm a fish. This might be a problem if I can't manage to sneak us both back on the yacht come dawn.

I push the thought away with the shadow of a boat crossing over us. Ava stiffens, a blip of her fear washing over me. She might have human norms ingrained in her, but her mermaid essence flares. But no one can see us from the surface. The ocean bestowed magic into our essences to protect us from humans, from all predators, really.

I move my hand to her chest and press my fingers over her heart, feeling her relax under the pressure of my touch. "No human device can detect us. The light you see, our life force, protects us. It causes interference. It also disguises us from above. No one can see us as we are when we're underwater. It's surfacing that's dangerous."

Her heart beats against my palm, her essence drawing me in. I can't stop my other hand from gliding over the short dorsal fin running along her spine from between her shoulders to the ridge around her tail. I want to explore her entire body with my hands, familiarize myself with every curve, every muscle.

Gulping a breath of water to cool my desire, I guide Ava's body forward, getting her to move with the current only using her tail. She adapts to the swimming technique quickly, and pride swells through me. Ava makes an incredible mermaid. I long to see what else she's capable of...

I push the thought away. Ava's chosen the land. She might never reach her full potential if she doesn't remain in the sea. Guilt bats at me, thinking about how following her need to remain on the surface could hinder her, but I think forcing her out to sea would be much, much worse. I could never devastate her like that.

After a few minutes more of guiding her movements, I release her only to link my pinkie finger with hers so she can swim on her own and enjoy the feeling of cutting through the currents. We weave through the kelp, matching each other's movements, and her attraction to me grows so powerful that it's all I can think about. How close she swims, how gentle her touch is, how beautiful her wide eyes are, glittering in the moonlit ocean.

The world blurs around me as I watch her search the sea. Happiness floods through me when she spots a bat ray gliding along the ocean floor in search of its next meal. I love how her fear of the ocean vanished with her transformation. It's the best thing I could've hoped for, knowing how much her fear clung to her on the surface.

We reach a clearing past the kelp forest, and Ava slows. She won't be able to keep up with me all night, even at my slowest pace, and even though her eyes still remain wide and sparkling, I sense the exhaustion she tries and fails to hide from me.

I swim around her a few times to let her rest. Her hair

catches in the current of my making, spinning it in front of her, veiling her view of me. She floats up a few feet and gets caught in a current that tries to steal her away. Flicking my tail, I swim past her to catch her in my arms before motioning her to hook her arms around my neck.

Her smooth stomach presses into my back, putting pressure on my dorsal fin, sending a rush of tingles through me. Her body fits perfectly against mine, now sharing the warmth that blossoms between us.

I dart forward, swimming her at the speed gifted to me by the ocean. Every merperson has a gift. Some are exceptional hunters, others can heal, and me? I was made to be one of the king's warriors, though I've denied myself the position like my dad had.

The world blurs around me, and I focus on the world straight ahead. The ocean floor sneaks up on me as I enter shallow water to take Ava to some rocks not far from the harbor of Catalina Island, where the Ocean Jewel will dock for the day. It's too dark to be seen from the shore, and there's just something about wanting to see Ava on the surface in her mermaid form that pushes me to do so.

Ava spits out water and intakes a breath of air near my ear. A shiver rolls over me, and I tread water with her, waves swaying us back and forth. The full moon shines a glittering trail across the surface of the glowing ocean, bathing Ava's skin in ethereal, silver light. I swim us to the closest rock and hoist myself onto it before tugging her out of the water to sit next to me. She rests her tail over mine, her warm skin keeping the chill of night at bay.

I trail my fingers over the side of her tail, feeling the smooth yet tough surface of her scales. Now that we're out of the water, staring at the surface world around us, I can feel Ava's thoughts shift away from the magnificence of the sea and to something darker.

"For someone who was terrified of the ocean, you're doing surprisingly well," I say to break the silence and pull her from her thoughts.

She pouts for a second before smirking at the waves. "You're as surprised as I am. I never thought I'd ever go back in the water, let alone explore its depths."

"Why is that?" I can't stop myself from asking, though I know it stirs something sad in her. But I feel like I need to know everything about her—the good, the bad, everything— so it matches the rush of emotions the bond bestowed on me when I gave her part of my life. My soul. I need to let Ava know that I'm here no matter what. I want nothing more than to do everything I can to see to it that she's always happy.

She bows her head, letting her damp hair shield her face from me. I'd yell at the ocean for making her feel this way if she wouldn't think the action was crazy.

"When I was a kid, my sister and I were playing in the waves late in the day. We got caught in a riptide, and she drowned. The ocean swept her away. It was a miracle that a neighbor managed to even save me."

Anger rushes through me. The ocean gives life but is quick to take them away. And knowing this isn't Ava's first encounter with the unrelenting ocean makes me believe it has wanted her all along. That it was fate for her to be here now. Ava never stood a chance. She would have never been given the choice. "And now the ocean finally got another girl it wanted," I say more to the dark water than to her.

"You hate that I'm here now." She says the words like she's certain they're true.

But the thing is, they're not. I would jump off the yacht and save her all over again. From the second I saw her, I knew she was supposed to be in my future. I just wish it wasn't this way. That the ocean would've had patience. Maybe it knew she'd have denied it.

I turn my gaze away from her, afraid how she'll react to my words. "I hate that you never had the choice—I hate that I'm selfishly enjoying your presence, how I got so lucky to have such a beautiful, smart, caring person with me now, sharing my world. I hate that I don't regret anything." Running my hand through my hair, I push it back.

Ava reaches for my hands and holds them in hers. I relax under her touch, thankful she doesn't reject me or despise me over my admission. Her cold fingers curl around mine, and I bring her hands to my lips to blow a breath of warm air on them, though I know the cold air wouldn't bother her in this form.

"I'm not going to lie. Everything about this terrified me. I'm still terrified. You wasted your one chance at transforming someone on me. You gave me, a girl you've known for so little time, the ring that was intended for your mate so I could return to my life back in Azure Waters." The words spill from her mouth as she bares her soul to me. Tears glass her eyes at her own admission. "And I don't even know what will happen when I get back."

"I didn't waste anything on you, Ava," I whisper, turning my gaze to the stars. Because I didn't. The ocean put her in my path. If I'd never saved her life, that would have been a waste—tragic. Unforgivable. I just don't know if she can see our future together yet, not when her human world dangles in front of her, threatening to be washed out to sea.

Her doubt combats my certainty, and one of her thoughts about a human boy trickles to me. But it's not a thought about her liking someone. It's about how she did and then didn't. She's afraid of her feelings for me. She's afraid that one day she won't like me anymore. And now I'm terrified at the thought. Because without our official bonding, Ava might never reciprocate the feelings I have for her born from the sea, from giving her a piece of me.

Instead of revealing her thoughts out loud, she says, "The sea air might be getting to your head."

I shake my fear away and laugh. "It clears my mind if anything. You make me think past the day that's ahead of us."

She doesn't smile, her eyes still shining with tears as she struggles with her thoughts. Thoughts I'll prove to her are unwarranted. Because I have faith in the ocean. It wouldn't have given me to her if this wasn't meant to be. I know it. I can't let her doubt take that from me.

When she doesn't say anything, I wrap my arms around her, holding her close. "Please, don't look so sad."

She rests her head on my shoulder, and I pull her even closer and into my lap so she can hear how my heart beats in sync with hers, just for her.

"It's just—I can't envision my future, Carter," she admits to me, and even though her words sting a little, I relish in her honesty. Her everything.

"Then just be with me in the now." It's what I want most. Because keeping her in the present with me will help her see more clearly. I'll make sure of it.

She nods. "Okay. I can do that. Why don't you show me more of your world?"

"You mean *our* world," I say, smiling. I love including Ava in my existence. I love everything about having her with me.

Shifting her off my lap, I adjust the waterproof bag across my side and then jump back into the waves. Ava dives after me, hugging her arms around my shoulders without me even having to ask her to do so.

I smile to myself, holding my hands over hers, and dive us deeper into the ocean's glowing depths. I can't wait to show her everything in our world.

Our world.

I love the sound of that, and with the warmth flourishing through me in waves from Ava, I know she loves the sound of that, too.

6

INTO THE DEEP

I ALMOST DON'T WANT THE moon to set. Ava hovers in the water in front of me smiling, her sky eyes sparkling with an excitement I want to devour in another kiss. Reaching out, I push her floating hair away and close the distance. She kisses me first, sending a dozen images of me in moments she can't stop thinking about into my mind. I gently pinch the ridge separating her tail from her luminous skin while sliding my tail against hers, and she hums a moan against my lips.

I break away and swim a circle around her, twirling her in a current of my making. She's unintentionally driving me wild with her desire, but I'm too nervous to let her feel mine, to let her know how much her transformation ignited my spark in feelings I don't know how to handle except to swim them off.

She grins at me, motioning me to come close again for another kiss. "I'm sorry. I didn't mean to show you that." Even in the glowing ocean, I spot the rosy blush tinting her cheeks.

I slide my fingers through hers, holding her in place, so she doesn't float away on my still moving current. "You don't have to apologize. I like it...a lot."

Giggling, she releases a few tiny bubbles from her lips. She responds to my comment with another smile, her cheeks reddening even more, and I swim the both of us in a circle before jetting along the sand.

Ava's voice trickles into my mind, but she doesn't speak to me directly. She keeps thinking to herself about how cute every animal is that she spots in the kelp forest. It's easy to forget she's never seen marine life outside of an aquarium, and I love showing her all of it. If she's this excited about some purple hydrocoral and mackerel, I can't wait to show her one of the mola molas that frequents the waters around Catalina Island, where the Ocean Jewel dropped anchor.

Flipping her in my arms, I hold her below me, swimming us down a submerged rock to the sand. She extends her arms, laughing in my mind.

"What is that?" Ava asks, pointing at something resting in

the sand.

I dive us closer and slow down, gliding through the water. "The human-given name is an angel shark."

"Do you know the names of every creature in the ocean?" she asks.

"The local stuff. We don't really need to know, though. Watch." I open my mind to Ava and envision the features of the angel shark, drawing a picture of it in my head from its flat, diamond-shaped body to the sandy color of its skin that blends it in with the sea floor.

"Whoa!" Ava says out loud, sending a bubble into my face.

I chuckle and swim us another few feet. "That's a torpedo ray."

She projects a cooing noise into my mind and stretches out to touch it.

"You might not want to get too clo—"

Ava jerks back, sending us up a few feet. She releases a yelp through the water, and I spin her around. She holds her hand to her heart, her spark blinking wildly through her fingers, making mine speed up.

"What the heck was that?" she asks, glancing at her fingers.

I tug her hand from her chest and bring it to my lips to kiss her fingers. "Are you okay? Torpedo rays are electric. If you were still human, that would've been a lot worse than a little shock."

She bobs her head, her blue eyes wide. "It surprised me is all." A blip of fear pours from her to me as she thinks of some of the ocean's fiercest predators.

Pulling her in close, I wrap my arms around her. "You're safe. Don't worry."

She nestles her face in the crook of my neck hugging me while I swim her away from the ocean floor and toward the surface. The sky lightens above us with the oncoming dawn, and all it takes is for Ava to think to herself about sleeping in a bed to get me to swim us to where the Ocean Jewel floats in a marina in a cove near the looming island.

"It should be safe to sneak back on in a minute. Captain Briggs and the others are most likely eating," I say, feeling Ava's trepidation.

I stop under the yacht and peer up. Ava tilts her head back, still grasping onto my shoulders. The movement presses her stomach into mine, and I wonder if I could convince her to stay with me another few minutes to watch the sun rise from here.

But she's already thinking about transforming back into a human.

"We'll enter on the swim platform," I think to her.

She watches a seal dart by us before looking into my eyes. "What if I can't transform back?"

I suppress her rising panic, doing my best to project my

assurance to her. "You will, I promise."

Floating a foot away, still linking my hands with hers, I close my eyes and will myself to transform into a human. Heat rushes through my heart and expands through the rest of me and then the water shifts, cooling what feels like several degrees, though it doesn't actually change. My chest tightens, my lungs now needing air, but I remain treading in place, hoping Ava can follow my lead. If she sees me as a human instead of a merman, she might will herself to transform easier than if I stayed a merman and waited. As my accidental, unofficial mate, her mermaid nature will gravitate toward the form I take and vice versa.

My vision blurs, but I can still see her vibrant eyes trailing down my body, just taking me in. Her spark flickers faster, and I tighten my jaw to stop myself from smiling. Her reddening cheeks get to me every time, and I wish I could kiss her blush away.

I puff out a bubble from my lips, my gills gone but the small amount of oxygen they pulled into my body remains. Ava pouts her bottom lip, flaring her nostrils as she breathes in the sea, and then she closes her eyes. Her expression speaks volumes, though her thoughts have been cut off from me with my transformation.

Pain sweeps across her face, twisting her features. She arches back and groans into the water as her tail splits and her scales vanish. A wave of fear crashes into me, and Ava thrashes, making me nearly lose my grip on her. She changed back as quickly as I had hoped, but she's now in shock from the cold water and not being able to breathe.

I hook my fingers to her waist and propel us to the surface, breaking through to the air. Ava coughs and spits, expelling the water from her lungs, her body still thrashing as she tries to stay afloat. There's no doubt in my mind she's exhausted. She doesn't even realize she's curled her naked body around me, using me to keep her head above water.

With one hand, I grab onto the swimming platform to keep us from going back under. Ava shudders a breath and freezes, a wave of her embarrassment pushing away my desire. I shift and hand her bikini bottoms to her, trying to make the situation less awkward for her. I hope she'll soon be comfortable enough around me that being naked to transform won't be a big deal to her. Though I like that it is at the same time.

Ava ties her bikini bottoms, using me to support her, and she releases a quivering breath. "Okay," she whispers into my ear when she's ready.

I lift her onto the platform with one arm, and she rolls onto her back, panting and flushing again when I climb aboard naked. I tug my clothes from my waterproof bag and get dressed, blocking the early morning sun from Ava.

Turning back toward her, I catch her gaping at me, and I clench my jaw to stop from smiling. I want nothing more than to scoop her up and carry her back to her room for her, because every time she moves, she groans. I offer my hand out to her instead.

She groans again and flops back to look at the sky. "I can't. My body's on fire, which means you lied to me, you know."

I smirk, rubbing my hand on the scruff of my cheek. "You asked if the transformation hurt. I find it uncomfortable, so technically I didn't lie from my experience."

Sighing, she moves her feet, wiggling her toes like she can't believe she has them. "You're just going to have to leave me here. I really don't think I can get up."

"I guess I'll have to carry you then," I say, chuckling while I lift her into my arms.

She giggles, batting my chest with her hand. "Carter, put me down."

I grin at her beautiful face lighting up with a smile, and she rubs her hands across the muscles of my chest and to my shoulders, memorizing the feeling of my body with her fingers. Spinning her toward the row of seats along the guardrail, I make her laugh again and set her in one to get her off the platform. I think if I set her on her feet she might fall overboard again.

Ava shrugs into her dress, peering at herself in the metal trim along the wall of the yacht. Her wet hair frames her face, dripping with saltwater, reminding me of us being in the ocean just moments ago. She's incredibly beautiful, her smooth skin flush and still glistening with sea spray. I step forward to sit next to her, hoping to kiss the salt from her pouty lips to show her how perfect she is, but voices trickle through the air from above, stopping me from moving.

It'll be strange to be around her friends now, considering they're more invested in Ava's new bond with me than I ever expected from humans. Human bonds are more complex and shift so often. It's hard for me to determine the norms of this group, but I'm guessing if they see us out here in clothes from last night, they'll pry Ava for details, and with details comes the risk of messing up, something Ava and I can't afford.

"Come on," I say, reaching out my hand to her.

She teeters on her feet, and I hold her weight without picking her up. It's not normal to carry her around like I would in the sea, and I doubt she'd let me yet. She straightens her shoulders with determination, pushing through her exhaustion. We stroll to the elevator, thankfully not running into anyone along the way.

"You sure Ava's not in her room?" It's Sapphire's voice coming from the stairs, probably waiting on the elevator I called down.

Instead of getting on the elevator and risk getting cornered in a tiny box by her friends, I nudge Ava toward the stairs. She grimaces, groaning every step of the way up to the sundeck, though she keeps pace with me. I feel bad that she's aching so much, and if her friends weren't looking for her, I'd offer to give her a massage.

I shake my head, pushing the thought from my mind with the hum of the elevator about to stop on the sundeck. Tugging my shirt off, I set it on top of the cabinet and grab two towels. Ava strips from her dress and sighs while wrapping the warm towel around her shivering body.

Her eyes widen as the elevator door slides open, and Giselle and Sapphire stand in front of us, gaping like we were the last people they expected to be up here. Their confusion morphs into something I can't determine, and I offer them a smile.

Giselle glances back and forth between me and Ava. "I was just at our room trying to wake your ass up, but the door was locked."

Ava tenses next to me, squeezing her eyes shut. "Crap. I must've accidentally locked it."

The sudden need to get out of the way of Ava's friends' line of questions washes over me, and I run my hand over Ava's shoulder. "Hey, don't worry. I can get the spare key."

She pouts at me, begging me with her eyes not to abandon her with her friends. I almost don't, but Giselle releases a weird noise, grinning at Sapphire, and I inch toward the stairs, so they stop studying me.

In the sea, merpeople from the same pod are naturally curious about someone's intended mate, but there isn't the same need to impress anyone or go through all the social norms humans do when bringing an outsider into their families—which Ava's friends feel like to me with how close they are to her.

And the pressure gets to me. I wish I had tried harder to form bonds—friendships—growing up in San Francisco, but it always felt too risky. Still does. I like to enjoy the benefits of being on land without getting involved with people, though now I have the need to learn more about Ava and every facet of her life.

Rushing down the stairs, I run toward the dining terrace wanting to do something to impress her friends without missing much of the conversation between Ava and her friends. I only make it halfway to the dining terrace when I run into Keith, carrying a tray.

"Can I?" I ask, motioning to the array of fruit and muffins in his hands.

He laughs and gives me the tray. "You look like you're having a good time."

"It's something." I leave him chuckling and take the stairs two at a time, not even bothering to get the spare key to open Ava's door. I thought I wanted to escape her friends, but something inside me draws me right back to Ava.

I laugh to myself, glancing at the tray. I guess I can leave the water, but my merman instincts still linger inside me in the form of wanting to feed Ava and take care of her after a long night. I don't go all the way on the sundeck though and hover in the stairwell, listening to Giselle and Sapphire laugh.

"It's not a big deal," Ava says, her voice failing to stay even, revealing that whatever they were talking about is definitely a huge deal to her. "If you think we had sex, think again."

Oh. I tilt my head back, closing my eyes. Hearing her mention sex, and then feeling her emotions rise with the thought, nearly makes me rush onto the sundeck to launch over the railing and into the sea to cool off.

My merman instincts make it hard to stand on my legs. I knew I'd feel like this when I met my intended mate, but feeling everything I've only heard about gives me an understanding to why mates jump into everything so suddenly. It's easy to submerge myself in every hot emotion Ava projects to me even without me being next to her.

"Hey, I wasn't thinking that," Giselle says.

"But now I am," I whisper to myself.

"But we did kiss...and I saw him naked." Ava's voice draws me from the stairwell, but no one glances my way. The three of them sit in the hot tub, grinning and laughing. Ava's face burns with the same flush I feel rising into my own neck.

"Oh, my God. I bet he's so damn sexy," Sapphire says, smacking the water with her hand.

I can't stop myself from grinning because Ava smiles, sinking lower into the hot tub, clearly thinking about me.

"You have no idea," she says, fanning herself, her face

glistening in the steam of the bubbling water.

Giselle's eyes meet mine, and she waves to me. "Oh, but I think I do."

I straighten my shoulders, smirking at Ava as her eyes leave my face to travel down my chest and to my stomach like she hadn't just seen me a minute ago. Setting the tray down on the table, I close the distance, all three of them laughing now, and Ava sinks underwater.

"The water's great," Giselle says, still laughing. "Join us."

I step in and slide next to Ava still holding her breath underwater. Reaching down, I touch her chin until she relents and surfaces. We hold each other's gazes, her spark flickering in the same quickness as mine.

"You heard everything, didn't you?" she asks, flicking her eyes to her friends and back to me.

I open my mouth to tell her it's not a big deal, but Giselle splashes water at us and says, "Look, Carter. Just so you know. If you want to hang out with Ava, you have to know that I'm her BFF, and we talk. Actually, all of us talk, and you're new, so we're going to talk about you."

Ava touches my leg underwater. I'm not sure her cheeks will ever return to normal, her embarrassment making me want to figure out how to get her away from her friends so she can relax around me. Get comfortable.

"Only the good stuff," she whispers.

"Especially the good stuff," Sapphire says.

Ava splashes her friends, leaning into me more, and I slide my arm over her shoulders to let her sink against me. She hides her warm face against my chest, brushing her lips to my skin with each of her deep breaths.

"And another thing," Giselle says. "If I start to hear anything bad, you better watch out. I know people."

I chuckle.

Ava groans, tilting up to look at me. "She doesn't know people."

Giselle presses her lips together without smiling. "Oh, you know I know people, Aves."

I match her fake seriousness with my own, nodding my head. "Got it," I say, instead of what's really on my mind about how I'm the last person she has to worry about. Ava already has my spark, and I'd never do wrong by her. I want to give her the world. I'll break every law in the sea to do so.

"Good."

Sapphire grins, laughing. "Now that everything's settled, are you joining us for a day of adventures?"

She's talking about their plans at Catalina Island, which I know include snorkeling, something Ava wouldn't have wanted to do, and we can't reveal her sudden lack of fear of the ocean. It'll draw too much attention.

"Whatever Ava wants to do," I say, turning to Ava. "I'm pretty sure all ocean activities are out, right?"

Sapphire raises her brows. "Just because Ava doesn't go in

the ocean, doesn't mean you can't."

Ava lifts and drops her shoulders. "She's right."

I can tell she doesn't mean it, and I want her to know that being with her, even doing nothing, is a hundred times better than any activity her friends could come up with. "I live most of my time on the ocean, but hanging with you is something I haven't had much time to do."

She smiles, her eyes and nose crinkling with the happiness I've stirred in her. I could survive on her feelings, just being with her, holding her to me, losing myself in the blue of her sparkling eyes.

"Okay, you're definitely not invited to go snorkeling with us. Ava, he's all yours," Giselle says. "I expect him to show you a good time, too."

I reach up and brush Ava's hair from her face. She smiles at me, another wave of happiness mixed with lust and something new—trust and certainty.

Leaning in, I kiss her in front of her friends. "I will," I whisper into her lips.

She releases a tiny breath. "I know."

7

MERMAN NATURE

"YOU'VE CLEANED YOURSELF UP. YOU goin' out with Ava again?" Keith asks, coming up next to me in the galley.

I finish packing the picnic basket and close the top. "Yeah."

Keith reaches into the storage compartment and offers me a blanket. "You've been hanging out with her a lot."

"She's amazing."

Patting my back, Keith says, "Gotta love a fling. I'm surprised, actually. I don't think I've ever seen you give any babe a second glance since you joined the crew. I thought you might've had a girlfriend at home, but I've only ever heard you call your parents."

I keep my gaze trained on the basket, trying not to let his words get to me. "Ava's the one, man."

He laughs. "Right."

I meet his gaze. "She is."

"Good luck, dude."

I bump my knuckles to his proffered fist. "Don't need it."

Leaving Keith laughing and shaking his head, I stroll to the stairwell, taking it up to the guest staterooms. I set the picnic basket down at my feet and knock on Ava's door. She greets me with a smile, her room smelling of some sort of tropical fruit fragrance that makes me intake an automatic breath, because I've never smelled anything as good as her.

She twirls once, showing off her smooth legs in her spin, and I wish I could close the space between us and brush my lips to hers, but I'm too anxious to even go into her cabin. She's sending me mixed emotions, and I don't want to rush things. I'm going against everything I've been taught to let her make the first move.

I stand in the hallway, unable to take my eyes from her pink lips. "You look beautiful."

"Thank you. I wasn't sure what to wear. I didn't really pack for hiking or anything." She shifts on her feet.

I nudge the picnic basket with my foot, drawing her attention to it. "You're perfect the way you are. Come on.

Keith's waiting to take us to the dock."

Ava steps closer, and I twine my fingers through hers. She surprises me by tugging me closer to stand on her tiptoes, sliding her hand over my side to balance herself to whisper in my ear. "Do you think I should tell my friends that my fear of the ocean isn't what it used to be?" she asks, her perfume making me inhale again.

She leans back, grimacing at my frown. I draw her hand up from my side and run my finger over the ring I gave her. "This stops you from a forced change, but it doesn't stop the transformation all together. Once it starts, you can't just stop it either."

"Oh."

"I'm not saying stay out of the ocean, but you have to be careful. You've only transformed once..." Damn, I hate myself a little for disappointing her and turning her nerves into full-blown anxiety that makes me doubt what the hell I'm doing.

"And I wasn't exactly that great at it," she says, putting words in my mouth—ones I completely disagree with.

I touch her cheek, getting her to look at me. "You did perfect, but something as little as a thought could trigger you to change. It's better to just stay out of the water for now unless you're going in to transform. The ocean will be more alluring than ever, and you might actually never want to return to shore."

She grimaces, cocking her head. "Doubt it but okay. I

don't want to risk messing things up."

I hope she's right about her doubt, because I want nothing more than a human life on land with her, but I'd understand if she chooses the ocean. And I'll follow her anywhere.

Pursing her lips, she loses herself in thoughts I wish I could hear because then I'd know what to say to snuff out the wave of sadness crashing over her.

I try to anyway and say, "It won't be like this forever, Aves."

It worked. Her glassy eyes clear, and she smirks. "You hope."

It's the only thing I hope for besides her falling madly in love with me. I don't say it, though. I kiss her instead, opening up my emotions to her just enough that she can feel the hope I carry inside me.

She laces her fingers through mine and pulls me toward the elevator, sending me a brand new emotion I've never felt from her—like attraction and happiness, desire and need, everything good about Ava woven together.

And it's just for me.

Ava sits on the blanket beside me with her legs over mine, allowing me to massage her calves. Every few seconds, she releases a moan and covers her mouth with her hand, laughing. I love seeing her like this, relaxed and smiling, giving me every bit of her attention.

"If you keep doing that, I don't know if I'll ever want to return to the yacht," Ava says, biting her lip as she smiles at me.

I smirk. "Is that so?" She has no idea that her words make me want to try to convince her to stay here on this beach with her in my arms.

She hums her agreement and tilts her head closer to brush her lips to mine for a short moment, just a tease of a kiss that sends my heart racing.

"This might be my favorite day ever," she adds, shifting to slide her legs off mine to lie on the blanket.

I lean back on my elbows, leaving no space between us, and stare at the sea stretching into the distance. "Even though we're only sitting here?"

"Especially because we're just sitting here. I had no idea I'd ever enjoy the ocean again, but you picked such an amazing spot, and I'm enjoying getting to know you. I just wish I wasn't so—I want to know more, but..."

Her words trail off, and I turn my gaze from the ocean to her cerulean eyes the color of her tail as a mermaid. She turns her face away from me, letting pieces of her hair, loose from her bun, fall into her face.

"You can ask me anything," I whisper, pushing the tresses from her cheek. "I'll always be honest with you."

She clears her throat and blush sweeps across her face at whatever thoughts cross her mind. "I'm not sure I can handle..." Smiling, her nose crinkling, she surprises me by running her finger over my chest and down my stomach like she can't resist touching me. I close my eyes for a minute, relishing the sensation as much as her company.

"What is it?" I inch closer, twisting to look at her straight on.

She giggles, combing her hair behind her ear. "I'm struggling with my feelings, and I want to know if it's because—or how—or if you..." She heaves a breath, fumbling to put her thoughts into words, and groans. "I feel like I don't know anything. All my questions are so embarrassing."

I chuckle, feeling my own cheeks warm because of her. "All of them?"

"Every last one."

I twine my fingers with hers and bring her hand to my lips to kiss her knuckles. "Can't be any more embarrassing than having your friends cheer us on every time we lea—" Another wave of heat cascades over me from her, and I bend down and rest my head on her shoulder. "Okay, how about you ask and I answer your questions without saying anything at all?"

"Oh, um." Her breath quickens, and she giggles again, knowing I'm referring to opening our minds to each other. Her musical voice wraps around me only to draw me closer. She waves her hand in front of her face. "Okay."

I move to close the distance between us, and her hand

flies up to touch my lips, stopping me from kissing her. Smiling against her fingers, I say, "How about I ask myself all the embarrassing questions?"

She grins and whispers, "Ask yourself what it's like when—" She squeezes her eyes shut, squealing at the same time she kisses me, flooding my mind with hundreds of scenarios that leave me kissing her harder in response, trying my best not to let my imagination get the best of me and turn her curiosity into a fantasy.

She pulls back, her eyes wide, her mouth hanging agape. "Whoa."

Reaching up, I touch my fingers to her chin, and her open mouth turns into the widest smile before she laughs. She shifts to her side and rolls half on top of me to hide her face into my shoulder.

"Too much?" I ask.

She shakes her head, still hiding her face and breathing her warm breath against my skin. "I need you to ask me another normal question or else my heart is going to break through my chest."

"Don't worry, I'll catch it," I tease.

She groans. "Carter."

Smiling, I ask, "What's your favorite season?"

Releasing a slow breath, she turns back over and away from me but still keeps her body pressed into mine. "Seasons? What are those?" She laughs and taps my arm when I raise my eyebrow before grinning at how cute she is, even making a bad joke referring to the mild temperatures Azure Waters has year round. "Probably the one where I'm not going to have to jump into freezing water on the full moon."

I bump her shoulder. "So same as mine."

"Favorite color?" she asks, running her feet over the smooth rocks of the pebbly beach.

I consider saying blue like her eyes to combat her joke with something as bad but then say, "Green."

"Mine's gray."

"Gray?"

She bobs her head, rubbing her lips together. "I know. Did I mention I'm boring?"

"Far from it." I don't think Ava could ever be boring, even her smile entertains me. "Favorite food?" I ask.

"Mexican. Cheese enchiladas in a red sauce to be more specific. Maybe tacos. Yours is seafood, isn't it?"

I tuck away the information for when we return back to Azure Waters. I doubt Ava will ever ask me to hunt a fish for her straight from the ocean, which I have to remind myself over and over that she's human born and would prefer something hot, in a chair, and not tasting of the sea. "You'd think, since I eat a whole lot of it but no. It's any type of dessert. I could eat it for every meal no matter what it is. I might even trade my tail for some if given the option."

Her whole face lights up, and she taps her hand to my

arm. "Well, it's a good thing I bake."

"Don't mess with me," I say.

She laughs. "I'm not. You get permission from the chef, and I'll make dessert tonight."

Her offer stirs my merman nature—not because she wants to feed me, though I'd love it if she did, but because she offers to do something specifically for me. I trace my fingers down her arm. "I'm holding you to it."

Leaning into her, I rest my head on hers, letting silence fall between us as I think about everything I want to experience with Ava. It's all I can think about—us and our future, especially watching my spark blink in her chest. If she were an ocean-born mermaid, we'd plan our coupling ceremony to officially vow eternity as mates to each other. From her rush of questions, I know she's already throwing her human rationale to the waves without even realizing it. But I'm afraid to explain how I feel. She would automatically assume it was because I changed her, and my feelings ignited the second I laid my eyes on her. I never want her to ever doubt my bond to her, and hopefully her bond to me.

Ava squeezes my hand, sitting up next to me. Peering at the horizon, she studies the vast ocean glittering white under the sun. A weird feeling rushes into me from her, darker than the constant happiness and attraction that has been pouring to me with every laugh and kiss, and I can't stop myself from tensing.

And then I see them.

In the distance, a pod of bottlenose dolphins play in the current of a boat speeding past. They break away and propel from the water, turning to face our direction. I realize what I'm feeling washing from Ava is jealousy as she watches the playful pod teasing her. Because dolphins, seals and sea lions, some whales, they love a mermaid's attention.

Her sudden urge to enter the water sneaks up on me so fast I can't stop the panic rising in my chest. She hops to her feet before I can reach for her and jogs to the waves, letting the ocean wash over her bare feet.

"Ava, what are you doing?" I ask, trying to bring her attention back to me, but it's no use.

The call of the sea summons her. I can feel it in my bones. She strolls deeper, and I get to my feet. But she's fast at unintentionally putting space between us.

She points at the dolphins. "Aren't they beaut—" Bending forward, Ava releases a cry. Her body reacts to the sudden transformation taking over her, triggered by the silent invitation from the dolphins wanting to play.

Under the white sun, her skin illuminates with a pearlescent sheen. "Carter! It's happening! I can't stop."

She releases a sob, her jewel eyes turning from the ocean to glance in my direction, but she doesn't get a chance to look at me. Her muscles spasm, and she arches her back, wobbling on her feet. I rush to her, my own panic stealing my breath. I need to get her in the water. I need to make sure no one sees. This could be it. I might have to take her to sea.

By the time I reach her, scales already sprout on her legs, sparkling the same blue as the sky. She cries again, frozen in place, and I hook an arm around her back and the other behind her knees, stopping her from falling into the surf.

Her agony hits me hard, and I push my legs to carry us faster into the waves. She gasps air she can't breathe, and if she doesn't get underwater, she could suffocate. It takes a breath of the sea to complete the transformation. This is the reason human-born merpeople move into the sea. They have to be fully connected to it to control their transformation. The longer Ava stays away, the worse it might get. I was stupid for thinking I could even control the situation when her heart drifts from land to carry us both into the deep.

But there's no turning back. I made her a promise that she could maintain her human life. The idea of breaking her heart like that kills me. I can't do it. I have to figure out another way. I have to protect her and take care of her and see to it she's happy.

My own guilt chills my insides at not being able to do anything but carry Ava into the water. Her pectoral fins brush my bare stomach, her muscles still rippling. Her tight dress stretches at the seams as her dorsal fin erupts from her back, and I tug the fabric over her head as fast as I can before it rips free, leaving her with nothing to wear apart from her bikini.

She groans, pressing her face into my chest, struggling to shimmy out of her bikini bottoms in my arms. The side strap frays from the ridge swelling from her smooth waist, and I hook my fingers around the fabric. Ava's panic is far worse than her embarrassment of me undressing her, so I tug her bikini bottoms off as fast as I can.

Her legs fuse together, and she thrashes, not giving me a choice but to let her go. She abandons me, flicking her tail, now submerged in the sea. Relief washes through me, coming through our bond, but it fades into sorrow that leaves me breathless even though my lungs continue to inhale the salty air.

I strip out of my board shorts and shove them into my bag with Ava's clothes and dive into the shallows, taking only a second to transform. Ava swims in a circle a few dozen feet away from me like she's afraid of going any farther. Her need for me pushes me to swim faster, and I feel like a failure for not coming up with a plan, for preparing her for the worst in a moment like this where she accidentally transformed.

But this isn't the worst. We're okay, and no one saw us. I send a silent prayer to the sea for helping me protect Ava's heart, for protecting my own. For not forcing us to disappear to a place I know she'd be unhappy. The colonies lack everything she's comfortable with on land. I couldn't imagine dragging her from her luxurious lifestyle to live in what is basically a hollow rock within shimmering walls containing powerful, protective magic. She deserves more than such a life. She deserves more than what I can offer in the sea.

"Ava, calm down," I manage to say when my nerves finally settle enough that I can think straight. "There's no one around, and if they were, they can't see us. We're safe."

I swim around her, twirling her in a quick current that draws her into my arms. Burying my face in her floating hair, free of her hair tie, I suck in a calming breath of the sea, doing my best to settle her panic for her.

"But I can't change back," she thinks to me, fighting my attempt to overwhelm her with all the best emotions inside me.

I never considered such a thing. Her heart could long for the sea against her mind. It may never let her transform back into a human. The only thing I can think to do is to let her heart win, to get it out of her system. Maybe then, we can return to land. At least I hope.

I close myself off a bit, fearing the foreign-to-her emotions might only make things worse. She's confused and scared enough already. "Then why don't we go for a swim? I could tell how much you wanted to see the dolphins."

I lace my fingers through hers and swim us deeper into the surf. She doesn't try to swim, just letting me carry her on a current, peering around the sunlit waters with wide, jewel-eyes. Her fear transforms into wonder, and I pick up my pace to dart us along the bottom until she finally flicks her tail and swims beside me.

Small fish jet around us, daring to get close enough to swim in the current we create. The creatures are drawn to Ava as much as I am, and I grin at the laughter that sends bubbles from her mouth and toward the surface.

Her mind wanders from the ocean life around us to settle on how much she enjoys the feeling of touching my body, of how it feels when our bodies align in the sea. I turn my attention to her, wanting with everything in me to lose myself in the lust stirred from her mermaid nature as we're closer than ever in the sea, with our minds open to each other. I swim faster, ignoring my very nature to pull her into my arms and hold her against me. I'm trying to get her to remember how much she loves the land and not how incredible being in the sea with me is in this moment.

Dolphins chatter, sending their musical voices bouncing around us. Without having to see them, I can sense them speeding up fast to greet us. It helps push Ava's desire from my mind. Diving us deeper, I take her to look at the leopard sharks on the sandy bottom, wanting to show her everything I can to keep her attention split so she's not concentrating solely on me. If she continues to do so, I'm afraid I'll never take her back to land. I'm afraid she'd let me.

"We have no predators in the sea." I interrupt her wavering thoughts so I can concentrate on something apart from our skin touching. I run my finger over one of the sharks without grazing it before flipping to swim under her, facing her so I can see her smiling face. Bringing my hand to the spark in her chest, I say, "Our essence protects us."

My distraction works as she thinks to herself about all the biggest predators in the sea and how she never considered them to be a threat with me by her side. I press my lips together, swelling with so many emotions, thankful that she trusts me enough to always keep her safe. Instead of saying anything, I pull her to me and propel us forward without letting any space get between us. She buries her face in my neck, just holding me without looking at the sea around us.

The dolphins call to us, sending their bell-like voices through the water. Confusion washes over Ava at the musical songs of the animals, because she's never heard them like a mermaid before. And I love how much she loves it.

I swim us up to the dolphins, slowing down to join the playful pod. A few dozen dolphins close the distance, letting us swim with them, and I let Ava pull away from me to join them on her own as they rub against her, letting her pet them as they swim.

A few more dolphins get between us, calling out to each other in a game that turns into a race. I groan to myself, annoyed by how enthralled they are with Ava that one of the larger males pushes me away, now playing keep away with my mate. And they swim faster, caging her in, wanting her to follow along with their games that push her toward the surface.

I spot the silhouette of a boat cutting the water ahead, and the dolphins jet right toward it, drawn to the wakes created by the propellers. If they continue as they do, they'll force Ava to break the surface with them, and out of water, there is nothing to protect Ava from being seen by the people on the boats. The ocean magic remains in the sea, and it might very well rise up to knock any potential threats from discovering the merpeople secret. Because King Attilonious controls the seas. He doesn't even need to be around to protect every merperson when his ocean magic does it for him.

"Ava! I yell, realizing she's starting to freak out because she's trapped in the pod's current. "Dive. There's a boat up ahead."

Some of the pod breaks away and launch through the surface to jump in the air. There's no doubt that the entire boat of people watch their acrobatics. The dolphins jostle Ava between them, and she can't free herself.

"They think this is a game," she calls to me.

One by one, the dolphins breach until its only two male dolphins flanking Ava. They squish her between them, releasing happy calls as they head to the surface. But I'm faster. Flicking my fin, I hook my hands onto Ava's tail, yanking her back at the same time they yank her forward to breach. Diving down, I swim space between us and the pod. I hover next to Ava as she drops her hands from her face, her expression scrunched with pain I can nearly feel in my own tail.

I release a few bubbles and sink down to inspect the base of her tail where her caudal fin now looks slightly dislocated. I put pressure on it for a second but don't get the chance to try to shift it back in place. Ava's muscles spasm under my fingers. The pain from me pulling her away from the dolphins triggers her to transform back into a human.

I swim up and meet her startled eyes.

"Carter!" she shouts at me, her body changing faster than ever.

Her words disappear from my mind, her humanity cutting our telepathic connection. She's so out of control that there's no way she'll be able to transform back into a mermaid, and as a human she'll need to breathe. And soon.

If she doesn't, she'll drown.

8

SINKING INTO DEEP WATER

I SCOOP AVA INTO MY arms, jetting us as fast as I can to the surface. I've seen a few free divers reach several hundred feet below surface without getting decompression sickness. And since Ava only carries the air brought into her lungs from her gills, the last thing I'm worried about is how she'll handle the ascension. I just need to make sure she gets the air she needs.

Stopping short of the surface, I give Ava the extra push she needs without surfacing myself. She kicks her legs, bobbing up and down, trying to stay afloat. I inspect her swollen ankle without touching it. It looks bad, but it could've been far worse, and I hate myself for not thinking of another way to free her from the dolphins. She's hurt because I was careless. I got lost in her happiness instead of thinking of her safety. I just—

"Carter? Carter, no one's around." Ava's muffled voice sounds to me from above and she waves her hands to get my attention.

I pop up next to her and release a breath of water from my lungs. She automatically grabs onto me, using me to buoy her to the surface so she can stop kicking her legs. I comb her wet hair from her eyes and study her face, dripping with salt-water.

"I'm too tired to swim. I'll never make it," she whispers, her breath shuddering.

I fan my tail to keep us both above water and cup her face in my hands, trying my best to suppress my nerves to give her more confidence. "Try to transform back. The distance might be too far for me to swim you back in my human form, and it's not safe for me to coast the surface. You can do this."

She pouts her bottom lip, her eyes shining under the sun, and then closes her eyes. "I can't concentrate. My ankle hurts pretty badly. It's what triggered the transformation back."

Her words confirm what I had been thinking, and I frown. We're in this position because I've failed her. How will she ever trust me to take care of her or be here for her for the rest of our lives if I can't even do something as simple as keep a pod of playful dolphins in control? Living on land all my life hindered my ability to be a great mate.

I can't stand staring into her sad eyes a moment longer, so I sink back under to look at her ankle once more. I'm not a healer like my mom, but I know for sure it's not broken. A small blip of embarrassment cuts through Ava's worry, and I jet back to the surface to face her. I've felt her awkwardness over me seeing her naked as a human enough to recognize the cause behind her shift in emotions.

Instead of mentioning that I didn't look at her, which I'm sure will make things worse, I say, "It's bruised, but I don't think it's broken. You're still moving it well. You'll probably heal within an hour or so—one of the benefits of being a mermaid."

"Think we should wait it out and see if I can transform in a bit?" she asks.

Treading out here in the middle of the ocean for anyone to find us, especially with her in pain, is the last thing I want to do. "We might be missed."

"Then they'll have to miss us, because I can't swim or transform," she snaps, her annoyance hitting me in a hot wave. "This whole situation is ridiculous. I probably deserve to be found out here floating half-naked."

I clench my jaw. I would never let such a thing happen to her, and there's no way I'm allowing her to carry the guilt of something I'm at fault for. "Don't blame yourself. I should've been more careful. If I hadn't grabbed you the way I did—"

"Those dolphins would have forced me out of the water. This isn't your fault," she says, touching my cheek.

I swipe my hair from my forehead. "But I—"

She shuts me up with a kiss, pressing her naked body against me while sliding her arms around my neck. My muscles relax under her touch as my mind wanders from the situation to the way her legs feel against my tail.

Slowly pulling back, she says, "Stop. Blame isn't going to help me get back to the shore."

"You're right. But I will. I have an idea." She doesn't need to swim. She doesn't even need to transform. Not with me. I'll risk the surface to see to it that we can go back to land together.

Shifting my bag on my shoulder, I open it and pull out her ripped bikini bottoms to hand to her. If things don't go my way, I'm going to make sure she isn't mortified if someone sees her in the water.

Ava bobs next to me, holding onto my shoulder with one hand while trying to dress with the other. I consider offering to help, but she looks incredibly determined to do it herself, so I wait until she finally manages.

She releases a small breath and meets my smirking gaze. Her cheeks redden with blush, but she doesn't turn away. She drinks me in with her beautiful eyes as I smile at her. In one quick motion, she sweeps her hand across the water, fake glaring, splashing me in the face.

I sink under and swim a tight circle around her, brushing my tail against her torso, sucking in a deep breath to push the memory of her body against mine from my head. I want so badly to transform into my human self, because being this close to Ava in her human form is driving me crazy.

I emerge in front of her so close that she's all I see. Reaching out, I brush her loose hair from her face. "You have to stop looking at me like that."

She smirks, licking the saltwater from her lips. "Like what?"

Her wave of desire and amusement quicken my breath, and I inch closer, leaning in without kissing her.

I clear my throat. "Like you don't want me to take you back to the shore."

"Maybe I don't."

I sink under again at her words, my heart beating in sync with hers so quickly that it's hard to see the pauses in beats as our sparks flicker. In the water, with no land in sight, it's easy to forget that there's more to the world than each other. And I don't think she realizes the weight of her words and how much they burrow into me.

I can't handle such musings or jokes. "Ava," I say, my voice low and throaty as I suppress my very nature as a merman to remind her that she might like the idea in this moment, but it's not what she really wants. "Be careful what you suggest. You have friends—you have family—all waiting for you on land."

She blinks a few times, letting my words sink in. "You're right. I guess we should get back." But she doesn't sound completely convinced, and I'm afraid I'll lose the part of her that loves the land to the sea. I'm not even so sure I care anymore. I love the land, but if Ava can't ignore the call of the sea, I can't either. "You said you had an idea?"

I nod, focusing on my plan instead of how Ava feels as she hooks her legs around me to hug me with her whole body.

"I'm going to need you to hold your breath for a bit, okay? It's not safe to swim the surface with you, but I can take you under. It'll be slow going, but unless you transform back, I don't know of a better way," I say.

She puckers her lips. "I'm sorry for being so much trouble, Carter."

I close the space between us, splashing water as I envelop her in my arms to kiss the pout from her lips. Because she's not trouble. She's learning how to live in my world. None of this is her fault. And I wouldn't change it.

"You're worth the trouble, you know. Like I said before, I don't regret anything," I say, feeling her worry shift into something that warms me inside out.

She smiles into my lips. "How did I get so lucky?"

"Lucky?" I can't stop the question from escaping my mouth. "I—"

"You saved my life. Given me so much more than I ever thought possible." She trails her finger along my jaw. "I don't know how I'll ever repay you."

"You don't owe me anything," I say.

Before I can say anymore, she cuts off my thoughts with a kiss. Ava projects an image of herself running her fingers down my chest and stomach, making me moan into her mouth. Her surprise interruption sends a shudder through me, and I sink under the cool water. I need to swim. If I stay here with her a second longer, I know we'll never make it back.

It takes everything in me to surface to face her, and I refrain from getting lost in her eyes. I'll save that for when we're back on dry land without the ocean beckoning us to stay. Turning my back toward her, I motion for her to slide her arms around my neck. Her breasts press into my back, and I fan my tail a few times, dying to swim and inhale cold water into my lungs.

"Ready, Ava?" I ask in a whisper, my voice trying to betray me.

"As ready as I'll ever be."

"Okay, take a deep breath and hold on."

Ava wraps her whole body around me, pressing her cheek between my shoulder blades. I listen for her to inhale, and dive under. She squeezes me at the fast motion, her heart thumping against my skin. I silently count in my head, getting up to fifty eight before she digs her fingers into my shoulder to let me know she needs to surface.

She releases me to take a breath, and I only give her a few seconds before I tug her back under. As soon as this vacation is over, I'm going to help her build up her ability to stay submerged as long as possible without air. I never knew how important an ability it was until now. Swimming her to shore will take an eternity at this pace.

We continue on in a stop and go swim for miles until the shallows greet me. I release Ava to the surface and swim a dozen more circles around her to push the remaining thoughts of her body against mine from my mind. I transform back into my human form and slide my board shorts back on before I pop to the surface in front of her.

She nearly throws herself at me, making me laugh. "And you thought you were trouble. It's not every day I get to have a beautiful girl cling to my back."

A soft blush crawls up her neck to deepen her flushing cheeks, and I slide my arms around her, kicking for the both of us to keep her head above water as she continues to gasp. This wasn't exactly how I wanted to leave her breathless, but I still enjoy the way she breathes into my neck, holding me like she'll never release me.

I swim us the rest of the way back to shore, and Ava breaks away to stand on her feet, though all I want to do is carry her right back to the blanket I left on the beach. Taking most of her weight, I guide her from the water until she drops to her knees just out of the waves, pulling me down with her.

"Please, tell me it's not always going to be like this. I don't think I can handle being so out of control all the time. I thought this ring was supposed to help." She waves her hand at her ripped bottoms and then to her hurt ankle.

I lean back on my elbows. "It does, believe me. If you weren't wearing it, you'd never change back. Your body's adjusting, Ava. It'll take a while to figure it all out." I wish I knew how long for sure. Like her, I don't know how I'm going to handle her sudden transformations. No one told me how hard it would be. But why would they? No human-born mermaid ever returns to shore right away, if ever.

She sighs. "I don't have time, though. You saw how fast I ran into the ocean. What if that would've happened while we were on the yacht?"

We'd be screwed. I don't tell her that. That's my problem to worry about not hers. "Then we'd figure it out," I say instead.

I can't stand the pout stealing away her smile, so I shift over her, shading her eyes from the sun, and caress my lips to hers. I slide my fingers around her back, pulling her closer. She rubs her hands along my chest, making me moan. Arching into me, she begs me with her body to explore her skin with my fingers, to kiss her deeper, to... An image of us together, alone in the ocean, flits through my head.

I tug myself away, panting. "Ava. Ava look at me."

Slowly opening her eyes, she meets my gaze. Her chest heaves, her desire mirroring my own. If I don't stop her now I most definitely won't.

"Ava, your thoughts. As much as I want to carry you back to the water, I can't," I say, studying the shape of her mouth.

"Why not?" Her eyes widen, and she covers her mouth with her hand, surprised by her own question.

I suck in a deep breath, forcing my mouth to work. "I might regret this later, but you belong on land. You belong with your friends and your family."

"And you?" I ask.

"Right now, I belong where you are."

My words hang in the air, a thousand silent thoughts clouding her blue eyes. I wish we could hear each other's minds even out of the sea. I'm desperate to know what she's thinking. A mixture of excitement and doubt bat at my chest, and I plead with her to believe me with my eyes, nervous that if I say anything out loud, she might remind me about the humanity her mind clings to despite her heart sinking into deeper water.

She rubs her lips together. "What about when we return home?"

I consider making a hundred promises, assuring her that nothing will change between us when we're no longer on the Ocean Jewel. I think about our future and everything we'll do together, the places we'll visit, the adventures we'll share. But the words refuse to leave my lips. I'm afraid I won't be able to keep such promises, or she'll deny this dream I have of us straddling the land and sea, but always together.

Pulling her closer, I rest my head on her shoulder. "If you're worried about what happens to us, don't. We'll make this work, okay?"

She doesn't respond, sinking deeper into her thoughts that turn from a whisper of doubt to something indescribable. With her sudden change in emotion, I know we'll be okay. We'll survive anything.

9

LIFE ON LAND

AVA LIMPS NEXT TO ME as we make our way back to the dock to meet the others to ride the tender boat back to the Ocean Jewel. She stops, pulling me to a halt with her, and surprises me with another hug. It's the sixth one since we've come back to shore, and I'd be okay with a dozen more, even if it makes everyone else wait.

"I can't do this," she whispers. "How will I even explain?"

"Anything you come up with is more believable than spontaneously transforming into a mermaid," I say. "So, don't sweat it. Just take a breath."

Slowly tilting her head up, she meets my gaze and sucks in a breath before blowing it through her lips. The soft air tickles my collarbone, and I bow my head down to hers so she'll focus on me.

Before I can say anything else, she closes the space and kisses me, gliding her hands up my sides and to my chest. Her fingers travel upward, and I kiss her deeper, exploring her full lips with mine.

Easing away, she smiles at me, her nerves dissipating with every beat of our hearts. "What would I do without you? You're the best, you know. I'm so lucky."

I grin and quickly kiss her again because I'm afraid I won't be able to leave this spot if I let her sink anymore into me. Taking a step forward, I force myself to keep us moving. It's easy to get lost in everything that is Ava. Her beautiful eyes, her soft voice, the way she makes me feel like we will get through anything. She thinks she's lucky, but she has no idea how lucky I feel.

"At least for now. Brace yourself, Carter. Giselle's on a mission."

I don't let go of her as she tries her best to hide her limp that'll ease up once she can sit down to heal. Ava bares her teeth at me, making me chuckle. If I didn't feel her worry washing over me, I wouldn't be able to tell how nervous she was. She manages to hold her face expressionless at her fast approaching friend.

"Oh, my God, Aves! What the hell happened?" Giselle races from the others gathered on the dock, waiting for the boat to take them back to the Ocean Jewel.

Ava slides her hand around my waist, using me as a wall to block Giselle from performing what I think might be a good shoulder shaking. "You know me. I'm accident prone."

"You fell in the ocean again?" Giselle's amber eyes widen. "Seriously, maybe you shouldn't even be standing on the dock. Are you okay?"

Giselle's concern makes me like her even more. I half expected her to laugh and tease Ava about it, but she looks like she wants to turn and yell at the ocean.

Ava shifts her weight to her good foot, pouting her bottom lip. "Yeah, I'm okay now. My sandal got caught when we were walking down the beach, and then with my stupid luck, I got knocked over by a wave. I thought I was far enough away, but the ocean just snuck up on me. I warned Carter I don't do well with water. He believes me now."

Giselle's gaze lands on me, and she gives me a serious look like I should've done something to stop our fake incident from happening.

I smirk at Ava, nearly believing her lie even though I was there for the whole dolphin incident. "Hey, I've always believed you." And I hope Giselle believes her now.

With one more glare at me, Giselle tugs Ava away and links their arms together. "Don't you know you don't have to impress that boy? He's madly in-like with you."

I release a small breath, relieved Ava's best friend isn't as mad as I thought. I never knew someone could intimidate me, but I know how much Ava cares for Giselle, and I want all her friends to like me. I never dreamed I'd ever care about someone's approval, because it's usually freely given in the sea, and humans are hard. But Ava is worth it.

"In-like, Gi?" Ava asks, laughing.

"Duh. I read it in Teen Romance Weekly. It's like this instant attraction you have for someone. I could tell from the moment he brought your bag into our room—total in-like. Right, Carter?" Giselle peers over her shoulder at me, smiling.

"Right, Giselle." If only they both knew how madly and deeply I care for Ava. She's my soul mate. There's no changing it, not that I'd ever want to. I just wish I could tell Ava without scaring her.

"See, Aves. Now no more falling into the ocean. Saving your ass is going to get boring."

Doubt it. But I hope I don't have to. It's my job as a mate to make sure Ava can take care of herself. If I don't, then I'd be the worst mate ever. Protecting and caring for Ava also includes teaching her what she needs to know and how to deal. It's all I can hope for, even if things haven't been perfect.

"You always have the best advice," Ava says to Giselle, her voice sharper than she's ever spoken to me.

But Giselle only laughs again. "I know."

The tender boat couldn't have arrived at a better time to take us back to the yacht. Ava snuggles against me, hiding her face like the sea mist is enough to trigger another transformation. I remind her not to think about it, knowing that anyone who hears me would assume I'm talking about the ride on the waves and nothing more.

When we arrive back on the yacht, Ava invites me to her room to wait while she showers. And the wait feels like eternity. I sit on the edge of one of the beds, resting my elbows on my knees, afraid to do anything other than watch the door. I should've done more than dry off and change to pass the time, but there was no way I was going to be anywhere else and miss what she looks like after an activity I never even thought anything of until I thought of showering with Ava.

The doorknob turns, and I sit up straighter. My heart rams into my ribcage as Ava steps into the small room with a towel around her flushed body still glistening with the steam of the shower. I drink in everything about her, from her damp hair to her blue toenail polish. The intensity of her gaze makes something about this moment incredibly important—her shyness around me disappearing as she drops her towel to the floor to show off the sexiest lace bra I've ever seen.

She smirks, combing her fingers through her hair for a second to brush the strands off her shoulders. It takes me gripping my knees, digging my nails into my skin, not to jump off the bed and close the small space to her. Neither of us says anything, and she inches closer, pulling her shirt over her head.

And then she inhales a breath, crosses the room completely, and pushes me back on the bed.

Controlling my desire to touch Ava flies out to sea when her lust cascades over me in an unexpected, sexy as hell, heat wave that leaves my skin buzzing.

Leaning up, I kiss her, nearly crashing my mouth to hers because I can't taste the slight saltiness of her lips fast enough. Our tongues meet, and she moans into my mouth, rubbing her hands down my chest, feeling my muscles, grabbing at the hem of my shirt. An image of me as a merman sneaks in my mind from her through our kiss, and I tense, silently cursing the ocean for overflowing from her heart in a moment we both need to stay human.

My chest heaves, and I can barely whisper her name. "Ava...we should stop."

She sighs loud and long enough for the both of us. It kills me to disappoint her, and the second she rolls off me, my body aches to toss my caution to the sea, pull her back on me, and hope for the best. But I know better. I know the risk of giving in to her desire to be with me. Not only could it jeopardize her by triggering a transformation, it could change things between us. It will change things between us, and I want to make sure she's completely ready and not riding the current of our accidental, unofficial coupling.

I take a few breaths, hugging her close, and say, "Your thoughts are making it difficult to remember why I chose land over the sea in the first place. They might trigger your transformation."

She tips her head to look at me, offering me a breath of a smile. "I can't help myself."

"Then let me help you." I roll onto her, kissing her again, just lightly enough to open my mind to her with image after image taken from my memory of us together. Each snap shot captures a moment of Ava as a human, exactly as the girl I met on the dock.

Kissing me deeper, she shares her own memories with me, of her life from before us and the simple things she loves about the human world like her morning jogs around her neighborhood and how she loves to dance with Giselle. She even shows me her favorite pair of jeans—things she can't have as a mermaid in the water. Her memories swirl through my head until they stop on us in this moment and how much she enjoys the way my legs rest between hers and how she can see my spark beating through my shirt.

She gasps, breaking away from me, a serious look puckering her brows. "I think I understand now. I think I figured out how the transformation works for me."

She sounds so certain, I believe her.

I smile, touching my fingers to her rosy cheek. "Want to test it out?"

Glancing away, she considers it for a moment before saying, "No, not right now. I think I've had enough of the water for today. I just want to dream about the land."

I can feel the shift inside her and how she's gone from anxious and worried to confident and certain—and not just in her ability to know how her transformation works. In me as well. Her cerulean eyes sparkle, telling me what her heart sings to me—that she believes we'll be more than okay. That we'll be amazing.

I kiss her again, showing her how I envision life will be. I show her every little thing I look forward to experiencing with her. I lose myself to her kiss, showing her everything I love about her world and the life on land.

"You okay, Carter?" Ava asks, sliding her fingers through mine.

Her friends sit scattered throughout the cable car, all staring at the city as we pass by. Ava doesn't take her eyes off mine, giving me her full attention like she couldn't care less about everything else.

I shift on the seat, bumping my knees to hers. "I'm great. It's just weird being home."

Because this is the first time I haven't gone straight to visit my parents, and I don't plan to if I can avoid it. If I see them, they'll know immediately that I found my supposed intended mate. My mom would know from her mermaid instincts that I'm unavailable. Thankfully, neither will suspect Ava's a mermaid. She's too new—at least I hope. But it's best if I don't chance it.

"I couldn't imagine not seeing my parents every day," she muses. "This is actually the longest I've been away from home."

I swallow, absently bringing our intertwined hands to my mouth to kiss the back of her hand. Guilt trickles through me, knowing how different things could've been. I knew Ava was close to her friends, but I haven't thought much about her parents. Now that I know this is the longest amount of time she's been away, I realize how important keeping her on land is. It would devastate her if I had to take her to sea. If I hurt her like that...I don't know how I'd handle it.

"You probably think I'm so sheltered," she adds, filling the silence I let linger between us.

I flick my gaze at the buildings we pass by. "Definitely not. You're more worldly than many merpeople I know. Most never leave the colonies."

Ava's nose crinkles a second before she yawns and then laughs into her hand when she catches me staring. She slept as little as I did last night, but it was still the best sleep of my life. It was like Ava was made for my arms and how she fit so comfortably against me.

"I know you showed me them, but I still can't imagine," Ava says, resting her head on my shoulder. "But San Francisco? It looks exactly how I—you—it looks exactly like you showed me. I love it. I wish we had more time to stay."

"Thank the Ocean we don't," I whisper to myself.

"What was that?" Ava's soft voice sounds barely a whisper over the hum of city traffic as the cable car comes to a stop to drop us off at the Fisherman's Wharf.

Instead of answering her, I stand up and guide her to where her friends huddle together and peer around the busy boardwalk of the Fisherman's Wharf. I adjust the few shopping bags from our morning shopping in Union Square on my arm and tilt my head to peer at the hot sun overhead.

Sapphire spins in a circle, taking in everything. "Why didn't I pick a university here?"

Ava squeezes my hand, staring at a circular sign, shaped like an old ship's steering wheel with a crab in the center, which introduces the Fisherman's Wharf.

"Because you're going to UCLA with me." Matty kisses Sapphire's cheek, drawing my attention away from Ava.

Sapphire laughs. "Oh, yeah."

The busy crowd hums around us, and I listen to Ava's friends talk about their plans for after the summer. It's the first time I realize that Ava's life isn't all summer vacations and hanging with her friends. It's more than turning into an accidental mermaid and having a life with me.

Ava's friends start walking onto the boardwalk, but my legs refuse to move. I don't know if it's the realization of how complicated a life on land with Ava might be or if it's because I realize I'm still learning about Ava even though I know her on a soul-deep level—but whatever it is, I need to find out what she's going to return to when we leave the Ocean Jewel.

Giselle swivels on the balls of her feet, remaining by Ava's side. She smiles at Ava, releasing a small squeal, but I catch Ava's gaze in her peripheral vision.

I consider waiting until we're by ourselves, but I'm afraid of how I'll react if I'm alone with Ava about plans I was never intended to be a part of from her life before me. So, I ask, "Are you two going to college?" It's easy to stay expressionless including Giselle.

"Yup. UCSD," Giselle says, answering for Ava. "We're going house hunting when we get back. I want a place on the beach like I have now, but away from my parents. I know it'll take Ava some convincing. She already told me we better be somewhere she can no longer hear the ocean."

Sucking in her bottom lip, Ava responds with, "Actually, I think I might be okay with that idea now."

I had assumed I'd get a place with Ava and never thought about the possibility of any other way of life. And part of me is relieved that I'm not going to have to rush and figure out how the hell I'm going to make this work right away. I'm still not sure. My intense need to take care of her messes with what I know of human norms.

Ava and Giselle laugh, and I pull myself from my

thoughts, missing whatever it was they were talking about. I follow behind the two of them as they rush to catch up with the others. I regret mentioning coming here. But Ava was so excited to see things from my memory, and I couldn't resist her desire after feeling the excitement and happiness ignited in her, lighting up not only her face but her spark, at even the mention of sharing a part of my life on land.

Every so often, Ava peeks at me from over her shoulder, apologizing with her eyes because Giselle tugs her along and points at everything we pass by. But it doesn't bother me. I'm too distracted by the crowd of tourists, the caws of the seagulls overhead, the hum of familiar sounds of the boardwalk.

And then someone familiar waves at me. I quickly flick my hand up toward Nicole, the assistant manager of my parents' store, offering her a smile. Under any normal circumstances, I'd have approached her, but Ava calls my name at the front of a restaurant. Nicole notices, raising her brows, and without having to say anything, she shoos me away.

"This place good, Carter man?" Logan asks, pointing at a menu in a glass case.

I nod, even though I wouldn't know. I'd hope it was for the double digit prices. I've never actually paid for seafood on land. I can get plenty of that, which tastes a hell of a lot better when I catch it myself, in the ocean.

Ava makes her way to me, bumping her shoulder to mine. "Sorry it's not dessert."

I hug her to me, smiling. "I can catch you something a million times better than this."

Her face twists in a grimace, and I regret even mentioning hunting a fish for her. She almost looks offended at the idea. And damn. Because that's the best way to show off my skills as a merman. There's even competitions and everything during mostly every celebration in the sea.

I must make a weird face at her, because her grimace shifts into a pout that she forces away with a smile. "That would be interesting."

I chuckle. I can't help it. "It's a good thing there are plenty of restaurants I can take you to instead."

All through lunch, I listen as her friends chatter about some of the most random things. In the sea, merpeople only communicate when they have something to say and not to fill the silence. But I'm glad for the constant conversation. It allows me to get to know Ava and her friends and how they act together. For one, everything is a competition between Matty and Logan, and it's not even to impress their mates. And two, half the conversation comes in the form of a laugh, which makes me chuckle.

"What about you, dude?" Matty asks me. "I can't be the only one caught naked somewhere."

I'm taken aback by the gesture of including me in the conversation and how easily Ava's friends accept me without really knowing me.

Sapphire play smacks his arm. "Somewhere? Did you forget the time you and Logan thought it'd be funny to streak through the middle of my beach party last year? Remember how you left your clothes too close to the water and ended up having to leave in a towel."

I laugh. "That's happened to you, too?" I guess it's not only merpeople who accidentally lose their clothes. I might not run through a crowd naked and risk breaking a human law, but there has been a time or two that I had to wait for my parents to come looking for me when I lost my clothes on the beach or forgot to hold onto them when I was a kid. Now, it's the first thing I make sure I have. Wet clothes are better than no clothes on land.

Matty laughs and bumps his fist to mine. After Sapphire pays for the entire bill, refusing to let anyone pitch in, Ava drags me away from her friends and into the crowd. We stroll along the boardwalk, peering at the water.

Ava suddenly stops, cocking her head, and it takes everything in me not to groan when I realize she hears the colony of sea lions that have made their home nearby on the docks. I take her hands in mine, stopping her in place. She smiles at me, her sky blue eyes shining in the sun.

"What is that?" she asks, peering around again.

I relent and guide her down the pier to where a crowd has gathered to watch the sea lions. Ava smiles while I glare at the overly playful animals trying to lure her into the sea. One even has the nerve to approach us and jump from the water and grin at her. Animals know we're merpeople, and sea lions know that with us comes food. And from what I can tell, the fish love Ava.

I pull her away from the pier and jerk my hand at the sea lion. A few more jump into the water, turning the whole situation of encouraging Ava to join them into a game, and I'm terrified I'm about to lose. Our dolphin encounter hangs fresh in my mind, and the last thing I want to do is jump after Ava into the murky, green-gray water. It's not exactly open-sea fresh.

Turning to me, Ava offers me a smirk. "He was just being friendly."

I consider telling her that there's a huge difference between being friendly and going out of his way to attempt to trigger Ava's mermaid transformation to get her to play. Instead, I say, "Exactly. So were the dolphins."

She rolls her eyes at me. "I'm not going to jump off the pier to join them."

I raise my brows and twist my lips. "Until you start feeling the pull."

The expression she gives me, thin-lipped and serious eyes, makes me step closer to her. She's not even a little bit nervous, her confidence over herself and her ability incredibly sexy. "I told you I think I get how it works for me. Want me to prove it?"

I nearly say yes, but I shake my head, remembering we're near my home, and there's no way I want to risk swimming in these waters, though Ava's eyes dare me to toss her over my shoulder and dive in.

Sliding my arms around her waist, I hug her as I walk her backward away from the view of the sea lions. She grins, amused by my reaction, and then she surprises me by pulling out her phone from her bag to take a picture of the two of us. The small gesture of capturing us in a still does something to me. I can't stop smiling as Ava smiles at me. She wants to remember this moment outside her mind.

I close the space between us and kiss her, drawing her attention to me and away from the world around us. It's all I want right now—to be with her, showing her how important she is to me no matter what's happening in the world. Because even chatty sea lions aren't going to ruin this.

"Carter?" a familiar voice says from in front of me.

And like that, my happiness slides through the slats in the pier and into the murky water below. I stiffen in Ava's arms, feeling her sudden panic at my reaction. From over Ava's shoulder, I meet my mom's huge smile, her blue-green eyes crinkling in the corners. She strolls my way, now on a mission to meet Ava, who I can't deny that I feel is my intended mate. Merpeople don't date around. We just know. It can happen at any time.

"Who is it?" Ava whispers, dropping her hands from me.

Instead of answering her question, I say, "Why don't you go find Giselle? I'll meet you back at the yacht later, okay? And please, stay away from the water for now."

I kiss her forehead and leave her to meet my mom and intervene before she can start interrogating Ava. I need the chance to prepare Ava for any and all questions my mom might have for her. Mom has always been a bit nosey and firm on our merpeople way of life. Even if she would treat Ava like a human, because she doesn't know she's not, my mom might pull the truth from us. I'm not ready to deal with that kind of catastrophe. I know exactly what she'll insist on, which is to take Ava to sea.

It takes everything in me to force my legs to move, because Ava's confusion and hurt and anger crash over me. But then it all stops the second I hug my mom. Because Ava knows who my mom is. She would recognize her from my memory.

"My handsome son. It was quite the surprise to hear from Nicole that you disembarked the Ocean Jewel and didn't stop into the store to say hello. But now I see why. She's beautiful, Carter."

I hug my mom, letting her guide me farther and farther from Ava. "Her name's Ava. She's—"

"Perfect. I'm so happy for you. I can't wait to tell your dad. He's been waiting forever for this moment."

I inhale a deep breath, tempted to tell her everything

about Ava and how I changed her into a mermaid to save her life. But Ava's fear sinks into me again, and I steel myself. I can't risk it. I'll do everything to guarantee I get her back to Azure Waters.

"I insist you turn around and introduce me," Mom says.

"How about over dinner instead?" I ask, regretting the words immediately. The Ocean Jewel will set sail at sunset. But with how my mom's face lights up, I know I have to figure it out.

"I can't wait!" she squeals. I can almost hear her planning my coupling ceremony to Ava in her mind.

"Calm down. I just met Ava, and we've only started courting."

She claps her hands. "But it won't be long. I just know it."

I sigh. If only she knew. "Come on. I have to get back to the Ocean Jewel soon."

"But first, we tell your dad."

10

TRADITIONS

"I WANT TO KNOW all about her." Dad rushes me on the sidewalk outside the Stevens' Sea and Surf Shop my parents have owned for as long as I can remember. His muscular arms, twice the size of mine, open wide to scoop me off my feet just like he's done all my life. I could be a hundred and fifty and Dad would still spin me around like a merbabe. "Show me what she looks like."

I twist out of the way, grabbing onto the thick concrete light pole to put something between us. Holding up my palm, I say, "Dad, please. Not here. Remember, people might think it's weird if you kiss me. I'm not a kid." My parents follow human social norms most of the time and manage to be as normal as any parent can be, but something as huge as finding out that I've found my intended mate in Ava sets off his merman nature.

"You're my kid," he says, dodging around the pole.

I wish I had asked Ava to send me the picture she took of us together, because I never thought much about doing something like that with my photographic memory. Merpeople also tend to be cautious about being documented for safety. I've never taken more pictures than I've had to, but I'd take a million for Ava.

Dad swings out his arm, trying to grab onto my shirt, but I flip back to the other side of the pole. Unfortunately, I'm no match for his determination, and he fakes me out and hooks an arm around me. Lifting me off my feet, he envelops me in a bear hug tight enough to make my chest heave. I arch away from his puckered lips, pressing my hands to his broad chest. Mom's musical laugh sounds from beside us, and I swing my gaze to her.

"Mom, you saw her. You show him," I say, pleading with her. It's not only that kissing my dad on the lips might be considered weird, but I'm also afraid I might slip up and accidentally give away the fact that I transformed her into a mermaid. If I can get away with not telling them, I will. They don't have a reason to suspect she's anything but human. But if I know my parents, it'll be a long shot. "There's no way I'm bringing her for dinner if you guys can't manage to keep yourselves together. She's human. You're going to scare her."

"Don't be silly," Dad says.

"Oh, Mateo, put him down," Mom says. "I think he might be serious. He wouldn't even introduce me at the pier, and I'll be so disappointed if I can't meet our daughter."

Dad sets me back down, his face softening as he looks at my mom. "Okay, okay. I cannot stand the thought of a pout stealing away your stunning smile. Now, come here and let me assure it."

I glance at the passing cars as my parents make out on the sidewalk longer than it would have taken for my mom to send my dad the memory she has of Ava and me on the pier. Dad finally pulls away, and my mom sighs, smiling, and both my parents turn to look at me with so much pride any normal person would think I won an award or something—but this is a billion times better. I can't help the smile crossing my face. They look even happier than they did when I graduated high school or told them my desire to leave home.

"She's incredible, right?" I ask.

"Perfect," Dad says. "I cannot wait to meet my daughter."

His words bring me back to land and away from the customs of the sea. "Dad, please don't call her that to her face. We just started court...dating."

Mom wraps her arms around me. "It won't be long until

I'm a grandmer. Your father and I have been saving up to help you since the day you were born, so you could have the chance to extend our pod on land the way we never could. I'll be right beside Ava for all of it."

I shake my head, pushing her words from my mind. It's far too early in my relationship with Ava to even consider such a thing. Starting a family with me would mean leaving hers, and I can't ask that of her anytime soon. "We haven't officially coupled. Stop it with that. She's sensitive about her family, and I—"

"Oh, son. You'll both feel quite different when—"

"Dad."

Mom takes my hand. "He's only trying to prepare and guide you, Carter. Our life on land is different than that in the sea, especially with you choosing a land-born mate, but tradition is tradition, and it's important. Since you don't have another newly courting merman to support you, please accept your father's knowledge. He will assure you sweep Ava off her feet into the waves to start a happy life."

Her words bother me more than they should. Guilt bats at me at the fact that I never got the chance to sweep Ava into the waves with every bit of romance she deserves, and the ocean made her plunge headfirst into a life that leaves the both of us flailing. Not to mention that my mom's implying that my love should be enough to convince her to give up the land, but what she doesn't get is that because I feel so deeply for

Ava, I could never ask her to do that no matter the laws of the sea. My parents won't understand. They were both born in the water. They've never had anything to lose with love—only everything to gain.

Dad whacks me on the arm. "Knock it off with that face. You look like you don't believe you're capable, and trust me, son, she'll reciprocate those feelings I'm sure are driving you mad."

"You should've warned me," I say. "I can't imagine them getting worse."

He laughs. "Not worse. Better—stronger. Your mom manages to summon my desire with one look, especially—"

Heat erupts on my face. "Okay, Dad. I get it." More than he even knows. I already feel everything at the intensity a coupled mate feels, and Ava's lust leaves me in a constant state of wanting to get to know her on every level but also knowing that she might not be there yet.

"Oh, honey. Love in all its forms is nothing to be embarrassed about."

I clear my throat. "I'm not embarrassed. I just—I'm trying not to—Ava and I aren't—" I can't even get the words out.

Dad pats my back. "In time. You'll make her an extremely happy and satisfied mate."

I can only hope. "I just have to survive bringing her around you two." And survive them finding out that I changed Ava into a mermaid. I know I have to. If they figure it out before I get the chance to stand up for the decision Ava and I made about the land, it might shatter everything. They'll assume I'm not responsible enough to handle the situation and could insist on forcing Ava to go. I'll at least have to tell them she knows our secret if anything.

Mom clicks her tongue. "We'll behave. I promise you a nice, relaxed dinner. We won't even serve fish."

I smile and nod, thanking the ocean, because Dad would never buy seafood from the store and Mom hates it cooked. "I should probably get back to the Ocean Jewel and tell Ava."

"How's seven?"

I tighten my jaw. There's no way I could sneak Ava off the boat and back here that early. "I can't until after eight." I feel bad for lying now, but I need the chance for them to see that Ava's doing fine on her legs. I also need time to prepare her. At least the Ocean Jewel sets sail after sunset to head down the coast, so if I do need a getaway with Ava, I know they won't bother me there with so many humans.

Mom nods her head. "Then we'll see you and Ava at nine."

The second I saw Ava when I boarded the Ocean Jewel, I wanted to kick myself for abandoning her on Pier 39 like I had. What made it worse was having to tell her that even though I stopped her from meeting my mom that I didn't do a great job, because I accepted a dinner invitation without even asking if she was okay with meeting my parents. I could barely handle her nerves when I implied that my parents would find out the truth as well. Dinner will be interesting if we can even get through the door.

"I'm so nervous," she says, bouncing on her feet. All through dinner, she pushed food around her plate, and her anxiety seems to grow by the second. "I'm going to change again. I think this is too much." She shrugs out of her black dress and tosses it on the floor.

"You'll look beautiful in anything. They're just my parents. You can count on them being ecstatic to meet you. Merpeople are welcoming and accepting of bonds—especially one like ours. I'm more worried they'll freak you out and you'll abandon me."

She inhales a deep breath and surprises me with a hug, sliding her arms under mine to rest her head on me, listening to my heart through my shirt. "You know that won't happen, right? Sorry, but you're stuck with me..." She turns her face to whisper into my neck. "I mean, for as long as you want. I don't mean to get ahead of myself. I'm just—the ocean isn't scary with you."

I swallow, clenching my teeth into a smile to stop myself from overreacting when I want nothing more than to twirl her off her feet and onto the bed feet away to show her that I'm far ahead of her, prepared to swear my eternity to her if she asked no matter how crazy it seems. She carries part of my essence in her after all.

"I hope it will never be, Aves," I say, staring into her worry-lined eyes. "And so you know, I'm holding you to your word about not letting my parents scare you away. My mom can be...a little overbearing. But if they start to make you feel uncomfortable, just tell me, okay? I'll get us out of there faster than I can swim to Hawaii."

"I bet that's crazy fast," she muses, finally picking up a teal dress with white floral embroidery over the bodice to put into the bag while remaining in what she calls her new least favorite bikini because of the torn seam on the side.

"I'll show you sometime." I help her pack the rest of the bag with everything we'll need to walk to my parents' apartment. I'm not too worried about them thinking we've emerged from the sea. It'll come out. I can't hide much of anything from their instincts. It's how they knew I found my intended mate.

After waiting for Ava's friends to leave their rooms to head to the saloon for a movie marathon, I sneak her to the pathway, avoiding all main areas. It's better if people think we're still in her room, and we left music on the TV to hopefully help.

Running her hands up and down her arms, Ava shivers in the cool night air. She stares at the bubbling wake as the yacht cuts across the bay to head back to the open water. She's not only worried about meeting my parents and them discovering what I've done but also about the swim back no matter how many times I've assured her that the Ocean Jewel won't go off course, and I'll be able to catch us up.

"You should undress here," I say to break her from her thoughts.

I give her the waterproof bag with a towel and our clothes. Ava watches me untie my board shorts and take them off without averting her gaze. My heart pounds as she familiarizes herself with my naked body without even blushing. I pick up my shorts off the deck and close the distance between us. Her eyes widen for a second, and I realize she's just become aware that she was gawking at me, but I don't smile or react. If I do, then she will, and I want her to be comfortable enough to trust me in a form she feels vulnerable in.

Ava releases a small breath and shimmies out of her bottoms and tosses them to me to put in the bag. We stand together on the swim platform, and I adjust the waterproof bag around my chest, glad the decks are empty and we don't have to resort to jumping from the sundeck.

I hold out my hand to Ava. "Ready?"

I can tell she's not, but she nods anyway, and I don't give her the chance to think more about it. I launch us from the platform and dive her down into the glowing sea. I transform before Ava does and take in how beautiful she looks in the water with her blond hair swirling around her face. Her wide eyes meet mine, but she's not afraid. Her determination to follow my lead crosses her face, and she arches through her rippling muscle spasms, transforming faster than ever.

Ava amazes me by the second, and I dart around her before she opens her eyes and swim up in front of her. "That was much faster. I knew you could do it."

All she does is smile, her jewel eyes flickering in the light from our chests. She doesn't say anything as I jet through the water at a speed she can match. Her movements mirror mine but more graceful, her body rolling through the current. We reach the shallows of a beach in walking distance of my parents' apartment, and I stop to take in the sight of her as a mermaid again. I wish we had a few extra minutes so I can show her the manta rays that favor the calm waters.

Instead, I ask, "Think you can transform here and swim the rest of the way with me?"

She pushes a bubble through her lips and nods. I hold her hands, waiting for her to transform, because the look of longing for the sea that pinches her face makes me nervous. I wouldn't doubt something like the idea of meeting my parents might stop her from transforming to follow me to land.

She crinkles her nose, rolling her shoulders. Nothing happens.

It's not that she can't, but she doesn't want to. I can feel her nerves tightening my own chest.

"Ava?" I ask, letting go of her hand to touch her cheek.

She opens her eyes, baring her bottom teeth at me. We both know what the holdup is.

"Please, try. For me." I use my own pout against her.

I wasn't sure if it was going to work, but she runs her finger across my bottom lip and transforms into a human as quickly as she had a mermaid. I swim us to the surface and keep my arm around her, feeling her bare hip against mine. The heat of my intense need to keep Ava close pushes away the chill of the water, and I glance at her a few times, seeing the city lights reflect in her gaze like a dozen stars in her glassy eyes.

If she didn't remain on her feet to trudge through the surf, I'd have let it carry us both to the sand to lie with her for a moment under the moon. I shake out my drenched hair, making her laugh as it pelts her. She shivers on the beach, covering herself, and I yank the towel from the bag and wrap it around her, standing close to her naked body and dry her off for her, pushing away the goosebumps prickling her skin.

She stands utterly still, her breath panting with the rise and fall of her chest, the moment feeling so important because she doesn't turn away or hide from me. I run the towel down her back and to her waist, stopping there before I get carried away with myself in seeing to it that every droplet of water dries from her skin. With the way her eyes hold mine, her breath quickening, her tongue sliding over her lips as she tastes the saltwater still streaming from her hair into her face, I know she'd let me.

If I had my phone, I'd cancel dinner with my parents altogether, and they might even understand.

I inhale a breath of the ocean air and take the towel from Ava to wrap around my waist and grab her dress from the bag to hand to her. She turns her back on me and pulls the strings on her bikini top, letting it drop to the sand. Moonlight sets her bare body aglow, and I drink in the smoothness of her skin as she shrugs into her dress, letting it cling to her damp skin.

Closing the distance between us, I help her tie the halter straps while she lifts her wet hair from her neck. As she puts on her bikini bottoms, I throw my clothes on and run the towel through my hair.

She turns around and shrugs that she's as ready as ever. I grin, taking in how amazing she looks with her hair waving over her shoulders, her flushed cheeks making her eyes bluer, her cleavage peeking out of the V-neck of the dress... I swallow, pulling myself together before I lose myself to her.

My heart beats to the snap of her flip flops as she strolls the sidewalk next to me, holding my hand for a block and then moving closer to nestle under my arm. She runs her fingers across my lower back to settle on my hip, sneaking them under my shirt to graze softly over my skin.

The green lawn and colorful flowerbeds of my parents' complex comes into view, and Ava smiles at me, recognizing it from a memory I shared with her from growing up here. Mr. Mooney, the neighbor upstairs and the man who keeps an eye on my parents place whenever they head to sea, which he thinks is by boat, smokes a cigarette outside his door.

He waves at us in greeting, his eyes turning from me to Ava and then back to me.

"Hello, Mr. Mooney. How's it going?" I ask as I tug Ava along, who now drags her feet to glance at the pool in the center of the complex.

"Good, boy. You haven't visited in a while. Your mom says you're working on a boat? Fishing?"

It's always the first thing anyone assumes. Laughable if he knew my merman secret. There's no fun in fishing with a net or pole. I only hunt what I can eat and with my bare hands. "No, sir. Luxury cruises."

He snuffs out his cigarette, laughing. "Whatever pays the bills."

Ava smiles politely at Mr. Mooney, and we watch him enter his apartment. We make our way to my parents' front door. Nerves wash over me, some my own, but mostly from Ava, and I slow down to give Ava a moment to prepare.

But who am I kidding? I need one too. This could end badly. I didn't even think things through completely. I know my parents will feel my forming bond with Ava, because they'll form their own to her as well with her being my accidental mate. I just hope we can make it long enough before having to tell them. I want them to see Ava as I see her.

"What if they don't like me?" she whispers, hugging me even closer, begging me to hold her.

I turn away from my mom singing and dancing around the dining room table, not even noticing us outside the open window, and wrap her in my arms. "They will."

"Then why are you nervous?" Crap. I've failed to hide my feeling of impending doom from my expression. I have to have hope that it'll be okay. Maybe I could just see how things go without telling them.

"Because I've never introduced anyone to them. Merpeople are different. I'm worried they'll scare you away." At least, those are just some of the reasons. No way am I going to give her the full list and make this any worse. She already knows there is a chance they'll recognize her as a mermaid, but we're both hoping they'll be too excited to realize they're playing human for no reason until I manage to say something.

She laughs, her musical voice turning my nerves into something manageable. "Not like I'm going far."

Ava puffs a breath of air through her lips and smiles away from me, and I realize her laughter drew my mom's attention to us. Mom sways across the living room in her own little excited bubble I want to steer clear of in fear of bursting it.

"Mateo, they're here," she practically squeals, throwing the door open.

I guide Ava inside before Mom can pull her away from

me. Ava shifts on her feet, her eyes widening as Dad strides into the room. Even though I've showed her what my parents look like, I can tell she didn't expect my dad to be taller and buffer than me. But he's been swimming in the ocean longer and stands by for the call of King Attilonious as one of the ocean's warriors.

My parents stand a little too close, crowding us. "Mom, Dad, this is Ava Adair. Ava, meet my parents, Mateo and Starla."

Dad breaks first, unable to help himself, and scoops Ava up into a hug, rocking her back and forth. She giggles into his shirt, clearly surprised by the action, but she accepts the greeting in stride, hugging my dad back. He grins at me over her shoulder, wagging his eyebrows.

My mom steals Ava from my dad, hugging her twice as long as Dad. She looks like she's planning on doing so all through dinner like she's missed Ava all her life though she just met her.

"Mom, please," I say. "You're smothering her."

Ava peers at me from over her shoulder, still caged in my mom's arms. "It's fine, Carter. I'll take a hug any day." She says that now, but it won't be fine when the hug turns into my mom whispering about how she can't wait for the day Ava joins our family and turns her into a grandmer.

"See," Mom says, finally releasing Ava only to hook their arms together to pull her into the living room, accented with things that remind my mom of the sea.

"I still can't believe you were passing through and weren't going to stop in to say hello," Dad says to fill the silence falling over everyone. "Already forgetting your poor parents."

His smile shows he doesn't mean the words, and it's his attempt to sound like a normal human parent. I almost don't believe he doesn't realize Ava's a mermaid.

I play along with his fake guilt trip, taking all the extra time I can. "Dad." I sigh for good measure. "I didn't expect to even leave the yacht. Plans changed, though." A lot.

Mom strolls into the kitchen to check on what smells like pasta sauce and garlic—lasagna—and peers at Ava. "Do you work on the Ocean Jewel, Ava?"

I don't know why she asks. She knows Ava doesn't. I'd have mentioned her much sooner. I have a feeling she's just trying to make Ava comfortable enough to answer all of her other burning questions. She might even be a little annoyed with me that I purposely haven't given her Ava's life story yet.

"No, just a passenger," Ava responds, her voice hitching under Mom's sudden scrutiny. "I live in Azure Waters with my parents, but I'm moving out with my best friend before college in the fall."

Uh-oh. Both my parents snap their gazes to me. "Oh, you plan to attend college?" Dad asks first.

I close the space to Ava and hug her from behind, so she can't see the glare I give Dad to stop him from even considering saying what's on his mind. "I've considered going myself."

Mom returns my look, her expression turning from excited to curious, and then suspicious as she sets the casserole dish on the table. "So, you two are pretty serious?"

Crap. Crap. Crap. They know something is up. I can see it splashed across their faces, but it doesn't dawn on either of them yet. They already know I haven't gotten to familiarize myself with Ava's body yet, because I've admitted as much, but they can tell I'm hiding something.

Ava's anxiety pours over me under my mom's questions. Her eyes give herself away, though she forces her mouth to remain in a smile. She looks ready to bolt toward the nearest door to avoid any more questions. And now I regret not preparing Ava more. She can sense something is off with seemingly normal questions from my parents.

I steel myself, concentrating on sending calming emotions to Ava as I turn to my mom. "Mom, can't you give us a moment to sit down before the interrogation?"

She forces a small laugh. "Sorry, sweetheart. It's just we have so little time with you and Ava."

Now that is a real guilt trip unlike my dad's teasing.

"And there will be plenty of time to get to know her." I pull out a chair for Ava to sit in. "Maybe we can visit later in the summer and stay longer than a few hours." It's what they expect. Courting merpeople spend a lot of time with each other's families. But since Ava's human born, all her time would be unfairly dedicated to my pod. Her ties to land are supposed to be severed. Everything she knows stays on shore while she's to start her life in the sea.

I hang my head, losing myself in my thoughts. I know it's what my parents will tell me. I know the traditions and laws. The importance of our secret and the consequences for a human to find out unless they're intended to be a mate.

"We'd love that, son," Dad says, kicking me under the table so I look at him.

Mom dishes out the food onto our plates, giving Ava more uncomfortable attention. I can see she's trying to figure out what's wrong with us and why both me and Ava continue to shift in our seats. "You're always welcome in our home, Ava. We're so happy that Carter has found you."

Ava smiles and nods, barely managing to speak through the weirdness of the invisible wave ready to wash us all away with the news I'm still deciding to go through with telling them. "Thank you so much for inviting me. Carter's an incredible person, and I'm lucky he asked me out. I like your son a lot."

Ava's words pull my parents from their suspicious glances toward me, hearing her fondness of me radiating from her voice. Thankfully, I don't think Ava realizes that they're much more than curious. But I know my parents, and they know me. We've never kept secrets and have always been honest with each other. They're now officially waiting for me to tell them what's going on.

Mom and Dad take initiative to get Ava to talk and tell her all about the shop and how much they enjoy living in San Francisco. After an hour of meaningless conversation that does nothing but help me avoid telling them the truth, Mom finally wears me down and asks me to tell her about the moment I set my gaze on Ava.

From the surprise crossing Dad's face, I wish I had started when she was already aboard the yacht. I guess I'm alone in my pride of convincing Ava to get on the Ocean Jewel.

I smile at Ava, trying to pretend it's still okay. "Obviously, she got on."

My parents gaping expressions silently scream that things are in fact not okay and far from it. I think they assume I might've told Ava I was a merman, which would be too soon to even know if Ava reciprocates the bond I felt the moment I saw her.

"You're afraid of the ocean?" Dad questions Ava, his voice rising with his disbelief. "But Carter loves the ocean."

I'm pretty sure the second they can corner me alone, they will. They'll question the entire situation to warn me that I had better be sure that Ava is my intended mate.

And it pisses me off. I don't think I've ever been so mad. It takes everything in me to stay calm for Ava's sake. They don't trust that I know what I'm doing, but they won't say their thoughts in front of Ava in case they're misinterpreting the situation. They'll only wish me revealing what I was to Ava was the only thing.

Ava doesn't need all these questions and assumptions. She doesn't need to know that even for a second my parents might doubt we're supposed to be together. Obviously we are or the ocean wouldn't have allowed me to save her life. I'd have never been allowed to swim in the unsaid wave of love I know Ava's starting to feel though her human rationale might force her to deny such an instant devotion is possible.

Ava shifts in her seat, drawing my attention to her. "When I boarded the yacht, yes."

"Dad, please," I beg, afraid he might say something that could hurt Ava's feelings. Or worse, say something that'll make Ava get up and run.

I know at any moment, I'm going to have to tell them about the accident and about changing Ava into a mermaid. I know it. I'll say the words, grab Ava's hand, and leave. I'll not allow them to question what I'm doing or what's best for me and my mate.

Mom stares at Ava, making her so nervous that her body trembles, sending pieces of her hair into her face. The second Ava tugs her hand from mine to pull the strands away, I know it's over.

Mom gasps, her mouth falling open, her blue-green eyes widening and lighting up with recognition and overwhelming excitement that has her leaning across the table and closer to us.

"Ava, your hand," Mom says.

She's shocked silent, unable to form the million thoughts I know are flitting through her mind. I can see her idea of mine and Ava's future lighting her face, turning her from suspicious to the happiest I have ever seen in my life. It's not exactly what I was expecting, but I'll take it. She's not mad at all and thinks Ava's accepted my merman secret and what it means for her life as a human.

Ava pulls her hand out from under the table and stares at it.

"The ring," Mom says, pointing at the sea stone glittering in the light. "You gave her your ring, Carter?"

I clear my throat. "It's not what you—"

"Oh, Ava. I'm so happy you've accepted my son's proposal," Dad says, speaking up.

Damn it. My parents' excitement doesn't give me a chance to explain anything as they talk to Ava over me. Dad grabs Ava's hand and looks at the sea stone ring glittering in the light. He jerks his head up to me, smiling, and I open and close my mouth. I thought there would be more yelling. More questioning of what I was doing. More of anything other than their excitement, stealing the color right from Ava's face as my dad's words sink in.

Ava blinks. "Um, I—"

"There's so much planning to do," Mom says, interrupting Ava before she can say anything. "Summer is the perfect time for the transformation ceremony."

Ava sinks into her seat, clutching the table with one hand. Her wild eyes dart around the room, and she blinks a dozen times, trying to control the anxiety battling inside the both of us.

"Mom."

"And it'll give you just enough time to say goodbye to your family," Mom adds, ignoring me.

"What? I'm not leaving my family." Ava grips the table, her head lolling. It's too much. The whole situation leaves her gasping, unable to process anything.

"But—"

"Mom! Stop! You need to listen." I slam my hands on the table to get my parents to look at me, but they're already lost to everything that Ava turns into for them—they don't see her as my intended mate. They see her as the girl who I've swept off her feet with the promise of a life in the sea beyond anything she could imagine. They envision how Ava will be their daughter after our promise, and how I'll have the life every merman prepares for.

But they can't see the heartbreak stealing Ava's smile.

They can't see the horror crossing my face.

All they can see is their idea of how their future for the two of us is without even considering it's not what we want.

Ava groans, covering her face with her hands, snuffing

out my fear and anger. Her eyes roll to the back of her head, and she tips over in the chair too fast for me to catch her. Silence falls over the room, my parents in as much shock as Ava.

I drop to my knees, pulling Ava into my lap, touching her face in an attempt to get her to look at me. "Ava? Ava, please don't transform, okay? We're too far from the water. Please," I beg, half expecting her skin to sheen over in a luminescent glow.

But Ava doesn't transform. All she does is gaze at my chest and my blinking heart for a second before passing out.

11

DISAPPOINTMENT

I'VE NEVER FELT LIKE more of a disappointment in my life until this moment. I carefully carry Ava to the couch while my mom runs for a cool cloth. Dad sits on the floor beside me, watching me absently brush Ava's hair from her face, waiting for her to come to. I don't know if it was my mom's sudden excitement overwhelming her or if her fear of having to give up the land that got to her, but whatever it was, Ava's not ready to deal with it.

"You're so lucky she only passed out, Carter. This could've been much worse. The transition on a human is hard.

This is why you should've taken her to sea, son," Mom says, gently pressing the washcloth to Ava's forehead while checking her vitals.

Out of all the places to succumb to Ava's newly intense emotions, enhanced by mine, my parents' apartment was probably the best one outside the sea because my mom's a healer. She's been gifted with the ability to care for others using her instincts and the magic controlled by King Attilonious in the ocean.

"Her body has gone through a traumatic change. She surely feels out of control and scared. There's only so much you can do, son. She needs the support of another mermaid that she can talk about things she might not be comfortable doing with you yet."

"She's fine," I say. Because she is. Ava might blush like crazy through certain questions, but we get through them together. It's brought her closer to me more than anything.

Mom sighs. "She was human-born with no time to prepare herself. I know you've bonded with her, and you think she's fine, but that's probably because she's too nervous to tell you otherwise. She doesn't know our ways. She probably thinks you'll abandon her at any second."

I scowl. "I'd never. She knows that."

"You gave her your ring without a promise to fulfill."

But I did, and I intend to keep it. My parents won't see it that way. "Mom."

Clicking her tongue, she shakes her head at me. "This would not have happened in the water. She'd have our family's support to get through the grief of losing her human life and to teach her our ways. It'd be an adjustment, but you'd both get through it. You'd make her an extremely happy mermaid, son."

"She's happy now and has been doing great, really."

"And you, Carter?" Dad asks. "This could not have been easy on you. You had no time to create the bond you need with Ava. Humans require long courtships for a reason."

I blow a puff of air through my lips. "I'm fine. Ava's been great to me. She's perfect."

Mom rubs her hands together. "Nothing about this situation is fine or great or perfect, sweetheart. You took her last breath as a human."

"She drowned. I couldn't let her go. She is my intended."

A ghost of a smile plays on Mom's lips, hearing my words. "So treat her like she is. There are laws for a reason. King Attilonious would expect you to bring Ava to Pearlestria. You *need* to take her. This isn't fair for her, and I hate to say this, but it's incredibly selfish of you. You are keeping her from the beautiful, fulfilling life the ocean bestowed on her as your mate."

She says it like I haven't thought about it a thousand times. Because she's partly right. I am selfish. It's not only Ava's desire to stay on land that makes me think twice about taking her into the deep, but it's my own. I grew up on land. I've been working to create a life of my own here. I don't want to give it all up to live in a rock house in the sea—a simple life that is boring as hell. Ava deserves better than that.

"And because you so selfishly kept her from her new nature, you might've ruined your chance to return to land when she's ready. You also jeopardized our lives on land, too. If you disappear with Ava now, the human police will get involved. We cannot afford this sort of attention. You know the consequences."

I hang my head. "You don't understand."

"No, you obviously don't," Mom says, rubbing my shoulder. "This is serious. It's more than what you and Ava want. It's what she needs and what you need to do for her. She's your responsibility, Carter. She's our pod's responsibility. If we act now, we can get her to the water without her putting up a fight."

"Are you kidding me?" I ask, turning my gaze to my dad. "I'm not allowing you to take Ava to sea."

"Be reasonable, Carter. Look at her," Dad says, speaking up. He reaches up and touches my heart. "Feel her with everything inside you. You can't actually want to live like this with her. I know you. You have a good heart, but she needs more than that."

"Well, sorry to be such a disappointment, Dad." I don't mean to say it, but everything my parents say does nothing to help me.

"Carter, don't say that. I'm not disappointed. I'm upset you didn't reach out to us to help you. I thought you knew you could no matter what."

Ava stirs in my arms, but she doesn't open her eyes. As I look at her face, all I can think about is how I wanted to do right by her. I couldn't bear—I still can't bear—the idea of ripping her from her family, from her friends, from her bonds on land, which are just as important to her as the bonds merpeople share in the sea.

"I just couldn't, okay?"

"You could have," Mom says. "We're your parents. You know how humans are. If you don't take her away, you risk never establishing your eternal bond. She might never reciprocate your feelings. A life of unrequited love would damage your soul, son. I can't stand here and watch you risk everything."

None of that matters to me. I'd deserve it if Ava hates me after everything—if she denies me her love. I'm afraid doing what my mom asks will do just that. How could Ava ever love me if I take away everything she loves? I can't. I won't. I might not have made the kind of vow I would have if we officially coupled, but I still swore to her she'd get the life of her making.

Shaking my head, I whisper, "I promised Ava she could go back home. I'm not going to take her away from her family because of some stupid tradition. She didn't agree to any of this."

Dad rubs his hand across his forehead, clearly as lost as I am, but for reasons I'm unsure of. "Oh, son. You should've called us sooner." Draping his arm over my shoulders, he reaffirms my mom's words. What I should've done doesn't make a difference because what I've done is done. I can't change it no matter how much they think I can. I thought Dad would be angry. I thought he'd be disappointed. But he's as sad as I am. And if I know my dad, I know he's blaming himself for my shortcomings.

"What difference would it have made? I stole away Ava's choice to decide. I'm not going to steal her decision of what happens to her future as well. I'm letting her make the choice if she wants to be with me, and I doubt she'd know for sure after a few days." I can only hope things continue as they do, though the more I sit with my parents, the harder it is to see things so clearly.

Ava shifts, avoiding opening her eyes. I won't call her out on it if she's not ready to face the disaster I made of things. She should hear how sorry I am for everything she's going through.

"For your sake, I hope so, son," Dad says.

I sigh, brushing my fingers across Ava's cheek. "I'm ready to accept whatever happens, even if it doesn't happen how I imagine."

A wave of emotions rolls over me from Ava stronger than ever. Somehow she manages to light a flame of hope to brighten my spark, beating for her. She doesn't have to say anything or even open her eyes to look at me for me to know that she believes in me and this life we want together. The warmth now erupting in my heart is enough for me to straighten my shoulders and stop feeling sorry for myself. Because I still wouldn't have changed things. Ava is my mate, and even if it didn't happen how everyone expects two people to tether their existences, it happened, and I'm grateful for it. I'll fight for her. I'll break every damn law in the sea if I have to—and I might.

I think my dad sees the shift in my eyes to know I've made my decision. He gives me a serious look, his brows lowering on his forehead. "I think you really need to think things through. You can't just hope for the best."

I meet his stern gaze with my own. I don't like that my dad doubts my ability to be a good mate. "I'm not hoping, and I can handle this. We have things under control." I have enough money in my savings for a deposit on an apartment, a good job, and the determination I need to see to it that Ava's taken care of. Ava's getting the hang of her transformations. She'll adapt with my help. I'll assure it.

"But Carter, she's a liability," Mom says, clearly not wanting to accept that I don't need her help. "She needs to be in the sea. She needs to be with our people until she adjusts.

You can't just put the sea stone on her finger and expect her to master the transformation without really knowing what she's capable of. What happens if she loses control in the car? Or in the middle of a mall? She said she's going to college. Could you imagine what would happen if she changed in the middle of a lecture hall in front of hundreds of people? We've survived so long by remaining a secret. As her mate, it's your job to protect her. This isn't a game. It's her life."

"I am protecting her. It's more than just the transformation and keeping our secret. It's about protecting her heart too, and you don't feel her like I do. I can't devastate her like that. You two should know this."

I realize Ava's staring at me with such sadness that it snuffs the anger Mom dragged from me and summons a wave of grief and doubt within me. Because what if my parents are right? What if I fail Ava? Bowing my head, I close my eyes, trying to stop the tears triggered by Ava's sorrow. But who am I kidding? It's not all her. I screwed everything up, and I can already feel my life with Ava crashing with the cresting waves of a stormy beach.

Warm fingers dry the dampness under my eyes. "Carter. Please, don't be sad." Ava's soft voice wraps around me, blanketing me in her unsaid love. Love I can't ignore. Love I'm not worthy of.

"But I've ruined your life." My words hitch in my throat as I try to summon the strength of the sea to talk to her.

"How could you have ruined a life I wouldn't have had?" Though her words are intended to make me feel better, I can't ignore her grief, thinking about everything that led us to this moment. She doesn't have to tell me what's on her mind for me to know that she heard my mom's words and that they got to her. Her hands squeeze mine, and she stiffens, bracing herself for what she thinks is the end of her world.

"See, son," Dad says. "She understands. Ava's a reasonable person. She wouldn't want to put our people at risk."

Her grimace deepens. "Of course not, but you can't expect me to never see my family again, especially if I can live on land." My dad's words elicit something dark from Ava, and she turns her gaze from me to him. She might think the end of her human life nears, but she's not going to accept it without putting up a fight.

"But Ava—"

Ava surprises Dad by holding her hand up before he can even spit out an argument. Shifting upright, she swings her gaze to me. "Can we leave?"

Mom raises her eyebrows in astonishment, and Dad looks at me like I need to do something. I clench my jaw, thinking about what would be worse—ignoring my parents' warnings or risking seeing Ava fall apart. Ava wins without a question.

I help her to her feet, steeling myself to what I'm sure will be an onslaught of arguments and possibly interference from my parents. But they won't do anything crazy. Not here in their home. It's the only reason I move toward the door with Ava.

Mom touches her temples, closing her eyes, whipping her head back and forth. "Please, Carter. What you're doing...it's not right."

"It's right for Ava—and me." I kiss Mom on the cheek and don't acknowledge Dad. I half expect him to block our way, but Mom sinks into his arms to stop him from doing anything that'll risk Ava freaking out and drawing attention from the other tenants in the apartment complex. "Please, respect our choice to live how we want."

As I guide Ava out, I concentrate on the quick blinks of her heart to get myself under control. I've never had an argument with my parents, let alone denied their guidance and help, and I feel like crap for doing so. But it would be worse otherwise.

Ava doesn't talk the entire walk back to the beach, and I try to ignore the feelings our disastrous dinner with my parents ignite in her. I'll do anything to change them. Neither of us should have to feel so badly for not wanting to give in to the traditions of the sea.

I pull her into my arms, doing my best to hug the negativity out of her. "I'm sorry about tonight, Ava. I thought my parents would understand. They haven't lived in the ocean all my life. I thought they'd respect our decision not to as well."

She breathes in the crook of her neck. "I don't blame

them for worrying. They don't even know me and were right about my lack of control." I was right about my mom's words getting to her, making her doubt whatever control she established, and now I'm even more angry at my parents.

"You're getting better. We'll keep practicing. We'll swim every day so you never have a chance to miss it. We'll figure this out." I just want her to know how incredible she's doing and how I'll make sure she stays in control.

She tilts her head up to me, holding my face in her hands, and kisses me in response. All her bad feelings disappear under the desperate touch of my fingers sliding around her waist to pull her closer. I lose control over my ability to block my emotions from Ava the second she sucks my bottom lip into her mouth.

"I'm so glad it was you who chose me as your mate," she whispers into my lips, opening her mind up to me to show me how truly grateful she is for me.

I smile at her admission, enjoying every second of her attention, so focused on me and my body that it's easy to forget everything else.

I kiss her deeper, trailing my fingers past her waist to explore her smooth skin peeking out from the skirt of her dress. She moans, inviting me to familiarize myself with her curves. She devours another kiss, panting while sliding her hands down my back while sinking her body into mine. She slips her tongue into my mouth, drawing her fingers along my skin above my board shorts under my shirt.

She arches her pelvis forward and rubs her body against mine with only the fabric of our clothes blocking us from touching in a way I've yearned for every time I feel her desire. And now, it's hotter than ever. Something shifts in Ava, and she gives in to her sudden need to be with me. She smiles through another kiss, enjoying my body as much as I crave hers.

I let my lust rush over Ava, giving into the feelings pouring through me. She gasps through my kiss as I lift her off her feet, her legs automatically curling around me, allowing my hands to explore the smooth skin of her thighs as I lay her in the sand. Her fingers explore my sides until she can hook them to my shirt to pull it over my head.

My breathing quickens when she shifts under me, giving me access to her body, her dress bunched around her waist. I touch my fingers to her bikini bottoms, her small intake of breath nudging me to tug her dress off, leaving her in only half her swimsuit. I yearn to look at her in a way I've been cautious about until this moment. Because this isn't out of necessity. This isn't about getting her into the water. It's about both our needs to be together in the closest way possible like we've never been with anyone before.

I lean back to drink in the sexy sight of her naked breasts, heaving with her racing heartbeat in bursts of light to mirror my own. Her blue eyes hold mine, her lips slightly parted as she sucks in another breath, her body trembling in a good way as she nods and invites me down on top of her for a kiss that steals my breath to replace with hers.

"You're so amazing," I whisper into her lips, feeling her bare body touch my taut chest with every intake of air, stirring desire that sends heat down my core. I graze my tongue over her jaw, tasting her salty skin as I suck and kiss her in places that make her squirm to hold me tighter. I trail my fingers over her skin and down her body to familiarize myself with what she likes, using the emotions washing from her to me to guide me along the way.

Gliding my hand over and between her thighs, I grin as she hugs me and kisses my neck through a moan that vibrates against my skin. Ocean spray mists through the air across us, and Ava reacts to the cold sensation, clenching her body and then shuddering until she relaxes and works her mouth from my earlobe to my lips, sending me her desire in a form of an image through her mind, one of how hot she thinks I am as a merman, her heart drifting to sea with another one of my kisses.

She tenses under me again, her need for me shifting to nerves, and I freeze mid-kiss and drop my hand from her body. Her wide eyes steal my desire only to toss it to the ocean stretching into the bay along with her humanity. She transforms so quickly into a mermaid that I don't even have time to react as her bikini bottoms rip free and leave her in the sand, sparkling under the moonlight, gasping for a breath of the ocean.

I scramble to my feet, the fear of someone catching sight of my beautiful mermaid mate cascading over me. "Hold on Ava," I say, scooping her from the beach and into my arms as she opens and closes her mouth, struggling to breathe the air.

Jogging her into the waves, I splash through the surf until she fights my hold and flicks her tail to dive under without me. I push away her annoyance with herself and her fear and try not to dwell in the sudden hopelessness rising in her. As much as I want to stay in the water and transform, I force my legs to carry me back to the beach to gather our belongings scattered through the sand.

I spot her spark calling to me in the sea and swim to her without transforming. She floats in the surf, her arms covering her chest. Water drips down her face, and I can't be certain she's not crying with the pout stealing her beautiful smile.

"That was close," I whisper, helping her tie her bikini top on because she's shaking so badly.

She waits for me to transform before she says, "I'm sorry, Carter. I really suck at this."

Suck? Definitely not. Having her fantasize about me as what I am makes everything so much better than I could've imagined. I knew she appreciated my body as a merman, but I also knew she wanted to get to know my body in the form she's most comfortable in first. But I love how much she enjoys me no matter what form I take as I do her.

I smile, touching her cheek. "You don't have to apologize. It's okay. It was probably for the best anyway." Because I want our first time to be more than a moment on the beach, ignited by the bad emotions we push away with the best ones we bring out in each other. I want it to be perfect where she's completely with me and not teetering on a cliff to fall into the sea.

Her eyes search mine, her own doubt trickling into me, needing me to say more.

"I shouldn't have rushed things like that. Your emotions are connected to your transformation, and you clearly enjoy me in both my forms," I add, smiling again at the thought.

"You have no idea," she thinks to me, covering her reddening cheeks with her hands.

"I think I do." I really, really do. And now I need to swim—far and fast until I can pull my thoughts away from the memory of Ava and the sea and take us back to the land. And it's exactly what I do.

12

SWIM

"DID I RUIN EVERYTHING?" Ava asks, flipping around in my arms to face me.

Neither of us slept since retreating to her stateroom after swimming with Giselle until well past two in the morning. I don't know if Ava realizes it yet, but I suspect Giselle's growing less fond of how much of Ava's time I steal from her. I don't want to mention it, because Ava has enough to worry about, and from her obvious pout, something hangs heavy in her mind.

"What do you mean?" I ask, cocking my head to give her

my attention. It's easy for me to assume, but I want to hear her say it out loud, especially after my mom made me feel like crap about everything. I want nothing more than to prove to my parents that I really can handle anything Ava throws at me, even without an established bond between us.

"I mean—with your parents. They're going to hate me forever, aren't they? Which sucks. I never imagined..." Her words trail off as she loses herself in thoughts I'm dying to hear. I need to know what she imagined with us and our future. If I know her expectations, I can figure out how to fulfill them the best I can. And she obviously cares about what my parents think of her. All I want to do is prove that she doesn't have to worry about it. They're angry at me for denying them the chance to accept Ava into our pod.

"Ava—"

"I bet the whole sea will hate me. I bet your parents are so offended by my manners. My parents would never let me hear the end of it if they knew the way I talked to your parents."

I chuckle. I can't help it. She feels incredibly human in this moment, and not only because she rests one of her legs between mine. Her words remind me that she doesn't understand the extent of a merperson's bond and how my parents already consider her their daughter because I gave her part of me, even unofficially.

She flicks my shoulder. "Don't laugh. This is serious."

"The last thing my parents were thinking about was your

lack of manners, which I doubt they even recognized. We're merpeople. Our customs are different."

Groaning, she says, "I'm the worst mermaid ever."

I knew she was working through her thoughts all night, tossing and turning in my arms, but I had no idea it was because of how she thought my parents felt about her. I should've pried, but I didn't want to remind her of the disastrous dinner that has me now peering at the ocean every time we're on deck, nervous about whether or not my parents will actually leave us alone.

"You're not even close to being the worst of anything." I absently play with the tips of her blond hair, twisting and releasing them in my fingers over and over again. "And my parents love you, Aves. They wouldn't fault you because of the choices I made."

"Love me? I don't think so. Didn't feel like it, at least. I'm pretty sure they've declared me the girl who basically took over their son's life. You'd think we told them I was pregnant or something." She rolls her eyes and sighs. "Actually, with the way your mom acted at the sight of your ring on my finger—" She buries her face into my neck, her lips vibrating against my skin through her sigh.

I laugh, my voice booming through the room, making her look up to smile at me. "Can I apologize in advance for everything that comes out of her mouth from now on? When she realizes it's not something you want, she'll...forget about it. She'll survive."

Ava scrunches her nose, an expression I have trouble reading crossing her face. I regret even responding to her remarks. It's not exactly normal human conversation to talk about having kids. I know what she has planned for her life with college and moving in with her best friend. I know I wasn't part of her plan to begin with no matter how she's adjusting it for me, which I'm grateful for. She just makes it so easy to forget that we're not in the ocean, living for only each other. That we won't go through our official coupling ceremony under the light of the next full moon like normal mates would have.

"I won't let her harass you about it, either," I add, though I know I'll never hear the end of it. It's all Mom has talked about since I reached maturity.

We're so few in numbers that it's nearly expected to extend our pods the moment we couple and agree to tether our eternities together. Not every merperson finds their mate right away in the sea, and my parents were lucky enough to have ties to the land passed down from their parents. After the last year of full moons and meeting every prospect in all the colonies, I was pretty grateful for what they assured, especially because I now know it's because Ava was far away from the waves.

"It's not something I want now, but maybe in like ten years," she says, keeping her eyes trained on the spark in my chest, picking up pace at her words. Because she implies that she would consider such a thing with me. And the thought pokes at my nature as a merman, as her mate. It gives me hope to know that my parents were wrong to assume she might never love me. "If I can even manage to keep my legs with you long enough to..."

Her gaze shifts from my chest to look at me when I'm not quick enough to respond, now lost in my own thoughts about being with Ava.

She swallows. "God this got awkward, didn't it? I'm sorry."

I smile and shake my head. "It's far from awkward for me. And you know, you don't need your legs. You're a mermaid," I muse, running my finger over her hot cheeks, deepening in color at my words. "So, don't worry about that."

She licks her lips, her wide eyes searching my face as she thinks about what I've implied, and it leaves her flustered and speechless, and incredibly sexy even with her sudden embarrassment reminding me of my mom's words about Ava needing a mermaid to confide in. I bring her hand to my mouth and kiss her knuckles, trying to ease her sudden wave of mixed emotions crashing over me.

I clear my throat. "I'm sorry. I didn't mean to make you uncomfortable." I don't even know why I say it. She's embarrassed, but I don't think it has anything to do with me or my words. She's working through her own thoughts and fighting with her new mermaid nature that's vastly different than who she was as a human.

"Oh, I—I'm not uncomfortable. I just—I knew that. And I'm having trouble...I never, I mean..." Squeezing her eyes shut, she inhales a deep breath that shudders through her body.

I tighten my jaw, stopping myself from smiling again, though it's all I want to do as she bounces around a dozen thoughts in her mind, trying to spill her heart to me, no longer thinking about my parents or the disaster dinner but about me and her together.

Leaning closer, I brush my lips to hers, and she unintentionally sends me an image of us on the beach last night, confirming that I was right about where her thoughts shifted to. "It's fine," I whisper, nuzzling my nose to hers. "There's no pressure from me, Aves. Last night was—"

"I'm mad at myself," she admits, interrupting my attempt to calm her racing heart. "I don't even know what came over me. My mind was begging me to stay human with you, and then..." She groans, her voice lowering to a breathless pitch. "What's wrong with me? I messed everything up."

I almost tell her we can try again right now, but I hold back because her emotions are all over the place. "I was flattered, to be honest." I run my fingers along her jaw and up to push the hair she keeps trying to hide under behind her ear. Flush sweeps across her face, and I fail to keep my mind from wandering to Ava lying beneath me in the sand on the beach, the way the moonlight drenched her skin and lit up her eyes. How her warm body felt as I familiarized myself with every inch of her. It was one of the best moments of my life. "And you definitely didn't mess anything up."

She releases a small laugh, pressing her hands into my chest to bow forward. "Pretty sure I did. I—I've never been with someone like that, and I just felt…" She turns her gaze to the ceiling, searching for an answer she doesn't know.

"Out of control?" I find myself leaning closer, twining my fingers with hers. I wasn't expecting her to open up like this, but I'm glad she does. It says a lot about where she's at and how closely our wants and needs align.

"Yeah, a bit. With myself at least. Not with you, though. You make me feel like even if the tide rose to drag me out to sea, I'd be okay. And that's what makes me nervous. I like you—I mean, I can't even explain how much, and last night at your parents, you said…" She closes her mouth without finishing her thoughts.

I feel bad for not realizing it was more than sex and the new experience we were going to share. But as much as I feel bad, Ava makes me feel like I'm not a failure. She doesn't even realize how much what she said means to me or how much I needed to hear it.

Sitting up, I pull her with me, so I can look into her eyes. "I was serious last night about making things right for you and making sure this all works on land. I know you might doubt me, because you—"

She silences me with a surprise kiss I gladly accept along with the rest of her body as she scoots closer, resting her legs outside my hips, sitting so close that her weight sinking into me stops me from even trying to finish my thought. "I don't doubt you no matter how impossible this feels, Carter. I'm nervous is all. It's like I'm standing on the ledge of the sundeck all over again, bracing myself to jump in, except it's not the ocean I'm afraid of. It's me. The sea is getting into my head, and I don't want to let you down. You are perfect, and I'm an utter mess."

I smirk, feeling completely opposite than she does. "You're not. You amaze me. Everything about you. I—"

She kisses me again, cutting off my words before I can tell her how hard I've fallen for her over these last few days and not only because I gave her part of my essence. She always says exactly what I need to hear and seeing her, being with her, I feel like the world is better for it. "Thank you," she whispers. "I mean for everything. I'd be lost without you."

I open and close my mouth, my admission now lodged in my throat, because I realize she might not be ready to hear the words. She might not believe them. So instead, I show her. I kiss her and summon everything I love about her, giving her snapshots of moments where I could barely believe I got so lucky to have her with me.

She gasps and pulls away, her chest heaving. "Carter, I—"

A knock sounds on her door, drawing her attention away from me, interrupting whatever she had planned to say.

"Yo, Ava-babe. You better get your ass up," Matty yells through the door, pounding his fists on it again. "We're hitting the beach the second we dock."

Ava clings to me without moving. "He'll leave us alone if we don't respond."

I consider doing as she asks, pretending we're asleep, but I hear Giselle bang on the door next, reminding me that I need to make sure Ava doesn't unintentionally sever her ties to the people she loves on land. It's them who keep her human, not me. Because I'll follow her anywhere.

"I've never got to disembark here," I whisper. "Always had to work."

She flops off me and stares at the ceiling. "Okay, fine. I could use the distraction."

I almost tell her I could distract her, but she's already on her feet and crossing the small room to open the door.

"Damn, Aves. You look—"

"No worse than Sapphire," Giselle says. "At least Ava's quiet."

Matty tips his head back and laughs, and Ava slams the door in his face and turns to rest her back on it.

"You sure?" she asks me, banging her head on the door a couple times. "Because my friends—"

"Are great. I'd like to hang out with them more."

"You say that now."

I laugh and get up to hug her. "I'll say it later, too. Because really, after last night with my parents, nothing will ever be that bad."

"You really like her, don't you?" Chloe straddles her board next to me, bobbing over a small wave.

I don't know what happened, but one second I was planning an afternoon with Ava, possibly taking her to a Mexican restaurant near the water, just hanging out and experiencing a normal date with her away from the waves my parents could emerge from to surprise us, and then the next second, I found myself renting a surfboard with Ava's friends to hang out with them while Ava sits in the sand. If Giselle didn't take a wave to shore, I might've done so myself, because Ava looks miserable staring at her phone. I should've stayed on the Ocean Jewel like Ava had wanted.

A stream of seawater splashes my face, yanking my attention from Ava and Giselle on the beach. "Earth to Carter?" Chloe flicks water droplets at me. "I was talking to you."

I run my hand over my hair, pushing it from my face. "Sorry, yeah."

"Can't even take his damn eyes off her for a second," Matty says, shooting an arc of ocean water from his direction. "Witch craft, I think."

"Or something." Logan reaches over from my other side

and punches my arm. "I've seen all the candles in her room. And now this? Dude's a goner."

"Seriously, you guys?" Chloe says. "Have you not seen my room? You guys have both bought us all those damn candles for our birthdays and Christmas for the last few years."

"What about the potions?" Matty says.

Daisy rolls her eyes. "That's your doing, too. Candles and lotion." She turns to me. "I bet you'd never buy Ava either."

She's right about that, but I shrug, knowing that Matty and Logan expect me to take their side. "Maybe a recipe book for cakes around the world. She likes baking."

"See?" Chloe says. "You should take lessons from Carter. Do you have a brother?"

"I could be just as romantic," Matty says. He looks at Sapphire, who stares at the beach. "Right, babe?"

"Oh, no," Sapphire says instead of agreeing with him. "Something's going on between Giselle and Ava."

"They seemed fine this morning," Daisy says.

I jerk my attention to the beach where Ava scrambles to her feet. She peers around and turns her gaze to me once, and then rushes away, leaving Giselle yelling for her to stop. But Ava doesn't stop. She runs faster, hitting me with a bout of anger and despair, leaving me paddling forward.

Chloe paddles up beside me. "Why don't you stay here, and I'll see if Ava was going back to the yacht. Sapphire will go to Giselle."

I shake my head. "I should go."

"But I think it's about you," she says.

"Me?" I ask.

She nods. "I wouldn't worry, though. I think Giselle's wrong."

My frown deepens. "Wrong? About what?"

Shrugging, she says, "She's just worried about Ava is all."

I turn my head to glance at the beach to search for Ava, but she's nowhere among the crowd of people. Her hot emotions suddenly calm, loosening the knot twisting my stomach. I don't have to see her to know she's taken a breath of the sea. Because the sea calms her. I feel it every time. And now I need to follow her more than ever.

I swallow, licking the sea spray from my lips. "I can handle Ava, okay? You stay here and enjoy the surf."

"You sure?" she asks.

I nod and ride the wave to the shallows, leaving my board next to the towels in the sand. I jog down the beach only far enough to enter back into the waves where Ava's friends can't see me. There are a couple sunbathers on the beach, and a few kids play in the tide, but no one pays me any attention as I swim out and disappear.

The moment I transform, Ava's mind opens to mine without her even realizing it. Sadness washes over me before a blip of fear, and she thinks about fish caught in the net of a fishing vessel, which means she's now pretty far from the shallows.

Her presence pulls at my spark, the need to find her overwhelming me. "Ava!" I call out through our telepathic link, letting her know I'm coming up on her as she floats frozen under the shadow of a boat.

She flicks her fin, jetting away from me through the open water. She sinks into grief and uncertainty the deeper she descends, unintentionally spilling her heart out for me to hear. She never closes her mind off from me, which makes me incredibly grateful in this moment. Because she's losing herself to the sea, her heart caught on an anchor to pull her farther away from shore and her humanity, where she's afraid she'll mess up.

I don't let her get far from me, but I don't stop her from swimming. I'd follow her to Hawaii or Australia, the places she currently dreams of fleeing to in this moment. She's so lost in her thoughts and the current surrounding her that she nearly crashes into the tail of a massive gray whale. I dart forward to get above her and hook my arm around her waist to pull her from the pod before she hurts herself.

But still, I don't stop her from swimming. I keep her pace, just holding her against me so she can feel me in the water, until she starts to slow down from exhaustion. Taking over for her, I flick my fin and glide us through the sea another mile.

"Carter," Ava whispers to me in my mind, her voice so

soft I almost miss it through my heart beating in my ears. "What are we doing?"

"Swimming."

Bubbles pop in my face as Ava laughs out loud in the water. She twists in my arms, pressing her blinking heart to mine, touching her whole body to me so I feel like we're one entity. It's not until we're too far from shore to ever make it back as humans that I finally stop swimming. She nuzzles into my neck, her loose hair flowing around my face, and hugs me tighter.

I want so badly to ask her about what happened with Giselle, but I'll wait until she's ready. I'll hover with her in the open ocean, letting her be who she needs to be in this moment, for as long as she needs to face what happened on shore.

She pulls away from me and stares at me in the water, her jewel eyes matching my gaze in intensity. "How did you find me?"

I reach out to her and run my fingers over her glowing chest. "I followed you."

Bringing her hand up, she cups it over mine. "I didn't know you could do that."

"You can do it, too." We're connected on a soul-deep level, our accidental bond more powerful than anything.

"Oh. I don't know how to do that."

I hadn't considered we'd be apart yet. "All it takes is you wanting to find me, Ava. If you want me, you'll find me. You might not feel it like I do, but we're connected."

Her sad features soften as she repeats my words to herself in her mind, and she doesn't have to say anything for me to know that she's feeling the deep meaning behind an action as simple as letting my spark pull me to her.

"Giselle thinks that I'm being selfish," she says, surprising me. I thought she was going to question our bond more. But she just accepts it with all her heart and soul, reminding me again how lucky I am. But even so, I can't stop myself from reacting to the hurt Giselle elicited in her. I knew I was right to suspect something was up with her, but I thought maybe it'd blow over after we return to Azure Waters.

"Ava, Giselle doesn't know what she's talking about," I say, suppressing my annoyance with Ava's best friend.

"That's what I thought, but it really got to me. She'll never know. I lost the person I told everything to. It's just— this is really hard." Her lip trembles as she thinks the words to me, hitting me with a wave of grief comparable to the night I told her that I transformed her.

And it guts me. Because my mom was right. Ava needs more than me despite how much I want to be enough for her. She didn't only lose her human life, she lost her identity. She lost the bonds I thought she could maintain, but I can't even see how. We could live on land and pretend to be human, but I ruined it. And I made things worse for her by giving her the hope that she could manage.

Bringing my hand up, I cup her face, peering into her eyes. "That's why you ran." It's not a question. It wasn't even about whatever Giselle said to her. It's about Ava and the damage I caused with promises I'm not sure I can even keep anymore.

She nods. "I want so badly to slip back into my old life like none of this ever happened. If I could just shut off my heart and turn my back on the ocean, I could make it work. I know I could. But then I—I'd be miserable. It'd be so much easier if I could tell my family."

"Ava..." I try not to react. I try not to give away how my heart shatters in my chest because I can't allow such a thing. If anyone finds out about our secret, if Ava decides she can't handle not telling her family, I'd have no choice but to carry her away to Pearlestria myself. Because I will not allow her to suffer the consequences of breaking the most strict law of the sea. King Attilonious would rise from the deep to kill her family to guarantee our secret is safe. It would destroy her worse than me breaking my promise.

"I know, Carter. I can't. I won't. It's just—maybe I'm better off not going back." She might say the words into my mind, but I can feel she doesn't mean them. But even so, if she asked me to swim her away, I would.

"You really think so?" I ask.

She shrugs. "Maybe."

"Okay then. We won't go back."

Her face falls at my words, and I know if we were above water, tears would splash her cheeks. Her sorrow sinks me down a foot, squeezing my chest, making it hard for my gills to pull oxygen from the water.

"No," she says after a silent moment between us.

She's all over the place with her thoughts that I can't keep up. "Ava, what is it you want?"

"That's the problem. I don't even know anymore. But this isn't just about me, Carter. You said it yourself. It's about us. Your feelings matter to me, too."

I'm so overcome with relief and love and everything good about Ava that I can only respond to her by closing the distance to meet her for a kiss. She's no longer worrying about her human life crashing in the waves to get dragged to sea, but she's worrying about me. About us. About making a life that leaves us both satisfied.

"I'd like to go back," I say, pulling away to meet her gaze again. "I love living on land. The beds are much more comfortable and the food is better. If you think it's too hard to be with your family. If that's what this is all about, we can move anywhere, Ava. It doesn't have to be your family or the sea. We have a choice."

A dozen thoughts flicker across her eyes as my words sink in. Her emotions morph from sorrow and uncertainty and to hope and love and happiness. Relief. "I don't want to say goodbye to my family forever. I want to stay with them for a while before we figure things out."

"We'll make this work," I say, nodding.

And I know we will. Ava's no longer struggling to keep her head above water. She finally realizes she can swim.

13

WELCOME HOME

I DIDN'T REALIZE HOW much I'd dread today. I knew it was coming. I knew the Ocean Jewel would make its way to Azure Waters, where Ava would disembark, ending what has been the best week of my existence. But knowing it would happen still didn't prepare me for how much I wish she could stay. Or for me to follow her and never return to the yacht. Neither can happen. Ava has her life to return to, and I have to see to it that she keeps it.

"I can't believe I'm actually going home. I wasn't sure I was ever going to make it," Ava says, folding a few of her dresses to fit in her bag." How am I going to sleep knowing you're not nearby?"

How will I? Because I've already grown so familiar with her body next to mine, enjoying how she flips back and forth a couple times throughout the night from wanting me to hold her from behind to wanting to hold me in her sleep.

I suppress the sadness trying to slip from me to her and say, "I'll be around so much you won't even have a chance to miss me."

I'll sneak back to her every day I'm away, even if only for an hour. She's done great since Santa Barbara without anymore accidental transformations and even worked things out with Giselle, but I still worry. Taking her into the water to swim is important, and I'm almost nervous that she'll do it alone. I can imagine what would happen if another merperson was near. It's unlikely, since most don't leave their colonies outside the full moon but still. I can bet my mom told my grandmer. She might've told others. Word travels fast in the sea.

It doesn't help that I have to return to work tomorrow for a trip to Orange County for some celebrity's birthday, but I'm willing to risk leaving for Ava. A phone call isn't enough. I've left the boat on full moons, so this won't be any different.

She drops her clothes and pouts at me. "I already miss you."

Without a word, I roll off the bed, feeling the truth to her words in my essence, and close the distance to hug her from behind to kiss the skin below her ear. She stops folding and shoves the rest of her clothes in her bag to give me her undivided attention, leaning back into me.

Gliding my fingers over her shoulders and down her clavicle, I map her skin all the way to her spark, feeling her breasts rise and fall under my hands with her breath and beating heart. Something about touching her where I feel a part of myself calms my nerves and reminds me that even if we have to leave this yacht, even if we have to re-enter the world that was so easy to forget, that we'll still always be connected through our bond, because we share our spark between our two bodies.

She turns her head to reach my mouth, and I kiss her softly, testing her, sending her an image of how beautiful and amazing she is. Her lust trickles through me at first before cascading in a wave that I react to, pressing myself against her while I hook my fingers under the straps of her dress and ease it from her shoulders.

In the mirror on the door, I watch the flush blossom up her neck as I tug her dress lower to admire how sexy she looks in her lacy bra. She shivers in a good way, meeting my gaze in the mirror, sucking her bottom lip between her teeth, just standing so still, waiting for me to continue.

Her emotions shift. She goes from lust and desire to something rawer that flows over me, warming me from my core to my heart far beyond the yearning to take our bodies to the next level to finally match our bond. I've never felt so wanted and needed in my life—not because Ava relies on me to help her as a mermaid. She now relies on me on a different level completely—to fill her up with everything I have to offer, so she can face the world with me by her side and not hiding behind me.

Baring herself to me in this moment in all her blushing humanity, her emotions so steady unlike anything I've felt from her, gives me the hope I need. Even though reality threatens to change our lives, it also greets us with a promise that we'll be okay. Better than okay.

Trailing my hands across the fabric of her bra, I brush my fingers over her breasts, feeling her body react with excitement I lose myself in as I continue to pull her dress down past her hips until it drops to her feet.

Ava spins in my arms and kisses me so desperately, so frantically, like she'll die if her lips aren't touching mine. I let her take control and follow her lead when she pushes me back on the bed to straddle me, running her fingers over my body while leaning down to kiss me again, sucking my lip into her mouth, tasting like the sugar and cinnamon of the breakfast we shared on the sundeck. She caresses her tongue to mine, deepening our kiss, her hips grinding against me enough that I moan into her mouth before flipping her over onto her back.

Her nails graze my sides as she yanks off my shirt like she

can't stand the fabric between us a moment longer. Her fingers work their way over my hips and up my back, gliding over my muscles to draw me closer, begging me to discover what she likes and what will make her gasp to match my panting breath. She arches her back and uses her body to explore mine, opening herself to me in a way that leaves us both breathless. Pressing her head into the pillow, she raises her hips to mine and makes me moan across her hot skin that I take extra care to explore with my fingers, tracing her body inch by inch until I know she's ready.

Easing away from Ava, I rest on my elbow to meet her bright eyes against the flush crossing her face and neck. I need to make sure our thoughts align, and she wants me to continue. A part of me needs to make sure I don't lose her to the call of the sea whispering around us to give in to who we are.

She leans up and kisses me again, sending me an image of the both of us right in the room, in this moment, in this second where she's ready to give herself to me as my mate, body and soul, with so much love neither of us has to say the words to know how incredibly important we are to each other, how perfect we are with our hearts beating in sync, our bodies now aligning to take us into uncharted territory we'll navigate together.

"Ava, are you sure you want to?" I ask quietly, holding my breath to listen to the rapid beat of her heart racing for me, because of me, while mine does the same for her.

Reaching over, she surprises me by pulling a box of condoms from her suitcase with a note from Giselle scrawled across them. The gesture reminds me of how human she still feels, how human this moment is to her, and how human I'll remain to spend our lives together. Because something like this doesn't matter in the sea. It doesn't matter to coupled mates. We're safe as long as she doesn't desire to extend our pod together.

"I do more than anything," she responds, handing me the box.

I smile to myself, suppressing my thoughts before I lose myself to my merman nature. I only want to lose myself to Ava. "You're the best thing to ever happen to me," I whisper into her lips, trailing my fingers over her skin to undress her completely.

She kisses me again, sending me a dozen images of us together, showing me how much I mean to her and how much she desires this moment between us. I don't stop kissing her, breathing in the sweet scent of her hair, holding her close, tasting and touching and feeling her body in a way that makes the both of us gasp and ache for more.

I open myself up to Ava, letting her experience the intensity of my feelings in a way I've never done before. Our needs and desires, every amazing burst of our emotions, entangle and entwine, blending as one until it's no longer me or her, but us together exactly how it should be.

How it'll always be.

★★★

Ava parks her silver BMW in the driveway outside of an enormous, sea green Victorian mansion nestled in a small beachfront community only ten minutes from the marina by car and even less by swim. Pink hydrangeas bloom in huge bouquets under the windows and meet a manicured lawn lit with solar lights. Tall palms line the circular drive long enough to fit a dozen cars, yet the only car parked is Ava's.

"This is home for me," Ava says, staring up at what I think is her bedroom hidden behind sheer curtains. The hum of the roaring ocean drifts through the air, calming my nerves, knowing that even if she's not with me all the time, she still has the ocean in case she needs it. "Are you sure you want to come in? You can say no."

I smile, raising my eyebrows like I'd ever consider such a thing. The fact that she invited me home with her to meet her parents speaks volumes about our now official human relationship. Ava doesn't realize it, but I already feel like her family is my family. It's another step I'll gladly face with her even if it might be slightly weird to her to bring me home. "It's only fair for me to meet your parents after the fiasco with mine. It can't be any worse than that, right?"

"Right, and you won't have to worry about an interrogation. My dad will be leaving for the hospital at any second, and my mom will soon lock herself in her office like every night," she says, reminding me that her dad's an emergency surgeon in the next town over. While I've seen doctors on TV, the only healer I've ever needed was my mom. In the ocean, only mermaids are gifted with such an ability.

I smile again, squeezing her hand, feeling her nerves seep into me. I don't pressure her to hurry up and show me the life she had before me, though I'm dying to see what lies behind the opaque glass doors.

After a minute, she finally gathers her nerves with the help of my calmness and pulls me up the red brick stairs and inside. Ava calls for her parents, guiding me through her house, decorated in warm woods and modern furniture, original artwork, and an entertainment room bigger than my parents' apartment with a TV big enough to compete with a movie screen.

Ava doesn't give me much time to take everything in, guiding me past a staircase and formal dining room to her kitchen, smelling of coffee and chocolate with the hint of ocean trickling in through a window.

Her parents sit at a small table in the nook of the modernized kitchen, sharing a piece of chocolate cake. They both turn their attention to us, looking from Ava to me, and her mom sets her fork down and tilts her head toward Ava's dad.

"Oh, Ava. You've brought a friend home," Ava's mom says.

Her dad lifts an eyebrow, taking in my appearance with a

sweep of his gaze. I half expect him to glare at me, but he surprises me by smiling and says, "I've never seen you before. Did you wash aboard the Ocean Jewel? I didn't think Ava would take me serious about the whole plenty of fish in the sea spiel."

Ava's mortification hits me as fast as she says, "Dad, seriously? Carter works on the yacht."

I chuckle with her dad, getting a cute, pursed lips look from Ava. Stepping forward, I offer her dad my hand to shake instead of the hugs my parents nearly smothered Ava with. "It's nice to meet you, Dr. Adair and Mrs. Adair."

Ava's mom takes my hand next, holding it softly for a moment. "It's a pleasure, Carter. Please, call me Beatrice." She looks from me to Ava. "Are you two hungry? We have some leftover Chinese food or cake."

"We already ate," Ava says, speaking for us.

"But cake sounds great." I can't help it. I've never denied an offer of dessert in my life.

Her parents don't interrogate me at all, just smiling like they're happy to see Ava with me. They're far different from my parents, seeming more laidback, and from what Ava's told me, I know that they've all done the best they could to work through their grief of losing Ava's sister, including not being overbearing in her parents case, or overly rebellious in Ava's.

Beatrice serves the both of us cake, and Ava's dad motions for us to join them, but Ava shakes her head and asks, "Is it okay if we take it on the back patio?"

Ava's mom twists her lips, cocking her head to look at Ava like she asked the strangest question she has ever heard. It's then that I realize that they know Ava better than anyone and the girl who left on vacation was deathly afraid of the ocean and would in no way go on the beach. Ava has even switched rooms when she was a kid, so she didn't have to look at the water where her sister was swept away.

"Uh, yeah. Sure, sweetheart." Beatrice shoots a confused look at Dr. Adair, who smiles at me. I can't be sure if they'll thank me or blame me when they realize how different Ava is now, even if they never see her tail.

Dr. Adair rises to his feet. "You feeling okay, Avie? You hate the beach."

Nerves bunch my stomach at his sudden scrutiny of Ava. Ava told me her parents spent thousands of dollars on all sorts of therapists until she refused to see anyone else as a teen in regards to dealing with her sister's death, and now to have her suddenly okay, worries me.

Ava closes the distance and hugs Dr. Adair. "I feel great, Dad. A week on the water has given me a new perspective on things."

"Really?" he questions, peering at me from over Ava's shoulder.

"Yeah," she says.

I don't know if it's because they're happy to see her and missed her after being away a week, which is the longest Ava's ever been away, or if it's because I'm standing here, shifting on my feet, but either way, Ava's parents accept her answer and excuse themselves for the evening.

I scoop up the two plates with the pieces of cake and follow Ava through the house and out the back door to an enclosed patio only a few dozen feet from the foamy surf. It's strange seeing the green cushions of the furniture that I had expected to be in a palm tree pattern like from a memory Ava shared with me.

"I haven't stepped foot on this patio since I was a kid," she says, answering my silent question. The sea breeze plays with Ava's hair, blowing it from her face, and she hugs herself and peers around to take in the sight of everything.

Ava watches me eat the cake, telling me she baked it herself, nearly making me throw her over my shoulder to dive us into the sea, so I can hunt her a fish she'd probably never eat all because I want to show her how much I love the idea that she promised to feed me more later.

I set the plate down and take her hands into mine, meeting her for a kiss she sinks into to reveal our afternoon together, focusing on a moment that makes me shudder with desire.

"You really are going to make it hard for me to leave," I whisper into her lips.

Gliding her tongue across my bottom lip, teasing me without letting me scoop her up like I want to, she says, "Is it working?"

I kiss her in response, moaning as she sends me the image again, and then she breaks away to pull me with her out the gate and onto the beach, leaving her flip flops in the sand. She lets me go to twirl in front of me, the wind lifting her dress to reveal her smooth skin of her thighs. She curls and uncurls her fingers, baiting me along, teasing me with her smile as she strips into her bikini, her spark blinking in sync with mine, and I know exactly what she wants to do.

I tug my clothes off and follow her into the surf, hooking my fingers to her bikini straps to untie them and pull her up to me to straddle my hips through another kiss. Ava's skin shimmers in the light of the crescent moon, her blue eyes like glittering stones as she starts to transform. I dive us under together and swim a few times around Ava as she completes her transformation. She hovers before me, drawing me closer with her hands, igniting in me passion and love and everything amazing about Ava.

She kisses me once and swims to break the surface, and I dart up after her, splashing water between us. I take her to some rocks near shore and help her out of the water to peer at the glittering lights of the houses on shore.

Leaning over, I kiss her softly, pushing the wet hair from her face. "I can see why you love it here."

A pout steals her smile from me. "It doesn't feel the same as it did when I left."

I nod my head, holding her against me. A dozen thoughts

cross my mind, feeling the bittersweet feelings emanating from Ava as she stares at her house in the distance. "Maybe that's a good thing." I can't help but think it might be easier if we ever had to go.

"Maybe it is. Either way, I don't want to think about it anymore."

So I won't let her. I propel into the ocean and hold out my arms to catch her. "Then come on. Let me help you forget."

Ava jumps to me, giving me a whisper of a kiss before taking off, laughing through my mind as I chase after her. Swimming a circle around me, she runs her fingers over my scales while gliding against me to hook her arms around my neck.

"How do you feel about the shallows here?" she asks. "Think you'd be okay calling them home?"

I hug her closer, brushing my lips to her neck, swimming her deeper from shore. "More than okay."

She smiles. "Welcome to our home."

Our home.

Nothing has sounded more right.

14

PROMISES

AVA FLOPS NEXT TO me in the surf, sinking into the sand to stare up at the glittering sky. A wave crashes over us, and she squeals, covering her hand with her mouth to muffle her voice. I laugh and kiss her, shifting on top of her to warm her cold body as she shivers in the tide.

She brushes her lips to mine and kisses me deeply in the surf. "I wish we could swim all night," she says, brushing her fingers through my sopping hair to flick it off my forehead. "It feels so perfect, like it's just us in the world."

I smile down at her, shifting her body in my lap to block

her from another cresting wave. "I haven't swum so much in a while. Usually only on the full moon and over the few holidays and celebrations this last year because of work. Before that, I used to spend a few weeks in the summer with ou—my pod." I correct myself, knowing Ava couldn't consider my family her own yet.

"How could you even resist?"

Her question swirls through my mind, and I can't think of a good answer to tell her. Because now that she carries my spark in her chest, now that I can feel how much she loves the water as a mermaid, no longer lost to the waves of fear, all I feel is my growing need for the sea, too. She ignited my spark in a way that makes it easy to lose myself in a world where only Ava matters.

"I think because my mate was on land," I say, twining our fingers together to kiss her hand.

"Me?" she asks. "Carter—"

I realize a little late that Ava's heart might float on the waves, but her mind is still human. She has trouble thinking past the weeks ahead of us. She freaked out at the idea that my mom thought I proposed to her with my sea stone ring. I doubt she could accept the possibility that we were fated to be together. The ocean brought us together after all. "Don't think too much into it, okay? It's just a term used in the sea. Like girlfriend." Or wife. But I won't go there. We're not officially coupled and probably won't be if we remain on land.

She nods, turning her eyes to the sea, stretching out into the night sky. "I think I like mate. Girlfriend seems...not enough. I mean, you transformed me into a mermaid."

I shake my head, smiling. "Kind of a big deal, huh?"

Tipping her head back, she releases a loud laugh, filling me up with the sweet melody of her voice I could listen to forever. "So mate it is. Well, at least with you. My friends would think we were weird."

"Our secret."

She laughs again, nuzzling her nose to mine, her heart soaring on a rush of the adrenaline from swimming and how simple things are in the water compared to how complicated our lives might be on land. It's easy to lose myself to her as she kisses me again before pulling me to my feet.

She saunters in front of me through the sand, smiling at me from over her shoulder, purposely walking with a sway to her hips that I admire, watching the rivers of saltwater flowing from her sopping hair to trickle off the smooth skin of her butt cheeks peeking out from her bikini bottoms.

"Wanna spend the night?" she asks, slowing down to fall into step next to me as we trudge the dark beach in the direction of her house. "I mean, it's a little late to go back to the Ocean Jewel, and I was hoping to get as much time as I could before..."

I wrap my arms around her, rubbing my fingers over her arms to smooth out the goosebumps prickling over her skin.

"If it's okay. I was just going to sleep in the surf."

Her nose crinkles at the thought, making me laugh. I don't think she ever imagined the idea and still can't envision it by the way she's staring at me like I've said the strangest thing she's ever heard. "What? The shallows? Like just out in the open?"

I nod. "I don't have time to build an underwater shelter."

"Carter, I—"

I grin, stopping in the sand to face her. I cup her cheeks, meeting her saucer eyes, sparkling in the light of the moon. "We're merpeople," I remind her. "It's not a big deal. We sleep wherever if we're outside the colonies. It's fine."

Shaking her head, she pelts me with droplets of water. It's obviously a huge deal to her and something I'll have to ease her into when she wants to explore the ocean outside these shores. And I know she'll want to even if she doesn't realize it yet. "No. You're definitely not sleeping alone in the ocean. You're spending the night with me. My mom probably won't even care if she notices. And don't even consider arguing."

I chuckle, sliding my arms around her back to pull her closer. "I wouldn't dare."

She nods her head. "Good."

We stroll together, her nestled under my arm, past the beach mansions of the elite of Azure Waters. Ava stands in the sand, staring up at the dark windows above her back patio and motions for me to walk with her around the house to a set of stairs that leads up to an apartment above the garage.

Twisting her hair in her fingers, she wrings out the sea-water and enters inside first, disappearing for a moment before bringing me a towel. The cool air of the AC blows around us, and Ava practically drags me to her bedroom and quietly clos-es the door without turning on the light.

Her king-sized bed sits under a wall of windows, made to perfection with a dozen decorative pillows. An open walk-in closet reveals what looks like hundreds of formal dresses to go with the built-in shelves of high heels and handbags and a glass case of jewelry I can't even imagine Ava wearing.

A flat screen TV hangs on the wall over an entertainment center, and a laptop sits closed on her desk with corkboards with what might be thousands of pictures of her friends. I glance at her dresser, spotting a picture of Ava as a kid with a girl I assume is her sister with similar blue eyes.

"That's Bailey," she says, padding across the room from me. I was right. "You've met everyone else on the walls."

"You look like you have a lot of fun with your friends. I hope they don't get tired of me hanging around," I muse, half joking.

She leaves my side to head to her dresser across the room. I listen to her rummage through her drawers and peer at what looks like a photo taken inside a limo. Possibly at prom. "I think they like you more than me," she says from behind me. "If they only knew you were a merman. I bet—" Ava snaps her mouth shut without finishing her thought, knowing that something like telling her friends could never happen.

"They'd make bets on how fast I can swim or something," I say, trying to ease her sudden worry.

"Or ask you to take them snorkeling."

"I'd have to practice with you as a human."

She laughs. "I'd like that, even if we can't actually tell my friends." She groans. "Oh, well. I don't want to think about it. I only want to think about you."

Ava flicks on a light, drawing my attention from the pictures on the walls to her. Sucking in a slow breath, I drink in the sight of her standing in the doorway. Sand peppers her naked body, haloed in the light behind her, and she offers me a smile, motioning for me to follow her in. She turns on the shower, filling the room with steam and stands in front of me without a word, something suddenly shifting in her eyes.

A small blip of sadness washes from her to me, making me study her gaze. "This sucks."

I frown at her unexpected words.

She flings her arms around me, hiding her face in my chest. "I don't think I can do this."

Pulling away, I reach up and brush the strands of sandy hair from her face. "What do you mean?" Her trickling fear enhances mine as I think of the worst thing she can possibly say.

"How can I pretend that my life is still normal? I'm

scared."

"Of what?"

"Everything. Of accidentally transforming. Of you leaving and realizing how much easier life is without me. How I feel like I don't even want to be here. It's just—it's harder than I thought. I wanted to come home, but now—"

"I'll never abandon you, Aves," I say, cutting her off. "I promise. I swear. I vow to you that I'll always be here, okay? And all that other stuff? You do belong here. And if you accidentally transform? We'll manage, okay? You will do fine. I will make sure of it."

She swallows, sniffling a few times as she composes herself. "Okay," she whispers. "We'll manage. I'll manage."

"I'll always be here. I promise," I repeat, holding her close.

And I mean it. I just wish she'd believe me.

Memories of last night linger in my mind, and I focus on Ava sleeping in my arms to push them away. Ava breathes into my fingers, her hand curled around mine, clutching it to her face in her sleep like how I imagine she'd hold onto me in the water. With the ebb and flow of the ocean, couples sleep entwined to stop the currents from drifting them apart. And having Ava cling to me instinctively seriously makes me never want to move again, even though I've been awake since before first light out of habit.

Sunbeams cut through the cracks in Ava's curtain, lighting her cheek aglow. She stirs, her calm emotions turning into happiness that makes me brush my lips against her shoulder until she wakes up enough to turn around to face me. After the best and longest shower of my life, I managed to calm down Ava enough to finally close her eyes to sleep. If only I could return tonight to be with her again. I'm afraid to leave now, though I have to go.

Tonight will be the real test, because once I board the Ocean Jewel, I won't get the chance to be with Ava again until I can manage to sneak away tomorrow night. It'll be the longest I've been away from her, and I know I should get used to it but damn. After last night, it's going to be especially hard. When I return, finding an apartment will be the first thing on my list. There's no way I can afford a place in Azure Waters, but I'll figure it out. I just hope Giselle doesn't mind if I crash at the condo they plan to get together in a few weeks. Because Ava needs to be walking distance to the water, and—

"I wish you didn't have to go," Ava murmurs, pulling me from my suddenly panicking thoughts about how I'm going to manage taking care of things to keep the lifestyle she's used to.

I envelop her in my arms, breathing into her hair as she rests her forehead on my chest. "I know what you mean, but working is now more important than ever. Living on land costs money, and you probably don't want me to live on the Ocean Jewel forever, right?"

She tilts her head up to frown at me. "Of course not."

I wish my mouth wouldn't have opened before I could think my words through, because I realize how they came out, making it sound like Ava doesn't understand our situation, and her annoyance pokes at me, the first she's ever directed a feeling I don't like at me.

Trying to clarify my thoughts, I say, "And while I have a pretty good savings already, I need to be ready to take care of—" I snap my mouth shut. Ava's grimace turns to full blown fear, her blue eyes widening at even the idea that things might not work out here.

"Carter..." Her voice comes out a whisper, her anxiety tightening my chest. She feels like she did at dinner with my parents when she thought life as she knew it would sink into the waves. "I hope you don't think that I expect you to take care of me, because I don't."

It's the last thing I know she expects, but it doesn't change the fact that I will. She's my mate, after all. But I'm afraid if I tell her so she might pull away from me, lost to her human rationale, and the thought of her suddenly distancing herself over something like this, especially after last night and after giving each other our bodies and souls—I can't even think about it. She wouldn't do that. I know it. I'm letting my own uncertainty get to me.

I brush my lips on her forehead, suppressing my emotions so she doesn't feel them. I'll only allow the best ones to drift to her if I can control it. "I know you don't, Ava. It was just a thought." If there's one thing I've learned about Ava, it's that she's strong-willed and determined but also considerate and empathetic to my wants and needs, even if I don't always allow her to feel me. All these things that make her incredibly hot to me, but she also has a side that I need to treat with care. She can only be so strong, and I'll lend her my strength and coddle her even if she glares at me. I know she'd do the same with me.

She tightens her lips, flaring her nostrils. "Okay, but to be clear, I'm capable of helping out. This isn't all on you. I'm not your respons—"

I interrupt her with a kiss to stop her from trying to explain to me why she thinks I don't need to treat her like my mate. She wouldn't understand the customs or traditions, and while we ignore them now, they still linger in me. As the one who changed her, she's my responsibility—everything we do together will fall on me in regards to the laws of the sea.

And honestly, I hate the way her annoyance feels. She has nothing to prove to me. I know she's capable of taking care of herself. I know that even if I couldn't provide for her how she's used to that her parents would. But when it comes down to it, I'll still feel bad if I can't. I want to show her I can give her the best life. I need to prove to the ocean that I'm worthy of her and that I'll always be the best mate, even if we never officially couple in the light of the full moon.

"You have enough to worry about. I don't want you worrying about something I was just thinking about. Let's just enjoy the morning before I have to leave, okay?" I say after she relaxes and gives into my affection.

She tilts her head back and peers into my eyes. "Fine, but only because I like you rudely interrupting me like that." She smiles as she says it, though I can see it in her eyes that she's still thinking about it.

After staying in bed for a few more minutes, Ava leaves me in her room to see if her mom's home. She calls out to me that we're alone, and I make my way from her room to find her in the kitchen with a plate full of muffins that I accept, eating one in a few bites, making her eyes widen. If she ever spends any time in the sea, she'll realize why I practically inhale things. They taste so good. I can't help it.

Ava shifts on her feet, staring at a sticky note in her fingers, glancing at the words scrawled across it. She holds it up for me to read. It's a note from her mom about dress shopping for the King's Scholarship Foundation Gala on Friday night along with the suggestion that Ava invite me as her date. My heart picks up pace at the thought that her mom likes me and wants me to join her family for what I think is a special occasion. It makes things feel more real. That Ava's not only going to get to live her human life on land, but I get to live it with her as well easily enough.

She rubs her lips together when I meet her eyes to respond, but she speaks first and says, "You busy on Friday? I know it's last minute, and you probably have to work..."

"I—"

"They're really boring anyway." I can sense that she's nervous, afraid that I won't want to join her, though I can see how much it would mean to her if I could make it possible. And I will.

I smile at her. "Then we'll be bored together, because I return to port on Friday afternoon and don't leave again until Saturday."

She grins back at me, excitement rushing through her. "You have to wear a tux."

"I look good in a tux," I say, making her laugh. I can see she's already thinking about me in formal attire because I'm always in shorts. While a tux isn't my first choice of apparel, and I don't own one, I'll adapt like any merman come to shore. I'll wear a tux if it means I get to be with Ava in her world.

"Then it's a date."

I kiss her. "I like the sound of that."

Ava offers me another muffin before relenting to getting ready to take me back to the Ocean Jewel. She clutches my hand the entire drive to the marina and parks in the lot and turns in her seat to face me. A dozen emotions pass between us, her pouty lips looking so kissable even as they tremble, and I bring her hand to my heart to let her feel how it beats in sync with hers.

"It's just until tomorrow night," I say quietly to myself through the sorrow pouring from her. Because now that we're sitting in the parking lot, gazing at the Ocean Jewel waiting for its crew to prepare the yacht for another excursion, all of this feels unbearable. I hate that I have a life outside of Ava I have to get back to, but it's the only way to make it. I want to be immersed in her world, not drifting in the shallows. I want to have a place that she'll call ours one day.

"I know," Ava says, squeezing my hand, shifting closer in her seat.

I chuckle. "I was reminding myself." Before I can change my mind, I hug her and meet her for a kiss, forcing myself to open the door to leave. "Call me if you need me, Ava. I'll figure out a way back if I have to."

She nods. "I'll try to think of a good reason."

Touching her cheek one more time, I exit the car and head toward the dock, looking over my shoulder to watch her watch me go.

"Dude!" Keith calls from the ramp, a bag slung over his shoulder. "I was almost sure you were about to call in your notice for some chick."

I tighten my jaw, stopping myself from reacting. "Shut up, man. Ava's my girlfriend."

He shakes his head. "Shit, man. You say that now, but wait until you see who's boarding next."

I sigh and stroll past to head onto the boat. "What did I tell you before?"

He laughs, and I know he remembers that I told him Ava was the one for me. He wouldn't forget with how he's hassled me over something he can't grasp. "Whatever, Carter. Hope it works for you, man."

"It will," I say.

From the main deck, I peer out over the parking lot, spotting Ava driving to the exit. My heart thrums against my ribcage, threatening to jump out of me to follow her, but I let her go.

"Just one night," I tell myself.

If only it didn't feel like forever.

❧15❧

DOUBT

"CARTER, YOU GOOD?" KEITH asks, watching me stare at two passengers gliding across the calm water on the jet skis.

I thought it was the erratic driving of the guy who swore up and down that he knew what he was doing making me nervous, but it's Ava. And now she's full blown panicking back in Azure Waters, and I'm stuck here, watching the liar attempt to impress his group of friends watching from the sundeck.

"No, this guy's going to eat it," I mutter, stretching my arms over my head.

Keith laughs. "That's all you, dude. I promised Ms. Hottie with the body I'd keep watch on her."

I open my mouth to tell him to knock it off with the nicknames. The last thing I need is for someone to overhear him and his underwhelming attempt at a compliment I guarantee won't land him a date. But the guy on the jet ski loses control as I predicted, and he tips the craft. I don't react, watching him float for a moment. He attempts to get back on the jet ski once before yelling out for help.

I sigh and shake my head at Keith. "What did I say?"

Keith slaps my back. "All yours, man."

The guy hollers again as I prepare to launch the jet ski from the hydraulic platform. Keith groans from his post, keeping an eye on the man for me. He's safe enough with his life jacket on, but he's growing impatient. The last thing we need is a complaint.

"Watch it, Carter. Looks like something curious is circling beneath him."

I turn my gaze to the water and swear under my breath. A mixture of emotions course through me. Keith distracted me enough to push Ava's wild nerves away, and then they vanished, so I thought she had everything under control. She was to call me if anything had happened, but I hadn't considered the possibility that she wouldn't be able to call.

And now she's here.

All I want to do is dive in and transform, to envelop her

in my arms and kiss her a dozen times to show her how happy I am to see her even if it could mean something awful happened back in Azure Waters that pushed her to find me. Suppressing my worry, I rush to launch the jet ski.

The man flails in the water, screaming and swimming as fast as he can, abandoning the jet ski altogether. There's no doubt he glimpses Ava beneath him, but he's probably imagining her to be a shark or something instead of my gorgeous mate who seems to be keeping a jellyfish bloom away.

I can't stop the smile from crossing my face despite the feeling of impending doom. No other mermaid in all the seas would get so close to a human in the water to try to protect them from pesky jellyfish. But merpeople are immune to stings. Jellyfish happen to be a favorite meal for merbabes before they learn to hunt.

"Help!" the guy shouts, waving his arms at me. "I was stung. Something else is in the water!"

I reach my arm out to pull the guy onto the back of my jet ski, but instead of grabbing my hand to let me do the work, he locks his fingers to my wrist and yanks me off and into the water. He yells again, splashing me in the face.

"Mr. Johnson, I know you're afraid, but you have to calm down so I can help you up. You're safe. The jellyfish are far enough away."

"But the thing!"

"The sea turtle is more interested in its meal than you." I

say the first jellyfish-eating creature that pops into my head.

"Sea turtle?"

I help the guy onto my jet ski by hoisting him up and out of the water. Now that he sees I'm not panicking, he settles down enough to stop trying to push me into his imaginary sea monster that happens to be my beautiful mate anxious for my attention. "Think so. You said you were stung by a jellyfish?" I ask, remaining in the water.

He nods.

"Can you drive the jet ski back on your own or do you need assistance?" I pray to the sea that he agrees to return on his own.

Loud hollers and cheers sound from the Ocean Jewel, and I signal to Keith that everything is good. The commotion draws the guy's attention, and he bobs his head. I can see it written all over his face that he's embarrassed by his panic and wants to prove himself to whomever he's trying to impress on the yacht.

"Great."

The guy takes off at a slower pace, and I swim the dozen feet to his abandoned jet ski. I sink under and inhale a breath of water. Ava snuck up on me and now swims close enough to kiss. I pop to the surface and cough, spitting out saltwater. She emerges next to me, her emotions flaring up again but not panic. Sorrow. Her sadness makes me think the worst, and I can't hide the frown overtaking my face. She doesn't even have to tell me that something bad happened, and I hate how I can't just abandon the jet ski to transform to be with her. Too many eyes probably remain in my direction, the only thing obscuring me is the jet ski.

I touch her cheek, forcing myself out of the water before Keith calls out to me. Sucking in a breath of air, I manage to ask, "Ava, what are you doing here?" despite wanting to ask her what happened. Because she doesn't need me to accuse her of messing up. Maybe she hasn't. Maybe she just couldn't ignore my absence any longer.

She twists her mouth, her brows pinching together. A dozen emotions crash over me. It takes her a second to work up the nerve to tell me what's wrong, and she blurts, "Giselle took my ring right off my finger in a moment of excitement while we were dress shopping."

I can't stop my own shock and fear from crossing my face. But damn it. If Giselle took her ring then it means she was forced into changing into a mermaid. "You transfor—"

"I made it to the water in time." She holds up her hand to show me her ring. "But she knows something was wrong. I was so upset by the whole incident that I couldn't force myself to change back, and somehow I ended up here."

My fear dissipates into something indescribable. Ava let her spark guide her to me. It's something mates can do, and she listened to her essence, my essence, in a moment of need, and it brought her right to me to help her. "Because you really wanted to find me."

Her eyes glass over with tears, and one splashes her cheek to blend with the saltwater dripping from her hairline. "I don't know how to get home. What do I do?"

I nearly dive in this second to guide Ava home, but if I do, things will turn bad for us. I'm already taking too long. Pain clenches my chest at having to ask her to wait, but I know she'll understand. "Give me a few minutes. I'm going to take the next group on the water, and I want you to follow me. There are some caves along the cliffs where you can wait for me until tonight, okay? I don't want to risk leaving you out here in case you trigger the transformation back." *Or risk someone from the colonies happening on Ava,* I add silently. While unlikely, it's not entirely impossible. My parents swim the coast all the time.

Without waiting for her to respond—because I'm afraid I'll lose my nerve and relent to follow my merman nature to abandon everything—I take off on the jet ski and back to the Ocean Jewel. I hustle to get the next group into the water so Ava doesn't have to wait long. I speed a little too fast for the group when we hit the water and purposely take a turn too quickly and knock myself off.

I motion to Ava toward the cliffs, wishing she'd come close enough to kiss me, but her nerves keep colliding into me, and I know all she wants to do is hide and wait until we can be together.

Dread sinks into my stomach watching her in the water without me. This is my fault. I should quit the Ocean Jewel. I should be near Ava in case something like this happens again. It's my duty to care for her, and I'm failing. My shortcomings will be the reason I have to take her to sea.

And then what?

I push the thought away. I won't let it come to that.

I drag myself through the narrow opening of one of the few untouched by humans caves nestled in an inaccessible part of a cliff that drops right into the sea. Ava's wild emotions eased a couple of hours ago, and I've been doing my best to share only my love with her through our accidental bond.

"Ava?" I call out telepathically, knowing she's fast asleep in an old mermaid hideout decorated with stones straight from what would be considered my home colony of Pearlestria. It's long since been used, probably before I was even born, but I've stopped here to rest once when a storm hit on a full moon and left me in rough waters, and my life on land doesn't grant me much time to migrate to others in the colonies. Not like when I was younger with my parents.

Ava's soft voice trickles to me as she thinks to herself about how much time has passed, flicking what feels like her never ending panic back on. I suppress it and make a promise to myself to figure out how to help her through another adjustment with my working.

"Ava, I'm here." I slide into the deep, sparkling pool, fanning my tail on the sandy bottom.

Ava hits me with a tidal wave of emotions—relief and joy, lust, excitement, and undeniable love—the second she spots me. She swims at me so quickly that I hit my back on the rock wall where she kisses me a dozen times, pressing her body to mine in a way that reminds me how badly I missed her closeness, her touch, us just being together. I cup her face, turned on and craving her in a way I know she's not ready for nor would be the best time considering our situation, but it doesn't stop me from kissing her deeply to show her exactly what she does to me and how much I enjoy it. How much I need her.

Forcing myself to pull away, I stop myself from getting lost on both our adrenaline and desire. "You okay?" I can see that she is, feel that she is, but I ask her anyway because hearing her confirm it will help ease my tense muscles.

She pouts her kissable mouth. "I don't even know if I am or not. What time is it anyway? I'm sure my mom's put out a search party by now."

I damn well hope not. I don't tell her so. Instead, I hook my fingers to her hips to keep her floating in front of me. "It's almost nine."

If I wasn't holding her, she'd breach out of the pool and injure herself in a rush to get back to sea. But I can't let her go. Not like this. Not until I prepare her the best I can. Because if she's right and her parents are looking for her, that will open us to risks we can't afford.

"We need to go," she says, pushing bubbles through her lips.

I pull her even closer until there's only an inch of space between us. "Okay. But I want you to be prepared. If your family has already put out a search party, we're not going to be able to stay. It'll draw too much attention and unwanted questions."

Ava squeezes her eyes closed, her whole face morphing into agony like my words cut out my spark from her chest, leaving me nearly incapacitated. I don't even know how to deal with the raging sorrow wanting to sink me to the bottom of the pool. I feel so lost as she breaks down in front of me. A good mate would never be such a disappointment, and I feel like crap. Nothing I can say will ease the pain inside her. So I hug her and try my best to keep her together with the weight of my arms.

"Carter." She hides her face in my neck, and to my relief, lets me hold her. She unintentionally shares her thoughts with me as she plays out all the possible ways to get through the what-if scenario of how to explain her absence.

I kiss her temple, smoothing out her floating hair against her back. "Please, Ava. Don't panic just yet. Everything might be okay. We might not have anything to worry about. I just need you to be prepared in case."

"Okay." Her words sound nearly inaudible in my mind.

If Ava wasn't so anxious, I'd continue to hold her right here in this place isolated from the rest of the world. Even the short time we've been apart affects me more than I imagined it could. No wonder my parents rarely ever separate from each other. It feels like my heart hangs outside of my reach, begging for me to find it, when I'm not close enough to touch her.

I help Ava out of the pool and catch her in the churning sea outside of the cave. She quietly hugs me the entire swim back to Azure Waters, her body perfectly aligned with mine that when she lets go, I feel as if a part of me is missing.

Jetting through the water, I make a point to get her close to any animal that piques her interest. It helps when I swim at a warrior's speed and flip her around a few times to make her squeal out loud. I'd do anything to keep her distracted, even breach out of the water, but the second I reach the familiar shallows of our home, she falls silent and serious, her worry threatening the very existence of her mermaid heart—and mine.

I break the surface with her near the jetting rocks offshore from her neighborhood. Ava releases a breath against my neck, her relief a sweet, much needed change from the tension tightening both our bodies.

"Can you transform?" I ask, holding her close to keep her from drifting.

She sinks under and hovers for a long moment before

popping up. "I can't."

With one look into her blue eyes, I know it's not because she can't. She's hung up on everything that happened that it's keeping her anchored to the sea. "Try harder." I dip under and transform into a human to encourage her mermaid essence to follow my lead. There's something deep-seated in our nature that makes us always want to be in the same form.

"Carter, I don't think I'm going to have to explain myself. I can't change. Something's wrong with me." I was right. If even a tiny part of her is hesitant, she won't do it. She sinks back underwater before I can react.

I tug her to the surface to stop her from losing herself to the sea. "What do you want to do? We can wait it out, or we can head back to the Ocean Jewel, and I can quit tomorrow. We'll head up to San Francisco to see if my parents will help, but you know what they'll say."

She grimaces at all my suggestions and covers her face. "I just want to change ba—"

And it worked. I knew she wouldn't want to go through with any of those things, not when she wants her life to be here with everything she knows. I stay underwater with her through her shuddering muscle spasms. She thrashes like the first time she transformed into a mermaid, but this time she looks as if it takes everything in her to find her human self. Finally, she pulls me back to the surface with her, curling her naked body around mine. The heat of her skin, even in the coolness of the water sets me off.

"It's a lot harder to come back when it's the lack of the sea stone that sets you off," I manage to say through my own ragged breath.

Ava nods, easing away from me to swim a few feet. It only takes her sinking under once to convince her to let me carry her the rest of the way. I make it to the sand and sink next to her, letting a wave crash over us. I drink in the sight of her in the soft moonlight. She stretches her arms over her head, not even caring she lies half naked beside me in a nearly sheer bra.

Reaching out her hand, she surprises me by trailing her fingers up the curve of my hip and to my stomach until she finally cups me face to pull my closer for a kiss just soft and sweet enough to leave me craving more.

I lie with Ava until she's ready to get to her feet. We stroll back into the waves just deep enough to help rinse off the sand to change into our wet clothing. Ava's ripped shirt looks like it's going to fall apart at the seams, but I know her well enough that she'd never risk being vulnerable in a state of undress that she's only starting to get comfortable with me.

I dust sand from her arms, shifting on my feet. "I'm not leaving until we make sure everything's okay. And if it's not, we'll stay around long enough for you to pack a few things."

She rubs her lips together, suppressing a groan by swallowing a few times. "Okay."

I hate having even to prepare her, but if people ask too

many questions, I won't have a choice. It's not only our lives at risk. The laws of the seas are in place for a reason, despite how I feel about them or what they demand I do with Ava.

Taking the lead, I guide Ava through the sand and to her beachfront property. Only the back porch light shines over the patio, but the rest of the house looks dark. Ava steers me around the side and to the front, guiding me up the stairs to the garage apartment. She tugs me inside her dark house, clutching my hand like we'll suddenly stumble upon a monster, but nothing happens. I don't hear anyone either.

"It's not unlike my parents to have drinks at the vodka bar near the marina with their friends on my dad's night off," Ava says to break the silence.

Ava leads me down the stairs and to the kitchen. She pulls a sticky note from her mom off the fridge and heaves another huge breath of relief, offering me a smile. "Everything's fine with my parents. Giselle covered for me."

I furrow my brows. That only solves half our problem. "But what about Giselle? She's going to expect an explanation, Ava. You can't tell her."

She crumples the note in her hand. "I know that!"

The sudden anger in her voice makes me startle and step back.

"Give me some credit. I know how important our secret is," she says, twisting strands of her hair.

And I feel like utter crap for doubting her for a second.

Feeling her anger directed at me is awful, but I deserved it. I know Ava would never purposely do something to jeopardize us. I can feel it deep inside me. But a nagging part of me feels like reminding her is the only way to assure it never comes down to having to take her to sea, a place neither of us wants to go.

"I'm sorry," I say, keeping my voice even to not show her how painful her anger is to me. "I just know how close you are."

Her shoulders slump, and she turns to face me. "And it kills me not telling her, but it is what it is. I get it, Carter. Don't ever doubt me."

"I don't," I say. At least I didn't mean to. Leaning over, I brush my lips to her forehead to try my best to show her so.

She searches my eyes for a long moment, reading into my half truthful admission. Because as much as I don't want to doubt her, I can't help it. Her bond with Giselle is comparable to bonds within a pod. And Giselle? She's vocal. She doesn't hold things back. I'm afraid if she pushed Ava enough, either Ava will give in or I'll have to step in and intervene, and the last place I ever want to be is blocking Ava from her best friend—a concept still hard for me to comprehend.

A dozen emotions race from her to me as she works through her thoughts, and I wish we were in the sea so I can catch at least a few that trickle my way.

But one thought shines bright enough in her eyes that I

realize she still sees my doubt, and the small blip of doubt is enough to make Ava step away and say, "I'm going to call Giselle and then hop in the shower. Want me to walk you back to the beach? I can handle my best friend without you."

Shit. I screwed up, and there's not much I can do. As much as even thinking about space between us kills me, I know she needs it, and I have to give it to her.

"You don't look so sure," I say, responding to her, wishing with everything in me that she'll change her mind and not send me away.

She bares her teeth at me, her grimace hard to overcome even as she tries to smile. "I am, promise."

I want to say a dozen things to her about how I can help her, but I know deep down that this is something beyond my capabilities. I don't know her friends well enough to handle this. This is Ava's world, the world she's sharing with me, and I have to trust in her to know she can handle it, even if it's without me.

Her annoyance dissipates as she lets it go, inching closer to me. I gladly accept her kiss, sinking into the affection she offers that make it easier to believe that things will be okay. That she's capable of succeeding at this life on land I want her to fight for, because I want it to. I need it to. I'm counting on her to fight for it for me. For us.

I pull away to smile at her. "You know, my life has gotten so much more exciting with you in it." I can't leave her thinking only doubt lingers in my mind, because it doesn't.

She laughs, beaming me a real smile, one that sends my spark racing for her. "It's safe to say I feel the same."

As much as I don't want to leave, I have to. I can't disappear from the Ocean Jewel like Ava can't disappear from Azure Waters. She walks me back out to the beach and kisses me in the light of the moon. Her emotions run hot from lust and longing to sadness I'm leaving, and I do my best to assure her it won't be for long.

"I'll come back tomorrow night, okay?" I say, pulling away before I pull her with me.

She responds with only a nod, her lip quivering for a moment. Turning my back on her, I stroll into the surf and undress, forcing myself to dive under. If I don't, if I even dare look back before I hit the water, I know I won't go.

From the surf, I watch Ava on shore, my heart begging me to run back to her, but she turns around and heads inside. I stay in the shallows outside her house for a few hours just in case, but she remains out of my reach and away from the sea. I know it's a good sign despite how bad it feels. I just can't wait until we get this new life of ours under control. I can't wait to see what our futures bring.

❀16❀

CAN'T STAY AWAY

THE SECOND I COULD SNEAK away from the Ocean Jewel, I did, and now I wait in the surf as Ava and her friends sit around a fire pit down the beach about a mile from Ava's house. I told Ava I would meet her tonight, but I couldn't wait. Despite how calm she's felt all day, I can't stop my own anxiety from getting the best of me over the situation with Giselle or how Ava made me leave last night. It was a hard adjustment for me knowing that Ava wants nothing more than to be independent and handle things in her human life without me. And I want to give it to her, but my deep-seated merman nature just wants to do it all for her.

Ava stands up from her spot in the sand and faces the water, searching the waves like her heart insists she finds me without even having to look. She waves to her friends and heads toward the cinderblock bathroom facility on the other side of the lifeguard tower.

I transform in the waves and rush to catch her as she rounds the building on the opposite side of her friends. I know I shouldn't risk emerging like this, but my heart can't take it as it pulls me closer to Ava. Catching sight of me, Ava's whole face lights with a smile and she rushes in my direction, throwing her arms around me. Ocean water soaks into her shirt, but she doesn't care. A wave of her emotions pours over me, and I'm thankful to the ocean that she missed me as much as I missed her no matter how things ended last night.

"I expected you later," she says, combing her fingers through my dark hair to push it away from my forehead. "I'm not alone."

I lick the saltwater from my lips. "I couldn't wait. I've been anxious all day."

She frowns for a second, misconstruing my words. "I told you I'd handle it, and I did..." Her voice trails off, stopping me from interrupting her to tell her that I've mostly been anxious because of how much I missed her not the other stuff I want to ignore. But I can't. Not with it on her mind now.

"But?" I ask, now needing her to fill me in, though I saw

for myself that everything was fine with her friends. If it wasn't, I doubt Ava would be hanging out with them on the beach.

She exhales a long breath against my chest. "Giselle kinda thinks we're involved in something awful. She asked me if I murdered someone."

My mouth drops open in surprise, and I laugh at the absurdity of it all. I'm certain Ava would never even kill a fish to eat let alone a human. To think that Ava's best friend even thinks of that possibility guarantees I'm never going to be on her good side now. At least it's better than the alternative. I'd rather her think I'm trouble and not a merman. "She's gonna hate me."

Ava pats my cheek with her hand. "She'll get over it. All that matters is that she won't ask any more questions."

"Good." Leaning down, I kiss her again, lifting her slightly off her feet, seeing if she'll let me pick her up to curl around me completely. If her friends wouldn't freak out, I'd take her into the waves. I want her to know how sorry I am for ever doubting her last night.

But we don't get the chance.

"Ava?" Giselle's voice cuts over the hum of the sea.

Ava stiffens and grimaces, pulling back from me. "You have to go!" she whisper-hisses at me, pushing me toward the water.

I don't let her run from me. Instead, I smile and grab her

arm, pulling her with me around to the back of the building. "One more kiss," I beg.

She smiles and relents, kissing me deep enough to make me really consider carrying her to the water. I graze my tongue over hers, and she reacts in such a way that speeds both our hearts up. Her desire keeps me in place, kissing her until she pants and smiles at me.

"Ava?" Giselle asks again, stopping Ava's mind from drifting to the sea with mine. "Where are you?"

I kiss Ava's cheek and drag myself away, though it feels like I abandon my heart on shore as I enter the sea. Peeking from the water, I notice Ava's friends pack up their stuff and put out the fire.

From my spot, I can see Ava and her friends stroll to the empty lot. She gets into her car and starts it, but the second her friends leave, the lights blink off, and she steps back out. Her mermaid instincts know I wouldn't have gone far, and I swim into the surf and closer. My breath catches at the sight of her stripping out of her clothes to leave under the lifeguard tower. She rushes into the waves and dives under, and I swim up to her, meeting her smile with my own.

"You came back," I think to her, swimming her away from shore.

"Everyone was heading to Sapphire's, and I told them I had to finish the cakes for the gala," she says. "Plus, those few kisses weren't enough for me. I've missed you all day."

I kiss her again, responding with a dozen images from moments of us together to show her exactly how much I missed her. We catch up on our lost time, showing each other what our days were like without one another.

"See how boring my life away from you is," she says, running her fingers up my chest, taking extra care to explore my skin as I swim us in the direction of a desolate beach in a spot humans don't usually go to because of the location at the bottom of a cliff.

"It's a good thing it won't be like this forever," I say, slowing down as the water gets shallow.

I consider jetting the both of us right onto the beach in our mer forms but instead trigger my transformation without letting go of Ava. She automatically follows my lead, letting me carry her all the way to the sand.

I pull off my waterproof bag and wrap a towel around Ava's shoulders before I put another on the sand. She does her best not to take in my body in the moonlight but fails miserably, making me smile at the blush deepening the color of her cheeks at the same time her heart picks up pace to carry mine along with the rhythm of her palpable desire.

"You're so prepared," she muses, smiling at me.

I nod and pull out a sealed container of cookies Rita, the Ocean Jewel's chef, saved for me. Ava's eyes crinkle in the corners with a smile, and she takes a bite of the chocolate peanut butter cookie from my fingers.

"If I promise to bake you a few dozen, will you get this recipe for me?" she asks, taking another bite, closing her eyes to savor the flavor.

I grin. "You bet."

Ava takes another cookie from the container and waves it at me. "You don't want any?"

"I brought them for you...as an apology. For last night." My voice barely comes out a husky breath, because I don't want to think about last night ever again, especially because Ava's already forgiven me.

She presses her lips into a thin line and shifts on the towel closer to me, resting one of her bare legs over mine. "I'm sorry, too. You had every right to react as you did. You barely even know me, so how could you possibly really trust me?"

I blink a few times, the surprise of her words washing over me. "I trust you, Aves. Out of everyone in the world, you're the one I'll always trust." Reaching out, I touch my fingers to the towel covering her heart. "And I hope to win yours over too. I know this is all new and confusing—"

"And incredible, amazing, magical even," she says, cutting me off. "Everything about this is just..." She sinks into me, meeting me for another kiss that gives me what I feel like I need to survive.

I know her human rationale stops her from saying any more, but her kiss and the dozens of images of us together flickering from her mind to mine tell my heart everything I need to know. Ava might worry about the newness of our relationship, but she's also aware of the level we sink into as unofficial mates. A level she finally accepts right here, kissing me on the beach.

She drops the towel from her shoulders, exposing her naked body to me with an intense gaze piercing me right in the core in a good way. Her startling blue eyes drink me in, roaming over my body in appreciation a second before her hands do. She takes care to explore my skin, working her fingers over my muscles, caressing her fingers over my nipples to ease lower.

Hesitating, she gathers her nerve to take things further, though I can feel how much she wants to. I brush my lips to her shoulder and run my hands down her body, testing her to see if she'll let me continue. I touch her in the way she craves, setting her off so much that her nerves vanish, and she takes control.

Her mouth explores my body, licking and sucking in a way that leaves me panting and wanting more from her. I pull Ava up and flip her over onto her back. Her fingers discover exactly what I like, and she smiles at my reaction. I shift her beneath me to feel the heat of her body and to push away the goosebumps prickling over her skin. She gasps against my shoulder, kissing her way up my throat to meet my mouth. I devour her kiss, trailing my fingers down her stomach to tease her for a reaction.

"Carter." My name comes out light and whispery from her full, soft lips. "I—"

I shift up to meet her gaze. "We can stop."

She shakes her head. "No, I don't want to, I just..."

"If you're too nervous, we won't, but remember what—"

Squeezing her eyes closed, she leans up to hide her face against me. After a moment, she meets my lips again, sending me a memory of our conversation about merpeople sex ed. that she couldn't stop giggling over. But she's not giggling now.

Her chest heaves, her emotions all over the place, battling it out for me to feel.

My mom was wrong about Ava needing another mermaid for this sort of thing. Another mermaid would guarantee Ava and I wouldn't be on this level because they teach how to get pregnant and not the other way around like humans. Coupled mates in the sea try to extend their pods pretty quickly, but those on land? There's a reason I'm an only child, partly due to the expense of it on land and partly because it's harder.

"We can wait," I say, running my finger along her jaw-line. "I'm perfect just laying here with you."

Her eyes search mine, boring into me as she sinks into the soul bond we share. She surprises me by kissing me deeper. Curling her legs around me, she throws all her human ra-tionale to the waves to experience every ounce of pleasure I'm determined to give her, my merman nature suppressing the human Ava knows of me. I whisper her name in question, and she licks her lips and nods for me to continue.

My heart beats wildly in sync with hers, and I lose myself to the wave of everything that is Ava as we connect on a level where I feel complete being so close to the part of my soul I gave her. I open myself up to her, so she can experience all the love and devotion I have for her as my mate, and she reacts by kissing me deeper, losing herself to me all the same. Nothing else in the world matters with Ava in my arms, with her heart against mine, her hands keeping me close.

I don't move until she lets me go, and even then, I pull her close to me, wrapping the towel around both our bodies as we lie on the beach together until the tide rises. I help Ava to her feet, her smile assuring tonight was as amazing for her as it was for me. She teasingly dances around me, tugging me back into the waves. Cold water splashes over us, and she jumps up into my arms with a shriek, letting me dive us both in.

Ava and I swim together, hand-in-hand, and I work on familiarizing her with the shallows outside her hometown until I feel her exhaustion sneaking up on me. We pop through the surface and clear our lungs of ocean water, treading in place.

"I hate that you have to go," she whispers, clinging to me.

"Me too." I brush her strands of sopping hair from her face. She has no idea how much I truly hate it. "But I'll be back tomorrow."

"Maybe we can skip the gala," she muses, her gaze wandering to her house.

"And miss my chance to experience a part of your life?" I ask.

She scrunches her nose. "It's not as magical as this. Or fun."

"We'll make it fun."

She kisses me, sinking me underwater with her while she transforms before me. I walk her to the lifeguard tower where she dresses, wishing with everything in me that I didn't have to leave, but being here is a risk already. We trudge through the sand and to her car alone in the parking lot, and we face each other, listening to the hum of the engine without her climbing in.

"So, I'll pick you up at the marina," Ava murmurs, hugging me again.

I nod. "I can't wait. I miss you already."

She breathlessly laughs and groans and pulls me close against her to kiss me a dozen more times until I force myself to step away. Ava locks herself in her car and waits for me to run back into the water before taking off.

Barely a minute after I transform and open my telepathic channel, a familiar voice sneaks into my mind, making me slow my pace from shore.

I was hoping with everything in me that my parents would respect my wishes and leave us alone, but my mom swims up to me, her fuchsia tail glittering in the glowing night sea.

"My son," she says, cupping my face between her hands. "Ava is stunning. As beautiful as I imagined."

I release a bubble through my lips and tighten my jaw to stop myself from beaming her a smile at her compliment. "What are you doing here? I have things under control."

"Can a mother not show her support? It hurts me deeply that you won't allow me to bond with your mate, Carter. Our pod should be together. What you're doing will only devastate your mate when—"

"Stop," I say, cutting her off. My chest clenches at the mere thought of hurting Ava.

"You need to hear it, son," Mom says, patting my cheek. "You've been far too removed from the colonies, and I'm sorry for that. I'm here for you. Your father wants nothing more than to assure you have a fulfilling life, but you have to do the right thing."

I swim back, tugging myself from her. "I am doing what's right."

"Carter."

I shake my head. "I have to get back to the Ocean Jewel. You should go home."

"Please, Carter. Give me the chance to talk to Ava."

It takes everything in me to hold firm in my decision no matter how much sorrow I see fill my mom's blue eyes. "I'm sorry, Mom. It's not a good idea after our visit. Maybe some other time when some time passes."

"Carter," she says again, begging me with her voice.

"Just go home. If I need anything, I'll let you know. Maybe I can ease Ava into the idea of visiting you and Dad some other time."

A look of despair mars my mom's features, making me feel like the worst son in the world. But it's far less agonizing than feeling like a failure of a mate. And that's what I'll be to Ava if my mom gets what she wants. Ava's proven that she can handle herself on land, even without me, and I know we'll adapt and overcome any obstacles that come our way.

"I hope you do," Mom says.

My mom hugs me once more, and I wait until she disappears before I swim to the stretch of beach outside Ava's house to assure myself she's safe and okay, though her contentment lets me know it.

Ava peers out her back window, her heart knowing I'm close without her even realizing it, and she smiles and presses her hand to the glass door.

I wave with a smile, and she blows me a kiss.

Taking a breath, I dive under and breach out of the water, feeling her happiness and awe crash over me in a warm burst I lose myself in as I head back to the Ocean Jewel. Her wave of emotion was exactly what I needed after the surprise visit from my mom. Because I know I'm right about Ava and our life together.

I know how amazing our future will be. I won't let anything stop me. Not my pod. Not the sea. Nothing.

17

SECRETS

"YOU'RE GOING TO A GALA?" Keith asks, raising an eyebrow at me. "Like a tuxedo, rubbing elbows with the rich and famous, overpriced party?"

"Mmmhmm, so I gotta go." I sling my bag over my shoulder and rush to disembark the yacht. I'm already thirty minutes late meeting Ava, and she anxiously waits for me in the parking lot.

Keith strides next to me to keep up and whacks my back before slinging his arm over my shoulders. "Shit, man. Why couldn't I have saved blondie? I thought she'd dump you the second her vacation was over."

I stiffen, anger rolling through me at his remark. "Her name is Ava, and I told you, she's my one. Don't disrespect me like that, okay?"

His eyes widen. "Chill out, Carter. I was kidding."

"And you know what? You'd both be dead if it were you who tried to save her." I don't know what comes over me, because it's unlike me to put myself out there like this, but I'm not in the mood to deal with someone who doesn't understand my bond. It doesn't help that I've spent the whole night stressing over my mom's arrival. I wouldn't put it past her to emerge on shore and talk to Ava anyway. She's the most overbearing person I know.

"Ouch, dude," Keith says.

I sigh and stop. "I'm sorry. I'm just nervous about tonight."

He whacks me again and chuckles. "Why don't you hook me up with her brunette friend? The other blonde? They're both hot. Then I'll have your back."

I shake my head. "Not a chance, man."

I leave Keith laughing on the main deck and run down the ramp to jog the rest of the way toward the gate that leads to the parking lot. Ava leans her back against her car, shading her eyes from the sun. Her shimmery pink lips part in a smile, and I stop in front of her and touch her cheek, surprised by how different she looks with thick lashes and glittery eyeshadow. I've never seen her wear makeup before. She looks like a model, glamorous and poised, the epitome of what I expect from the people attending tonight's affair.

"I almost didn't recognize you," I say, playing with the blond curls intricately woven into her low bun.

She bares her teeth at me in a fake grimace. "It's a bit much, huh?"

I shake my head, feeling her sudden nerves over her appearance and what I think about it coursing through me. "You're still just as beautiful."

I admire her with a smile before I kiss her, tasting the sweetness of her lipstick that I'm careful not to smudge. Finally pulling away, I toss my duffle bag on her backseat and slide into the passenger's side for the ride to her house. She only lets go of my hand once to let me get out of the car when we arrive, and her mom greets us at the door in the foyer, dressed in an expensive-looking deep burgundy gown with diamonds sparkling from her wrists and neck.

"I'm so happy you could make it, Carter." Beatrice hugs me instead of offering a handshake, making me smile. From growing up around humans, I know that unlike with merpeople, hugs are saved for those they're close to or their families are close to. It's a great sign that Ava's mom thinks highly enough of my relationship with Ava. "Ava told you that you could stay in the guest apartment, right?"

I can't stop smiling. The invite was unexpected but welcomed even if Ava said that she expects me to sleep in her room tonight, which I would never argue about. Just the thought excites me. We only have tonight and tomorrow morning together, and I don't plan to waste a moment. "Yes, thank you for the offer, Beatrice."

"My pleasure. Now, if you two will excuse me, I have to find Ava's father so we can head out. Ruby wants to go over her speech once more before the gala starts." Beatrice turns to look at Ava with a pointed look, her lips twisted. "Don't be late, Avie."

Ava tosses her hands up with a sigh. "Can't promise that, Mom. Matty rented the limo. He's in charge."

She shakes her head with a chuckle. "I'll see you two later."

Smiling at me, Ava practically drags me up the stairs to her room. I do my best to keep my face friendly the second I spot Giselle sitting at Ava's vanity table, snapping pictures of herself in the mirror.

"Our date has arrived!" Giselle spins to face us with a smile, though her eyes zone in on me, her distrust shining through enough that Ava's steps falter.

I remain calm, widening my smile. "How did I get so lucky to have two of the prettiest girls of Azure Waters on my arms tonight?" My dad taught me that a compliment is a must when it comes to mermaids, and it seems to work well on humans too, because Giselle's eyes soften toward me. I was worried that she would hate me after the incident with Ava, but I can tell now that she was more hurt than anything. Secrets are hard. I know this. Ava definitely knows this now. I wish with everything in me that things could be different for Ava, but the laws of the seas make it unsafe. King Attilonious would never trust a human no matter who they were.

"We're sure to be at the center of the gossip," Giselle says.

"Totally." Ava laughs. "Can you imagine Mrs. Goldberg's face?"

She and Giselle chat excitedly about all the different people who'll be attending tonight's event. Giselle insists I can't see Ava's dress yet, so Ava walks me to the guest apartment down the hall from her room.

I pull her to me and kiss her the second the door closes. She sends me a dozen images of us from last night, sending my heart racing. Her fingers slide under the hem of my shirt, and she pulls it up, teasing my skin for a moment.

"We don't have to stay long tonight," she murmurs against my lips.

I chuckle. "Whatever you want, Aves."

I love how hard it is for her to drag herself away from me, though she waits a moment, watching me undress for a quick shower. If Giselle didn't call her name, I'd have invited her in to watch me, because she obviously wants to.

"I'll be fast," she tells me, biting her bottom lip, slowly closing the door. "See you downstairs."

After showering and shaving, I get dressed and style my hair with wax, taking care to put some actual effort into my appearance. I head downstairs to wait, hearing laughter trickle through the room. Ava's excitement increases mine, and I rock on my feet, listening to the soft footsteps heading in my direction.

The second my eyes meet Ava's, my breath escapes me. The silhouette of her dress reminds me of how magnificent she looks in the sea. The color of her gown matches her shining eyes with intricate pearl beading that sparkles across the fabric in the overhead lights. Her heart lights up her chest, the beats speeding up to match mine, sending fractals of rainbow light through the room that only I can see.

"Wow." My voice barely manages to escape my throat. "Ava, you're—you look just like..." I let my words trail off, feeling the heaviness of Giselle's stare boring into the side of my face.

Giselle giggles and claps her hands. "So hot, right?"

"Beautiful, stunning, breathtaking," I tell Ava as I lean down to kiss her. I want nothing more than to gather her in my arms and feel her lips against mine, taste the sweetness of her kiss, the warmth of the blush blooming up her chest to splash color across her cheeks.

"Okay! Enough with the gushy stuff. We need pics. The limo will be here any minute." Giselle tugs out her phone and waves it at me.

Giselle drags Ava away and leads me to the back patio to use the sun setting on the blue water as their backdrop. I've never taken so many pictures in my life. Giselle takes more pictures than even my parents have of me, considering merpeople tend to remain cautious about something that could tie us to the human world forever.

Any weirdness between the three of us dissipates as Giselle gets swept away on her own excitement. I was worried that she might corner us and demand that we tell her what had Ava abandoning her a few days ago, but she manages to put her suspicion aside to enjoy the night.

The doorbell cuts Giselle's photo session short, and the three of us head out front to meet Ava's friends catcalling at us from the opened back door of a limo. Ava's friends talk with excitement as Sapphire pours champagne into glasses. I consider declining a glass because I don't drink. Merpeople can eat and drink anything, and our alcohol metabolism makes it impossible to be intoxicated. I don't know how to pretend to be drunk, so I usually go the other route and pretend that I'm a lightweight as my reason not to drink.

Ava sips her glass, and Giselle downs hers, already waving the flute to Sapphire to refill. I nearly snatch it from her hand to tell her to slow down, but it's obviously not my place, and the last thing I need is to give Giselle a reason to react to me since we've been okay with each other most of the night.

I shift to meet Ava's gaze and clink my glass to hers, and

we both take a sip. Her silent curiosity prods at me, and without her having to say anything, I can tell she notices that I'm not drinking like the rest of her friends. And weirdly, it makes her nervous.

She's not the only one to notice, because Logan tips his glass toward me and says, "You might want to finish that. Because these things suck. If my mom wasn't on the board, I'd have bailed and left Daisy to fend for herself."

I frown at his words, considering commenting on his lack of romance and also to offer a few tips to get his girlfriend to stop glaring at him, but then Daisy says, "I guess you don't want to have fun at *my* after party."

Logan laughs. "You know I'm just playing, babe."

I realize just how different humans can be. I nearly missed the fact that their teasing of each other came from a loving place, especially as they lean in and kiss like no one's watching. Now that is definitely something they have in common with merpeople.

I shift my attention away from them and to Ava, who leans forward to stare at Giselle gulping another glass of champagne. I groan under my breath. Alcohol rips the filter right off people and makes them do stupid things. It should've been more obvious to me considering that's how Ava ended up falling overboard at Matty's carelessness. And now? I fear Giselle's increasing intoxication is about to put us at risk. From Ava's sudden anxiety, I know she feels the same.

"You're my BFF, Avie," Giselle says in a child-like voice, arching forward. She pats her hand on my knee and meets my eyes. "And Carter, you're my BFF now because she's my BFF."

Ah shit.

The others laugh, grinning at Giselle's new affectionate attitude. Ava scoots closer, pressing her leg to mine to lean over my lap.

"I love you too, Gi," Ava says, squeezing her hand.

Giselle coos from her throat, swirling the tiny bit of champagne in her glass. "You know you guys can tell me anything, right?"

I tense at her words, struggling to keep my fingers entwined with Ava's instead of reaching out to cover Giselle's mouth to get her to shut up already. I can't imagine that going well, so I sink back in the seat to let Ava handle it.

"Yes, Giselle. I know we can," Ava says, keeping her voice low.

"Okay, because I hate secrets."

Ava huffs. "Giselle."

"No, Ava. I've been thinking about it a lot lately." Giselle swings her empty glass through the air.

Silence falls over the limo, the excitement dwindling away with Giselle's suddenly serious tone. Ava's spark blinks rapidly, and I shift uncomfortably under the gazes of her friends, stuck in the middle of a fight between friends that I'm the cause of.

"Giselle, please. Just stop," Ava says, reaching out for her friend.

Giselle sighs the most dramatic breath I've ever heard in my life. "Fine, but only because I don't want you to run away with Carter."

It takes everything in me to remain composed, but all I want to do is yell for Giselle to stop acting like Ava's the worst person in the world because of not wanting to share something with her that's none of her business. She has no idea that our secret, if exposed, would have dire consequences, but even if it was something else, a friendship doesn't obligate someone to spill their soul if they don't want to.

And now Giselle's words piqued everyone's curiosity, and all I can do is remain rigid, staring at my hands, because I know Ava might get upset if I tried to handle it. I feel stuck between wanting so badly to protect my mate and needing to see that she can manage on her own.

Sapphire arches her brows. "What the hell is she talking about? You two planning on eloping or something?" If only she knew that is exactly kind of what we did in the sea. Everyone in the colony would consider us bonded in a union far exceeding marriage on land, even if unofficially without the proper ceremony.

Ava immediately hides her sea stone ring with her right hand, though it looks nothing like the usual diamond rings involved in an engagement.

"Because that would be crazy," Chloe says from the corner of the limo. I watch her tilt her head to study me in my peripheral vision.

"You two just met," Matty says, pointing out the obvious like it actually matters when my essence blinks inside Ava's chest, forfeiting the whole idea that love takes time to grow and bloom between two people. We haven't told each other the words yet, but it doesn't matter when I can feel it in my essence.

Daisy smiles, tapping her sparkly shoe to Ava's. "I think it'd be romantic."

I can't stop the smirk from crossing my face at her words. She might be my favorite out of Ava's friends now.

"I know you all think love at first sight is cheesy, but I think it's possible. Right, babe?" Daisy asks Logan.

He shrugs. "Sure, babe."

Good man. I take back my idea that he might need a little help in the romance department. He clearly knows his girlfriend well enough to know exactly what to say to make her smile.

Ava heaves a breath, her face redder than I've ever seen it before. "Okay, you all need to stop. You're embarrassing me. Carter and I are *not* getting married. And if we were, you'd all be invited." Maybe except for Giselle at this point.

"Then why would you run away?" Daisy asks.

"Honestly? If I told you I'd have to kill you."

Everyone laughs at Ava's words, though I don't find them at all funny, and neither does she for that matter. She leans into me, trembling with both anger and fear, but none of her friends notice, quickly shifting the conversation now that Giselle just stares quietly at the floor.

I gulp my glass of champagne, trying to relax the best I can. Everything is going to be okay. Ava handled it like I knew she would, and now the limo pulls up to the Grand Le Mer, a swanky hotel on a cliff with a view of the ocean.

Sapphire pours everyone another glass, and then the valet attendant opens the limo door and everyone exits onto the glittery blue carpet, where paparazzi wait to snap pictures of some of the celebrities tied to the Kings and their beauty empire.

Giselle refuses to look at Ava, hopping out before she can stop her. Ava's blue eyes water, and she blinks a few times, shifting to look at me. Her sorrow digs into my soul, and I don't know what to say to her to bring a smile back to her face.

She sniffles and composes herself. "I'm sorry. I'll fix this."

I want to nod and tell her okay, but my expression gets the best of me, and I frown, my brows furrowing. "I'm not so sure you can. Suspicion makes people take a closer look. We can't have that. It's not safe." As much as I want to give Ava hope, I need her to be real about the situation. This could've ended badly.

She licks her lips, her heartache at my words nearly unbearable, crushing the air from my chest. "Will you please let me try?"

How could I not? I help her out of the limo to give me a second to pull myself together so she doesn't hear the pain in my words. "Yeah, of course, Ava. I just don't want you to get your hopes up. Secrets tear people apart."

Without having to ask her, I know that's what Ava's most afraid of.

"But I'll do everything I can, okay?" I say, hugging her close.

If only I knew what to do.

Ava's ready to go the second we step through the door and enter a grand room filled with a collection of art pieces on display. I peer at a few paintings and sculptures, trying my best to ease open my side of our bond to send her the wave of calmness I summon just from standing with my arm around her in a room full of Azure Waters' elite.

She relaxes her shoulders and eyes me, more composed now that a dozen people watch us stroll across the room. Ava told me we had to fulfill her mandatory round of greetings to all her mom's friends. Once we do that, the rest of the night belongs to us, which I'm glad for. She might want to leave, but I hope she changes her mind. I plan to ask her to dance to share our first one for everyone to see. I have the sudden need to show her off, to shout to the world that she's my mate and the best one in the universe.

"Ava, dear, don't you look stunning," an older woman says from a nearby table. The floor-length tablecloth matches the centerpiece of cascading purple orchids. "Your mother said you'd be here tonight."

Ava guides me to close the space to the woman. "Thank you, Mrs. Tenant. I love the color of your dress." Pulling me closer, Ava runs her fingers up and down my bicep. "This is my date Carter Stevens. Mrs. Tenant's husband is on the board of directors at the Betty Green Hospital where my dad works."

I bring the woman's proffered hand to my mouth and air kiss the back of her hand. "It's lovely to meet you, ma'am."

The woman nearly bounces in her seat, releasing a strangled, breathless laugh that makes Ava smirk. "What a charming young man you have, Ava." Mrs. Tenant turns her attention to me, studying me like she's trying to place me in one of Azure Waters' social circles. The small beach town probably knows everyone who's someone, except I'm practically no one—on purpose for the most part. "I'm afraid I don't know any of your family, dear. Are you new in town?"

"He's from San Francisco," Ava answers for me. She peers around, looking like she's ready to bolt away with me the second she has a chance, her discomfort only obvious through our bond. If I couldn't feel her, I wouldn't know. She's a master of keeping her face expressionless from all her years of having to pretend she was okay before I met her. "His parents own a business up there," she adds, not giving much about my life away.

"How interesting."

Mrs. Tenant looks like she's ready to interrogate me, but Ava's eyes lock on her mom across the room, and she says, "Oh, I hate to have to excuse ourselves, but I must check in with my mom. It was nice to see you again, Mrs. Tenant."

Ava drags me away, locking her fingers tightly on mine and keeps her gaze trained on the floor to stop anyone from even considering approaching us before she completes what feels like the most important mission of her life. I'm afraid she'll shout to her mom that she's here and then drag me away once more, though I want to take a moment to familiarize myself with the world Ava grew up in.

When we get halfway across the room, I spot Giselle swaying on her heels, talking to an older man who looks more invested in the conversation than she is. Ava must see her too, because a blip of sadness flares inside me, though watching Giselle's obvious boredom, that has her yawning, is nothing for me to be sad about.

I pull Ava's arm, forcing her to slow down. "Are you going to speak for me all night?" I ask, thinking of anything I can say to prolong having to face Giselle again. I keep my voice light and amused so she knows that I don't actually care if she talks for me. This is a distraction tactic I hope she doesn't realize I'm doing.

Ava's eyes widen at my question, rosy blush tinting her cheeks. Now I feel a tiny bit bad. She blinks a few times and swallows. "Only when it's someone nosey and gossipy like Mrs. Tenant. She has to know everything about everyone. It's better not to give her too much to go on."

I raise my eyebrows and decide against pushing the subject. I'd do the same for her if we were among a bunch of merpeople. If Ava thinks these people like to gossip, she'll be shocked that the colonies love gossiping probably ten times more. And word travels fast. If my mom or dad told anyone about my unofficial coupling to Ava, I'm sure the whole sea will know soon enough, and that scares me more than an old woman's curiosity about my upbringing.

"I suppose you're right," I manage to say, suddenly nervous by my own thoughts.

Ava touches my cheek and stretches to kiss me softly until we both smile again. Taking a breath, she guides me the rest of the way to Beatrice, who stands next to a woman who's undeniably Giselle's mom. They look nearly identical with bronzy hair and golden eyes with flawless tan complexions.

Beatrice kisses Ava's cheek. "The dress looks gorgeous."

"It's a shame you didn't stay around to give us your opinion on our gowns," Giselle's mom says from next to her daughter.

Giselle shifts on her feet, looking in every other direction away from us, clearly not over what happened in the limo and how she put Ava in an awful situation, calling her out like she had. It pisses me off just thinking about it.

"I think you did a fabulous job without us. I love the beadwork," Ava says, keeping the conversation focused and light. She glances at Giselle expectantly like she thinks her best friend might give something away about that day.

"Thank you, darling." Giselle's mom turns her attention to me. "This must be the boy who saved your life."

Ava gapes at her words in surprise, flicking her gaze to Giselle. I knew Ava wanted to keep her fall overboard a secret, but like in merpeople colonies, something huge like that couldn't possibly stay secret long.

Giselle finally draws her gaze to Ava. "It wasn't me, I swear."

Her words come out soft and pleading, nothing like the heated annoyance in the limo. A dozen emotions collide into me from Ava, despair and grief, loyalty and yearning. A dozen different things, but none of them seemingly over Giselle. She feels guilty about the situation.

Ava's mom's eyes glass over, and she reaches out and touches Ava's shoulder. "It's okay, Avie. Ruby told us when I asked about Carter. I'm just thankful for what he's done. I don't know what I'd have done if I..."

"It was nothing," I say, pulling myself from all of Ava's storming emotions, threatening my own cool.

"It was everything," she whispers to me. Her eyes lock on me, her flaring emotions dissipating into love and appreciation as she lets go of everything bothering her about tonight to focus solely on me and what I mean to her.

If I could get away with scooping Ava up into my arms for the kiss I want to give her that would leave her breathless, I would. But human parents are rather different than merpeople. My mom would be appalled I choose to kiss her cheek in a moment Ava opens her heart up to me in front of those she cares about.

"It's a shame you don't have a brother for my daughter," Giselle's mom says, swirling her glass of champagne.

I feel pretty bonded to Giselle in this moment, her shock and anger so palpable that I take an automatic step away.

"Mom!" Giselle yells, placing her hands on her hips. "I can find my own boyfriend, thank you very much."

I laugh nervously. "I have a few cousins, though I haven't seen them since I was a kid."

"I can't imagine why." Giselle hits me with the fakest smile I've ever seen, and I've seen a lot on the Ocean Jewel. She hates me. She probably thinks I'm the worst person in the world. She blames me for Ava not confiding in her, and I don't blame her. But hell.

Both Ava and I don't respond. I slide my hand around

Ava's waist and pull her closer, letting her sink into me. She's more annoyed than anything, and I feel a shift in their friendship. So does Ava. I don't doubt her anger will turn into grief. I want to be here for her when it does.

Giselle's mom places her hands on her hips and looks at Ava. "Don't let her get to you, Ava. She's been moody the last few days. It's hard when your friends start splitting their time with boys. Don't you remember how it was, Bea? We almost didn't talk for three months when I met Griffin."

Beatrice grimaces and nods. "She's right."

Tears cloud Ava's eyes as her agitation shifts at Giselle's mom's words. "I should go talk to her." Turning to me, Ava says, "Why don't you find Logan and Matty?"

Hurrying away, Ava abandons me with her mom and disappears out of the ballroom in the direction Giselle ran. It takes everything in me not to chase after her to stop her from a confrontation that might not end well. We're in public. Giselle's drunk. Ava's angry. The last thing we need is to draw attention to us.

A warm hand touches my arm. "Hey, Carter?" Beatrice says. "They're going to be okay. Ava and Giselle have been best friends all their lives. Practically sisters. They fight and makeup."

I bob my head, focusing on Ava's irritation turning into rage. "I feel bad. I didn't mean to get between them."

"I know, hon," Giselle's mom says.

Ava's anger suddenly turns to a fear so intense that it steals my breath. I bend forward, clutching my knees for a moment.

"You okay, Carter?" Beatrice asks.

I wave my hand, forcing my legs to work. I focused too much on Ava's emotions that they now feel like my own, and it's hard to close myself off. All I can think about is something terrible happened between Ava and Giselle. I need to get to them. I need to get to Ava. The intense terror suffocates me so much so that if it doesn't stop, I feel like I might die—but not me. Ava. It's her. It's what she's feeling.

I blink through the pain in my chest, my eyes burning with uncontrollable tears. "I'm sorry. Please excuse me," I call to Ava's mom.

Rushing through the crowded ballroom, I ignore the gazes boring into me. Sweat beads on my forehead, my breathing labored. I follow the pull in my chest that'll take me to Ava. The closer I get to her, the harder it is to focus.

I find myself running through an empty grand hallway with a sign declaring the terrace is around the corner. Condensation fogs the inside window, the air outside chilly this time of night compared to the heat of the building.

Ava's spark blinks so quickly in her chest—in my chest—that I can't distinguish the pause between beats. The light glowing from her is the only thing I can see on the dim balcony stretching over the side of the cliff and dark ocean.

And then I see Giselle. She holds her hands up to Ava, but I can't see her face. I can't hear anything.

I slam my hands against the door, pushing it open. Fear paralyzes me at the sight of Ava hiking up her dress. She swings her leg over the balcony to stand on the ledge. Giselle sobs and rushes forward to grab onto Ava's shoulder.

"Ava, please. Don't do this. Don't jump. We can work through this."

My head swirls at Giselle's pleas, and I focus on Ava. Her skin shimmers in the dim lighting, her body transforming right in front of Giselle. Ava's pectoral fins jet out from her forearms, and she releases a gasp and a groan.

From my position, I spot her dorsal fin protruding from her spine, pushing against her dress. Cerulean scales sprout over her bare leg, overtaking her smooth skin.

"You have to trust me," Ava cries. "I'm begging you. Don't tell anyone."

I barely have time to get halfway across the balcony before Ava leans back, seconds from letting go. "Ava!" I yell, my voice ringing through the air.

I'm not fast enough to get to her, and she doesn't wait for me.

She lets go.

18

FIGHT FOR LAND

GISELLE SCREAMS AS AVA DROPS from the balcony. I slap my hand over her mouth to stifle her high-pitched voice. She thrashes, fighting against me, but I pull her to my chest and hug her while we both watch Ava dive into the sea in her mermaid form.

If I thought Giselle could survive such a fall, I'd toss her on my back and jump with her after Ava, but I can't risk it. And I can't leave Giselle here either. She saw Ava as a mermaid. Our secret is now jeopardized, and I have no idea what I should do. The law of the sea demands that I put an immediate stop to the threat. Any other merperson would follow the king's law and give Giselle to the sea to keep our secret safe, but I've already broken so many, and no one else knows. If they did, the fate of Azure Waters wouldn't fare well.

"You need to stop screaming before someone hears you," I say to Giselle. "Please, I'm not going to hurt you, but if you continue, you'll hurt Ava."

Giselle stops fighting me, and I lean over the railing to peer into the rocky sea. Ava's head pops to the surface, sending a wave of relief through me. It was the good fate of the ocean that she missed all the rocks. If she hadn't, she'd have been injured enough to warrant a visit to my healer mom. We'd have no choice but to explain everything. And we still might.

"Oh, God," Giselle says, her chest still heaving. "What the actual hell, Carter?"

I don't answer her right away. I don't look at her either. All I do is stare at my beautiful mate diving under and disappearing into the sea, her tail cutting through the water once.

Giselle gasps. "A mermaid. A freaking mermaid."

I still don't respond.

"And I thought you were a cold-blooded killer. Or a cult leader." Giselle knocks me on the shoulder with her knuckles. "But you're a merman...right?"

"Shut up," I say, my voice low, nearly unrecognizable. "Don't say it again, especially not here."

Giselle snaps her mouth shut, her eyes widening with fear. "Oh, crap. Are you going to kill me? I thought Ava was joking."

My chest heaves as I inhale a few breaths.

Giselle takes a few steps away from me, looking ready to run.

Jerking my hand out, I grab her wrist and pull her back to me. "Don't run. We have to go."

"Carter, please."

I fist my free hand, trying to keep myself in control. "I'm not going to hurt you. I—don't talk. Don't run. You have to stay calm."

"How can I stay calm when my best friend is a—when Ava jumped—when...let's just get out of here. You can explain on the way," she says.

I shake my head. "No, I can't say anything. You know too much."

Tears burst from her eyes, and she swipes at her cheeks. "Then what? What are we doing? What do you plan to do?"

I scrub my hands down my face. "I have to find Ava. She shouldn't be alone out there. It's dangerous."

Giselle pales. "So, what? Are you going to jump now?"

I shake my head. "No, because I can't leave you here."

"Then I'll call a driver. If I know Ava, she's going home," Giselle says.

I nod. "We'll start there."

Giselle manages to compose herself long enough to get the tears to stop pouring from her eyes. Reaching into her clutch purse, she pulls out a compact mirror and swipes the streaks of tears from her cheeks and fixes her makeup the best she can.

Pulling out her phone, she quickly taps her finger across the screen. "Go wait outside. I'll make an excuse for Ava and tell her mom we're all leaving together."

"You sure she'll believe you?" I ask. "You were pissed at Ava only minutes ago."

"She's my best friend," Giselle says. "I can still be pissed at her and care about her. Our mom's know that. We once fought over some stupid game where we both thought the other cheated, but something was up with the cards. We didn't talk all night, but then Ava got sick and was puking her brains out. You know what I did?"

I shrug. I don't see where this conversation is going.

"I held her hair, sat in the bathroom with her all night, and sang her all of her favorite songs. But I was pissed the whole time I did it, but I did it because she's my best friend. And I don't care if she's..." She doesn't say the words out loud. "I love Ava, and I will do everything I can to make sure she's okay. Got it? Trust me."

I refrain from telling her that even if she's Ava's best friend that I can't trust her. Not now. Not after everything. One little story does nothing to help me trust her. The only reason I nod and agree to Giselle's plan is because I trust Ava, and it's Ava who trusts Giselle.

Giselle nods when I don't argue and pulls me with her back inside the hotel. I wait for her outside where the excitement and paparazzi have vanished. Giselle runs through the automatic doors, holding her heels in one hand.

"We're taking the limo back," she says.

All I do is nod.

After a fifteen minute, quiet and awkward ride back to Ava's, Giselle leads me up the stairs to enter Ava's house through the guest apartment. She pounds in the code and struts through the dark house like she lives here, and we make our way to the back patio.

"So, are you going to swim and find her or whatever?" Giselle asks me, shifting on her feet and crossing her arms.

"If she doesn't come soon. She should be here by now," I say.

"So, you never said what will happen to me. You know Ava won't let you kill me, right?"

I groan and turn away from her, lacing my fingers behind my head. "I should give you to the sea. You know our secret. It's the number one law."

"Rather extreme," she mutters. "I mean, how much threat am I really? I would never put Ava in danger by telling anyone. I've seen far too many TV shows where the government would swoop in and steal my best friend from me. And though my aunt could definitely fund a rescue mission, I'm not some powerful badass."

"You might have it in you." I don't know why I say it. Maybe to keep my mind off the fact that life as I know it hangs on a line, and Giselle will be the one to cut it or maybe because I nearly believe her. Either way, all I know is that I will do what it takes to make sure this works out for all of us, even if it means I have to do the one thing I promised Ava I wouldn't—make her leave.

But we can't stay.

It's too dangerous.

Ava's spark grabs my attention, and I jog into the sand and away from Giselle without another word. Dropping to her knees, Ava lands on her dress, clutching it in her hands. I don't let her lie half-naked in the surf for long. I shrug out of my suit jacket and drape it over her before I lift her shivering body to cradle in my arms. Relief trickles to me from her, and she sinks against my chest, clutching me as I silently carry her back to the house.

I set her in a patio chair and drop to my knees in front of her. "Are you hurt?" I ask, trailing my gaze over her body to assess any possible damage caused by the fall.

She shakes her head, hugging her arms over her chest to keep herself together. "No, I missed the rocks."

I exhale a long breath at her confirmation that my eyes don't deceive me and that she is okay. Wrapping my arms around her, I pull her to me and embrace her until she stops shivering, absorbing my warmth into her cold body.

Turning to Giselle, who has been utterly silent, I ask, "Can you grab a few towels?"

She runs inside without hesitation and returns with a stack of towels from a chest near the back door. I wrap Ava up first and dry her off, her whole body shaking, her mind still in shock as she processes what happened to her and what it means for her life here.

Keeping myself busy, I strip out of my wet clothes, not caring about the human norms or the fact that Giselle squeaks and twists away to stare at the wall. Ava watches me silently from her seat as I wrap a towel around my waist, tears blurring her eyes, her makeup smeared, yet she still looks beautiful crying.

All I can think about is picking her up and taking her to sea, the battle between my merman instincts and my learned human rationale for Ava at war with each other. Her wants and needs couldn't be more different. I should do what she needs—take her to Pearlestria to adjust as a mermaid.

I hate to admit that my mom was right. Ava shouldn't be here. The risk to her family far exceeds the wants we have for a life on land with her so out of control. If I were another merman, Giselle would be dead. But I could never. Giselle's not out to harm the colonies. She's Ava's best friend and part of her pod with the bond they share. If something happened to

Giselle, it'd ruin everything. I won't let that happen.

"I'm so sorry," Ava whispers, breaking the silence I let draw on as I try to think things through, silence that has both Ava and Giselle on edge. "I didn't mean for this to happen."

I help Ava to her feet to hug her, the soft defeat and disappointment in herself digging under my skin. "It could've been a lot worse." Like she could've transformed in the middle of the ballroom. Or in the car. She could've done so too far away from the beach and died. If something happened to Ava, I don't think I could survive.

But I can't tell her my fears. I can't tell her I have no idea how to handle any of this. I'm torn between what's right for Ava as a mermaid and what's right for her as my mate. If I do what I'm supposed to, she'll hate me forever. She won't forgive me. But she'd be safe and alive, and I could live with that. What I can't live with is knowing I'm responsible for putting her in danger. Putting her friends in danger.

"I'm sorry, too, Ava. I never imagined that this—this wasn't what I was expecting," Giselle says, apologizing.

Ava chokes out a strangled laugh. "At least you know we're not murderers."

"You're a mermaid," Giselle whispers, eyeing me, knowing that I told her not to say the words, but she risks it anyway. I respect her bravery. "I don't understand. How?"

Ava glances at me to see if I'll interject, but I don't see the point now. We're alone, close to the ocean, and Giselle already knows.

"When Matty knocked me off the boat...Carter saved me." Ava peeks at me in her peripheral vision, the admission sending both our hearts thudding in our chests.

Giselle frowns. "He couldn't save you without turning you into—into a—a mermaid?" She says it like there's something wrong with being a mermaid, though I know it's not her intent.

I bow my head, turning my gaze to the sandy patio. "I would've loved to have done that, Giselle. But in my human form, swimming that distance to get to her—the ocean already took her under. I tried, but it just wasn't possible. I was already too late by the time I transformed."

Her mouth drops open, her eyes wide. "I don't think I understand. Are you saying...?"

"Giselle, I drowned," Ava says, the words drifting to disappear into the hum of the waves.

A sob escapes Giselle's mouth, and she breaks down, bawling so hard that she shakes as much as Ava. The two of them hold each other. Ava comforts her friend, rubbing her hand up and down her back until Giselle calms down.

I step closer, needing Giselle to know that things could've been different. That I did what I could for Ava. I have enough guilt over the situation as it is that I don't need to feel worse. "I wasn't even supposed to allow her to return to the Ocean Jewel. I defied tradition and broke a few mer-laws. The only thing protecting us was that no one knew our secret. But now you do."

Ava shudders at my words as they elicit more panic from her. But she and Giselle have to know how bad this situation is.

Giselle huffs. "I swear on my life I'm not going to tell anyone."

Anger rushes over me, and I can't stop myself from saying, "The same way you promised Ava you wouldn't tell everyone we had a secret in the first place?" Because it's the truth. I'm trying so hard to stay cool, to do it for Ava, but they don't understand, and I don't want to scare Ava even more.

Giselle cringes and steps back. "You're right. That was messed up of me, but I was worried."

"You should've trusted Ava."

Ava releases a breath and steps between Giselle and me. She blocks her best friend and gazes in my eyes, clutching my face in her freezing fingers to hold my attention. "Just stop it. It's happened, she knows, and there's nothing we can do to change it."

"So, what now?" Giselle asks the question before Ava, but I don't look at her.

Clenching my jaw, I summon the courage to say what has to happen, answering Giselle while keeping my eyes on my mate. "Ava and I have to leave."

Ava stiffens at my words, and I brace myself for her wave

of emotions that'll surely sink me into the bottom of the sea, forcing me to drag her with me.

"Why? I swear I won't tell. You can trust me. For real," Giselle says, speaking first.

Her words stop Ava from reacting to the swelling panic inside her. "I agree with Gi. Now that she knows our secret, she won't be begging for answers. If anything, she can help. She can cover for me."

If only this were about Giselle.

Rubbing the back of my neck, I work up my courage to tell Ava the truth, something I know she'll have trouble dealing with. The truth that might destroy our relationship I've tried so hard to build in so little time. The truth that could obliterate my forever with the girl of my dreams. "Ava, it's not about Giselle knowing. It's you."

Her bottom lip quivers, her chin wrinkling with her grimace. "Because I'm the one who transformed?"

I nod and clear my throat, so she can't hear my voice crack under her sorrow. "You're too unpredictable. This is a small town where everyone knows you. It isn't safe. Bringing you home was a mistake. It's too risky to stay."

"But where will you go?" Giselle asks, automatically grabbing onto Ava like if she tries hard enough, she can force her to stay.

I nearly tell them both that Ava needs to be in the sea, but just the thought of feeling Ava's agony stops me. I have to think of something else. I have to. "I don't know. Living on land is expensive. It's not like I can continue to work on the Ocean Jewel. I'll be accused of hurting Ava if she disappears."

Ava stifles a cry. "Carter, I can't just disappear. You *promised.* You promised I could keep my ties to my family."

This is it. This is the moment I've been dreading. She'll never forgive me for ruining her life and failing her as her mate.

"You don't think they'll search for you if you run away?" I ask, hoping with everything inside me that she'll see my reason and not tell me to leave, so she can deal with this alone.

She surprises me by suppressing her fear, letting it turn into anger, but it's not directed at me. It's directed at the situation, the sea, the universe even. Placing her hands on her hips, she says, "I'm eighteen. I can legally do what I want, and there's nothing they can do. I'm not going to just dive into the water and disappear forever. When I get better control, I can come back."

Determination looks incredibly hot on Ava, but it still doesn't change things. Her parents already lost one daughter. I can't imagine them letting Ava do what she wants despite her age and the human law.

"And how exactly are you going to explain your absence?" I ask, needing her to really think about what she's proposing.

She hides her face with her hands, annoyance at my questions washing over her and spilling to me. "Who cares? They'll just be happy I'm back."

Giselle bobs her head. "She makes a good point."

I shift my attention to Giselle, nearly forgetting that she's standing behind Ava, taking in our entire conversation. "This is between me and Ava."

Giselle throws her hands up at the tone of my voice. "I'm only trying to help. I can't lose my BFF."

Ava steps closer and presses her cool hands to my bare chest, nudging me back, so I stop focusing on Giselle. The glow of my spark blinks through her fingers. Ava rubs her lips together, her emotions calming the longer she just feels my heart beating under her hands, which helps me relax and take a breath as well.

"Why don't we just pack a few things and stay somewhere else tonight? It'll give us a chance to think and figure things out." Ava's blue eyes plead with me to agree to her suggestion. And how can I not? This is her life on land at stake.

"My parents own an apartment in the city," Giselle says, still finding a need to interject in what should be a private conversation between me and Ava. "We can go there."

"Giselle, it might be better if you stay here. Make sure no one saw anything." Because the last thing I want to do is bring Giselle with us. She complicates things. Ava might resist leaving even more.

"No way." Giselle realizes my intent, and she might put up a bigger fight than Ava.

"Giselle," Ava says softly, surprising me. I was certain she'd take Giselle's side over mine. The fact that she doesn't stirs a wave of emotion from me, giving me hope that maybe all isn't lost. That maybe even if things turn out wrong, Ava might not reject me.

"Don't *Giselle* me. I know what he's thinking." Giselle waves at me, narrowing her eyes "The moment you two are away from me, you'll be gone." She's right. It's what we need to do.

Ava turns her attention to me for confirmation that Giselle is right, but I don't say anything. I don't deny it.

While studying my face, Ava responds to her best friend. "Okay, you can come, Gi. But I do have to leave. You know this, right?"

I don't react though a wave of relief at Ava's words floods through me. She's agreeing to leave with me. She's not going to put up a fight. Shifting, I glance at the ocean next to us and send a silent thank you to the seas.

"And I'm staying with you until then. Got it?" Giselle says, pulling my attention back to them.

Ava envelops her best friend in a hug. "Got it. I promise I won't leave without telling you goodbye."

"I wish you didn't have to say goodbye at all." Giselle swipes her hands across her cheeks.

"It won't be forever," Ava says. I nearly believe her. I can't tell her otherwise. "Now, come on. We have to hurry."

"You two get dressed, and I'll pack for you." Without waiting for our responses, Giselle darts inside, carrying our wet clothes wrapped in a towel.

Ava sinks against me, sniffling against my chest. "I'm sorry, Carter," she says, apologizing again. "I'm ruining your life."

Her words steal my breath away, because it was something that never crossed my mind. "Ava, no. Don't say that. You could never."

She licks her lips. "I know I'm a pain, and I know that you're afraid of what happens next, but I want you to know that I trust you. This is your life too, Carter. We need to figure this out together."

Pulling her close, I kiss her, tasting the salt of the sea on her lips. "Together," I whisper. "We'll figure it out."

"Don't think I'm going to let you give up the land without a fight, even if we can't stay here." She finally smiles, giving me the one thing I had no idea I needed.

And she's right. I'm not taking her to sea. I'm not giving up on our life together on land without a fight.

19

A PLAN

I WAIT FOR AVA TO drift to sleep next to Giselle on a king-sized bed in a swanky, penthouse apartment three times larger than the apartment I grew up in with my parents. A picture of the San Diego cityscape glowing on water decorates one wall and another of LA on the other. A floor-to-ceiling curtain covers the wall window that overlooks the outside world. I should get some sleep, but without the sound of the sea humming in my ears and Ava in my arms, the task seems impossible. And I can't get my mind to shut up.

I need to plan. I need to figure out where to take Ava.

Possibly south to Mexico. Maybe even farther and down to Costa Rica to waters I'm familiar traveling through from migrating to my dad's birth colony of Coralista, where my grandparents reside. If only I knew how the land worked there. I doubt Ava would want to remain in the sea...or leave the country.

Sighing, I stand from the chaise lounge across from the bed and shuffle out of the room as to not wake Ava. I wanted so much to avoid calling my parents, but I need my dad's advice. He understands me as a merman, unlike my mom. He can help me figure out a plan.

I perch on a barstool and force myself to call my dad. The line rings a couple of times before his gruff voice crackles into the line.

"What's wrong, Carter?" Dad asks without greeting me. He knows me too well. I wouldn't call him in the middle of the night otherwise.

"I need help," I murmur, keeping my voice low.

"Where are you?"

I shake my head though I know he can't see me. "I don't need you to come to me. Can I come to you? We need somewhere to stay, and I could use your advice."

"Son, no. Your mother asked that I remain distant until you come to your senses and go about your coupling with Ava properly. All I can tell you is to think about what you're doing. I mean, really think about it, Carter."

Groaning, I lean my elbows on the bar. "Hear me out."

Dad releases a breath into the line, creating static. "I can't, Carter. I'm sorry. Just listen to your mother. She knows what's best for Ava."

"Dad, please," I beg, keeping my voice low despite wanting to yell at him. "Mom can't be reasoned with. I called you because I need *your* guidance. Ava slipped up. I need to know what to do."

I regret the words immediately because I know exactly what my dad would expect me to do. Something I can't do. I just want him to know what I'm dealing with and for him to assure me that everything will be okay. I need him to act like my dad and not a warrior of the sea. I need to know how to fix this so we can stay.

"Oh, Carter. This was what we were afraid of. I will take care of it, so you don't have to. I'm willing to carry that burden for you. I love you, son. I vow to you that I will be swift. Just tell me who it was."

"No, you don't have to worry about the human. It was a stranger. No one will ever believe such a story." I pray to the ocean that he believes my lie. There have been mermaid sightings before—humans have their stories revolving around us—but King Attilonious would rather not risk the danger if we can avoid it.

Dad releases a breath. "King Attilonious will take that into account. He's kind and understanding. I'll take your punishment if I have to for not teaching you the proper way. But Carter, you have to take Ava to sea. Right now. We will meet you to travel to Pearlestria with her. Neither of you will be alone."

I was afraid he was going to say that. "There has to be something else we can do. She won't go for it."

"There is nothing else you can do, son. You must take her to sea even if she protests. It is your duty."

I shift, sensing Ava's panic rising. I know she's listening to my side of the conversation, but I can't bear to look at her hovering behind me. Not yet. "No, Dad. I'm not going to make her."

"You have to!" Dad yells into the line, making me tense. "If you don't, then you'll leave us no choice, Carter. You're being reckless. Ava's a liability on land. You can't let your bond with her muddle your good senses. This isn't the time to take her side. You're letting her human desires get into your head."

"That's not true. I'm taking her side because I love her, and I think what she wants is what's best for her. You out of everyone should understand. You chose the land over the sea. We chose it, too."

Ava gasps, her emotions flaring at my words to my dad. I realize that she's reacting to the fact that I told my dad that I'm in love with her, something we've never said to each other. I thought she could feel it already deep in our bond, that she knew how much I cared for her. What I didn't realize was how as a human, she needed to hear it out loud. She needed my confirmation.

"The land is a privilege, not a right, Carter."

I keep my anger in check, still concentrating on Ava. She's the only thing keeping me together. "I don't know why I bothered calling you. You might've chosen the land, but you still think like you live in the sea. Goodbye, Dad."

"Son, wai—"

I hang up the phone and slump forward onto my arms to calm down before Ava approaches me. Her soft footsteps thud across the floor. Inhaling a quick breath, I swivel to meet her gaze. She embraces me for a long moment, standing between my legs, running her fingers in circles until I lean back. Taking her hands into mine, I bring them to my cheek just to feel the weight of her fingers.

"Your parents don't want to help us," Ava says, her voice cracking.

"I asked if we could live there for a while until we got things situated, but my mom said no. She's too wrapped up in the mer traditions. My dad stands by her decision. He said if I loved you, I'd do the right thing, but they have no idea what that even is." I say it like I talked to my mom, though it was my dad who relayed the message. I don't want Ava freaking out about the possibility of my mom remaining nearby. Or how they expect me to take her to sea.

"You love me," Ava says, ignoring everything else I've said like my love to her is the only thing that matters. Our world could be falling apart, but the way she states the words makes it sound like it wouldn't matter as long as I confirmed what she feels.

I release her hands to touch my fingers to her glowing chest, her beautiful heart beating perfectly with mine. Something I'll never take for granted. "More than I could've ever imagined," I admit. "It's what happens when a merman gives his life to someone—he gives his heart, too. Have you ever noticed ours beat in an identical rhythm?"

"Oh," Ava whispers, uncertainty arising in her words. "But what if I never drowned?"

"Ava, are you questioning whether or not what I feel is real?" I smile, holding her gaze, thinking how ridiculous such a question is. My bond to her far exceeds what time could grow between us. I knew she was possibly my one the second I laid my eyes on her on the dock. And then the ocean cemented it, allowing me to give my soul to her.

"I'm just thinking about where we'd be if I didn't."

I bring her hands to my lips and kiss each of her knuckles. "We'd have a lot more dates away from the water."

Her laughter chimes through the air, the sweet melody of her voice matching her love drenching me as she accepts my admission as the truth she knows is real.

"You want the real reason I saved you? It wasn't only because I didn't want you to die. I gave you my life because I felt like we could have something together. I saw a future with you, living on the land with the girl who loved it as much as I did. And then when you went overboard, I saw it all being ripped away from me. I've never met anyone like you, Ava. That's why I did what I did. I had hoped that one day you could love me back." I never truly wanted to accept the possibility that she might have never loved me, and it hurts to think about it, but it's something she should hear. She should know that while my feelings are irrevocable and deep-seated, she still has a choice. Her love comes from her own heart, not mine.

"And if I didn't?"

I swallow. "It was a risk I was willing to take. I don't blame you if you can't ever love me, especially after all this."

Ava bites her lip, studying my eyes. And then she kisses me, teasing my mouth with hers. "Don't be ridiculous."

I smile, because that's what I thought of her questioning my love a moment ago.

She kisses me again and presses her forehead to mine, blurring her features at her closeness. "I wouldn't be standing here with you right now if I didn't feel something for you, Carter. You know, I think a lot about my life and my future but never once was it without you in it."

I didn't think I could love her more than I already do, but I was mistaken. Her words ignite something in me I didn't know existed, and now I'm more determined than ever to make a life on land work despite what anyone says. I'm determined to prove everyone wrong about Ava, too. We can do this. I know we can.

Pulling Ava onto my lap, I cradle her to me, kissing her and letting her snuggle against me as we both soak in what it's like to just be together without the complications the land or the sea bring. Ava remains lost in her thoughts until first light steals the night from us.

"Carter," Ava says, breaking the silence. "I think I know what I'm going to do about my parents. But it involves me going home. Just for a few hours. I can't leave without saying goodbye."

Going home. I shouldn't argue, but I worry about what could happen if we do. "A clean break is better." No one knows where we are apart from Giselle. We'll have less trouble this way.

Ava cuddles me, drawing her finger along my chest. "Not for me. I had plans this summer. I was supposed to move in with Giselle. We were going to start college in the fall, and my parents were going to pay for it."

I try not to react to the plans I ruined.

She continues, saying, "I'm going to ask them to give me the money for the rent instead so I can travel until school. And then when school comes around, I'm going to tell them I'm postponing and taking a gap year instead. Hopefully we'll have jobs by then, because taking a gap year wasn't on the agenda, and I doubt they'll just give us money without me being in school."

I knew Ava was amazing and smart and determined, but I've never been more proud in my life that the ocean picked such a brilliant mate for me. Her plan could work. It *will* work if she gets her parents to agree. That's the trouble we'll face. I don't know how she'll convince them to pay for her to basically run away with me, a guy Ava just met.

"And what about Giselle?" I ask, peering toward the hall-ways.

"What about me?" Giselle yawns as she strolls from the bedroom, her dark hair a mess of curls from last night's event.

"I need you to stay in Azure Waters. At least until the fall," Ava says. Giselle opens her mouth to argue, but Ava holds up her hand to stop her best friend from uttering a word. "Please, Gi. I'd feel a lot better about leaving if I knew you would be around. Plus, you're the only one I can visit if everyone else thinks I'm traveling the country."

Giselle eyes me. "Or I could just go with you."

"You can't exactly go everywhere we do," I say, nuzzling my nose to Ava's neck, just breathing in her sweet scent.

Sighing, Giselle says, "If only I could sprout a tail."

"Are you willing to risk your life for the chance? It's not always successful. Plus, you'd be stuck with whoever trans-forms you like Ava's stuck with me." Seeing if Giselle's fate lies in the ocean would be one way to solve our problem of her knowing our secret, but there would be no way to tell. If she was the future mate of a merman, I'd hope the ocean would see to it that he emerged to shore to meet her. But human-born mates are rare. Coupling in the sea is rare, even for the king himself. He coupled with a mermaid that wasn't his intended, and she disappeared from the sea without a trace. No one's willing to risk it.

Strange to think it, but in the sea, it seems we as a species just live for our pods and a simple life. I wanted more. So does Ava.

Giselle raises her eyebrows. "No thanks. I have commitment issues."

I laugh, the loudness of my voice surprising me. Ava smiles at me and slides from my arms to hug her best friend. Hearing her make plans with Giselle makes the whole situation less dire. Hearing them laugh eases the worry coursing through me.

Because Ava's got this. I thought all this time it had to be me to make this work, but she was always capable of doing it herself. She's my brave, intelligent, beautiful mate, and I know she'll be the one to care for me and get us both through it, and I'll do everything I can to guarantee it works.

20

UNEXPECTED VISITOR

AFTER TAKING AVA HOME TO confront her parents, Giselle drives me to the marina. As much as I wanted to stay with Ava to make sure it all goes smoothly, I have other things I have to take care of. Ava made a good point about trying to remain on good terms with Captain Briggs and the rest of the crew of the Ocean Jewel just in case even though I'm resigning and giving them Giselle's mailing address to send my last check.

"Carter, I know we haven't started off on good terms, but I want you to know that I'm here for both you and Ava no matter what. You're obviously going to be in her life forever, and so am I, and I'd like to start over with you for her sake."

I bob my head, keeping my gaze trained out the window. "I'd like that too. I'm sorry if I scared you yesterday, but—"

She waves her hand. "No apology needed. But I owe you one. I was a bitch to you for no other reason than I thought you were going to get my best friend in the entire universe in trouble. I don't know if you and Ava talked about this, but her feelings for you are clear—"

"I'm in love with her, Giselle," I say. "She's it for me. She's my soul mate."

She bites her lip between her teeth. "That sounds so crazy, but I believe you. And I expect you to take good care of her. I will hook you on a line and filet you myself if I learn she was eaten by a shark or something."

I chuckle at her threats. "Got it. And don't worry, sharks don't prey on mermaids."

She nods her head. "So, I have to ask. Megalodons? Krakens? Dinosaur fish? Are they still around?"

I shrug. "I don't swim away much from the coast."

"Well, try to find out for m—" She snaps her mouth closed. "Why is that gorgeous woman waving at us?"

Jerking my attention, I stare in the direction of Giselle's line of sight. My mom stands in the parking lot near the Ocean Jewel, smiling and waving at me as Giselle slows to park the car. Annoyance rushes over me. She's the last person

I wanted to see.

"Drop me off here and go around the block," I say.

Giselle hits the brakes a little too hard, locking my seat-belt in place. "Oh, God. Is that the queen or whatever? Is she here to—"

"No, it's my mom. Just drive around. I'll call you to get me after I send her away."

Giselle takes off the moment I close the car door, and I'm glad she doesn't argue. My mom strolls closer, her dark brown hair blowing in the breeze. She wears a sarong over her bikini with a small waterproof bag on her shoulder. Without having to ask, I know she talked to my dad last night. Though her mouth smiles, her eyes cloud with tears as she opens her arms for me.

"Oh, my son. I'm so sorry," she says, embracing me into a hug like I'm still a merbabe. If she could lift me, she probably would. "I know heading to sea will be a difficult adjustment, but you and Ava will find the happiness you deserve. I just know it. You'll have many mermen to guide you, and Ava will find exactly what she needs in our world. You two will better the colony, and you'll surely find everything your merman heart desires. After your official coupling, Ava will—"

"I'm not taking Ava to sea," I say, tugging myself away from her. "We have come up with a plan that will assure she can stay on land and connected to her family."

Mom frowns. "Impossible. It has to be this way. It's the

law."

"Screw the laws," I snap, anger simmering inside me, threatening to spill out in a tidal wave of rage. "I won't do it."

"Carter," my mom pleads. "I know this bond is new, and you feel out of control and want to do everything that Ava asks of you, but you have to think about what that means. You're lucky it was a stranger Ava transformed in front of with no way to track. It is selfish for you to allow Ava to risk the lives of people so that you can pretend to be something you're not."

I clench my fingers into fists, turning away from my mom. "You're a hypocrite. You and dad have played human for years. It's how you raised me."

She shakes her head. "No. I raised you on land so you could understand what the seas face. I wanted you to have the best opportunity to help our colonies flourish. Not many humans care for our oceans, and as much as King Attilonious tries, we're no match. We must do what we can. I remain on land so that if others in the colonies decide to emerge, they have the chance you had to find your mate."

I let her words sink in for a moment. She's never talked to me about why she and Dad chose to live on land, and I wish she had before now. But I didn't expect to find Ava so soon. I never imagined I'd already be unofficially coupled or that she could love me.

"I get it, Mom," I say. Because I do. I know exactly what

she yearns for me and Ava. She sees great importance in extending our pods so much so that she and Dad saved up for it so we could emerge from the sea later with a family. But I can't expect such a thing from Ava, and I won't allow my mom to. What she wants would guarantee Ava has to abandon her human ties and head to sea for years. And Ava was clear about her plans for our lives together. We will not be settling in the seas and having merbabes no matter how much my mom wants it to happen. This is our life and not hers.

"Do you, Carter?" she asks. "Because if you did, you'd—"

"Stop," I say, sighing. "Just leave. I let you speak your mind, but I have things I need to do. I'm not taking Ava to sea. That's final. Go home."

"Carter."

I push past her and head toward the docks where the Ocean Jewel waits. My mom doesn't follow me. She'd never. And I wait until she disappears from the parking lot to head back to the closest beach access a block away.

Her emergence from the ocean and her words leave me on edge. I can't shake the bad feeling coursing through me. All I know is I have to get back to Ava, and we have to leave immediately before someone besides my mom comes looking.

I just hope I'm not already too late.

"Go through the garage apartment," Giselle says. "You don't want Ava's parents to corner you for an interrogation. I'll be back in a bit, okay? Don't you dare even consider leaving without saying goodbye."

I nod without a word and exit the car. Strolling around the garage, I head up the stairs and do what Giselle asked. I was too concerned about my mom's arrival that I haven't called Ava to see if her parents will come through for us, but her emotions remain happy despite the blip of fear I felt from her earlier.

I quietly listen in the hallway for voices, but if Ava's parents are home, I don't hear or see them. Making my way to Ava's room, I tap my knuckles on the wood and wait. Nerves bunch in my stomach, and I almost call out to her, but I know she's here. I feel her closing the space to the door.

She greets me with a gorgeous smile that shoves all my worry away. I grin right back at her, my gaze moving past her to catch sight of her packed bags resting on her bed. "I came in through the guest apartment. I'm going to assume everything went okay with your parents?"

"Surprisingly well." Bringing her lips to mine, she replays her memory from earlier through a kiss, confirming that my suspicions were correct. Except for one thing. Ava told her parents Giselle would be leaving with us to make it less worrisome that she wanted to travel with me. Tugging out her phone, she shows me exactly how good it went from her five-figure bank account. "They were a little unsure when I told them we were leaving tonight, but I told them we wanted to go to some festival in San Francisco," she whispers, proving her parents are home.

I frown. "I hope they're not expecting pictures because San Francisco is the last place we'll be. My parents would never let us hear the end of it." Or let us stay. They'll guarantee we don't have any other choice but to go to Pearlestria.

Ava's nerves flare, and she shifts on her feet. "I don't think distance will stop them. Your mom showed up on the beach. She was trying to convince me to leave with her."

Ah, hell. Shit. "Of course she did. She just won't let this go," I say, trying my best not to freak Ava out, but if my mom came here after I told her to leave, we're going to have a lot more problems than accidental transformations. I just hope Ava can hold on long enough before she needs to transform, because the shallows are no longer safe here.

Ava pulls me into her room and closes the door completely. "Maybe we should head to the East Coast. It'd take her a lot longer to interrupt our lives."

"I don't know if you're ready for that kind of trip, Ava." Actually, I know she's not ready. I would never jeopardize her by allowing her on a plane. The car freaks me out enough.

Nodding in agreement, Ava says, "I liked Santa Barbara. We could just slowly make our way to every beach city."

I smile and kiss her. It's not as far as I would like to be, but we can plan better later. I just need to get us out of here. "That sounds like a good plan to me. We'll plan as we go.

Who knows, maybe we can even go to Hawaii."

Her happiness washes through me, pushing away my fear. I could survive forever like this if she'd just keep kissing me. "I'd like that."

"So, do you think you're ready to go then?"

Ava bobs her head and picks up her bags from her bed. "Yeah, I think so."

I take them from her and kiss her again. "Good, because I'm ready to start this new life with you."

Guiding me down the stairs, we meet Ava's parents in the kitchen. Dr. Adair waves us over from his spot at the table where he drinks a cup of coffee while Beatrice sits with her laptop in front of her.

"Carter, take a seat," Dr. Adair says.

Ava groans and nudges me forward to plop at the table across from her parents. "Is this necessary?"

I reach over and take Ava's hands. "Your parents just want to make sure you're going to be okay," I say to her.

Dr. Adair nods his approval. "You do understand our expectations, correct? I need you two to check in regularly, including tonight. If you don't, this trip gets cut short."

I nod. "Yes, sir."

"If you break any laws, and I don't care what—speeding, underage drinking, jaywalking, littering, whatever—you'll be facing more than a fine. Got it? If you want to be treated like responsible adults, that's what we expect you to be." Dr.

Adair's words are directed more toward Ava.

"And not just about the law," Beatrice says. She reaches into her bag and pulls out a round container. "Take these daily, Ava. Make it a routine. If you don't like them or have concerns, call me or your dad."

Ava turns red at the sight of the birth control. "Mom. You couldn't have given these to me in private?" I guess now wouldn't be a good time to mention that Ava's a mermaid and human medication probably wouldn't metabolize like expected.

Dr. Adair glances at me, and I freeze, wondering if I said my words out loud. "Those take a bit of time to work, so I have these for you, Carter." He hands me a paper bag, and I look inside without reacting to the condoms. "Wrap it up if you two are having or plan to have intercourse."

I'm pretty sure Ava's about to die out of embarrassment and take me with her, her face deepening into a color I've never seen on her. Even if her skin never recovers, she'd still be beautiful, the blush bringing out the blue of her eyes even more.

"Dad! This was completely unnecessary." It definitely was, but I respect Ava's parents for going out of their way to care for their daughter. I want so much to prove to them that I'll be the best son they could have ever wanted, even if they might never see me as such. Not like how pods in the sea treat a blending of families.

"Don't worry, Dr. Adair," I say. "We'll take every precaution if we get to that point."

Ava releases a deep breath at my flat-out lie over the fact that we've had sex. Just thinking about it stirs desire within me, and I rub Ava's leg under the table. I smile at her and then turn back to her parents. Beatrice stares at Ava, and Dr. Adair, while not obviously glaring, keeps his eyes trained on me with a silent threat that he's not giving me a bag of condoms to encourage us.

"Yeah, Dad. Now, can we go? I think you've made your rules clear to Carter. Giselle should be here at any minute."

Both Ava's parents stand from the table to come around to hug her. Dr. Adair shakes my hand, double checks that Ava gave me what feels like the whole town's contact information, and then Beatrice gives me a hug, rocking me back and forth.

"Have fun and be safe. Don't hesitate to call us," she says again.

Ava nearly drags me from the kitchen and to the back patio to watch one more sunset as we wait for Giselle to arrive. I keep my gaze trained on the water for signs of merpeople, but if they're here, they don't give themselves away to me. Soon, we'll be in a car and headed somewhere my mom doesn't know. We're one step away from freedom and another closer to figuring our lives out together.

Giselle taps her nails on the back door and opens it, greeting us both with sad eyes despite the smile on her face. She takes a long look at the water like she might somehow glimpse the world she can never be a part of.

"Everything's set, Aves. My mom arranged a hotel in Santa Barbara for the night and one in San Francisco for the weekend."

Ava hugs Giselle. "You know I owe you."

"I know you'd do the same for me. Plus, a night in a hotel in Santa Barbara? Amazing. I just wish I could go up to San Francisco," Giselle says, blinking away the tears that seem never to stop glassing over her eyes.

Leaning away, Ava says, "You have to stay far away from there."

"I know. I expect that I'll get sick and have to go home tomorrow afternoon."

I reach out and gently squeeze Giselle's shoulder. "And remember, if a stranger ever asks you about us, you don't know us. Understand?"

She blows her hair from her face. "Definitely. I think I'll give up talking to strangers all together for a while."

I hope she does. For her sake. For Ava's. For mine, too. "Good, then we should probably get going."

Hugging Ava from behind, I hold her close while she silently says goodbye to the shores that were supposed to be our home. I guide her away, sliding my hand through hers and stop her from entering the house right away.

"I know this is terrifying, but—"

Ava kisses me. "I'm not afraid, Carter. I know we'll make this work. And honestly—" She pauses, smirking. "I'm more excited than anything. I look forward to seeing the world with you."

❧21❧

LIFE IN THE WAVES

I FINISH PACKING OUR SMALL waterproof bag. Ava's been restless the entire drive to the hotel, and I'm afraid if I don't get her into the water soon, she'll trigger a transformation right on the couch. As long as we stay near the coast, hopefully no one will bother us. According to King Attilonious, the coast is human domain and not exactly a place many merpeople would choose to surface—if they choose to surface at all.

I adjust the bag on my shoulder and peer at Ava and Giselle, who take my cue that it's time for me and Ava to leave. I hope if we spend our nights in the water, Ava will be able to control her transformations and anchor herself to the sea to stop all possible accidents. We'll return in the morning for Ava's car and the rest of our stuff and slowly make our way north, skipping San Francisco.

"I'm going to miss you so much, Aves. You know the others are going to freak when they find out you left without saying goodbye." Giselle rubs her hands over her face.

Ava groans. "Tell them it was spontaneous, and I promise to call all of them in a couple of days, okay?"

"Okay."

Tears splash on Ava's cheeks, her sorrow trickling over me. "And I will come back to visit."

"You better."

I stand silently and watch the two of them hug and cry some more, but I remain in place to give them a moment. This isn't on either of them, and I know this will be the longest Ava's been away from Azure Waters. Because we'll be gone the rest of the summer and possibly fall. I just hope I can manage to find us a place we can call our home away from home where no one knows us, and we won't have to worry about our secret so much.

Giselle hands Ava a waterproof phone case. "I want you to have this. It's waterproof up to fifty feet. I expect a ton of awesome pictures."

Ava laughs and glances at me. "I'm pretty sure that might

be against the king's rules."

"The king?" Giselle huffs a breath, already disliking King Attilonious as much as I do, and I've never even personally talked to the guy.

Taking the case, Ava snaps it onto her phone. "Crazy, right? I wish I could tell you more, Gi. But just knowing about us puts you at risk."

"Well, I don't care about those stupid rules that keep us apart," Giselle says, crossing her arms.

I clear my throat. "Obviously we don't either, so don't worry. We'll send lots of pictures. Just not of us."

She bounces on the couch. "And to think I thought you were bad news."

Giselle surprises me with a short hug before nearly tackling Ava. Just when I think I'll have to peel the two of them apart, Ava leans away and wipes her eyes again.

"Ready?" I ask her.

She nods. "I guess so."

Lacing my fingers through Ava's, I guide her out the glass slider and onto the beach. She shivers in the cool air, the ocean breeze dampening our skin. The closer we stroll to the water, the more excitement rises in Ava. She picks up her pace, smiling at me, and my own nerves melt away. I can't wait to get her to the water and start our lives as accidental mates together.

Ava remains silent and happy and content, cementing in

my spark that we've made the right decision. Ava no longer has to stress about slipping up in front of her family, and I don't have to worry about leaving her while working on the Ocean Jewel. Every decision we make from now on will be for us together as it should be.

Cool water rushes over our bare feet, and I slide my hands under Ava's dress, pulling it over her head to tuck away in our bag. Tugging on the strings of her bikini bottoms, I remove them next, taking a moment to graze my fingers over her smooth skin. I strip down faster than she can help and lead her into the night waves of the glowing sea.

She hooks her fingers to my neck and kisses me deeply in the surf, the heat of our bodies pushing away the cold of the water before we can adjust. Something shifts inside Ava the longer we stand together. The weight of the land eases off her, and she now welcomes the sea. I can feel her spark drifting from shore, begging me to take her under.

I dive in first and transform, taking a moment to peer around the shallows. Opening my telepathic channel, I listen to the seas in case, but don't hear anything apart from Ava's excited thoughts as they drift to me.

Closing the space between us, I kiss her the moment she inhales a breath of the sea. Anticipation courses through me from transforming into my true form and at the enthralling beauty of Ava smiling at me. I swim around her a few dozen times, creating a whirlpool, trying my best not to give in to my desire to be with her in a way I'm unsure she wants yet.

I catch her in my arms, and she tilts her head to the side, running her fingers across my cheeks to burst the tiny bubbles of oxygen still clinging to my skin.

"What is it?" I ask her when she's not quick to open her thoughts to me. "You okay?"

She grins and kisses me. "It's almost easy to forget the land when we're together out here."

I cradle her face, treading in place for the both of us. "I know what you mean."

Sensing Ava's need to swim, I lace our fingers together and jet us off. She flicks her tail to keep up with me, and I dive us lower and along the ocean floor. Sea grass sways in the current, and Ava admires everything we pass, from the ropes of kelp to the different schools of fish and a few bat rays gliding along in the sand in search of a meal.

Ava brushes her lips to mine and pushes from me, using my body to propel herself away. She laughs in my mind, racing away from me. Her playfulness ignites my merman nature as she initiates a game of chase, weaving in and out of the strands of kelp reaching for the night sky.

Ava rolls in the water, swimming with her back toward the sea floor to watch the rippling surface above with moonbeams creating waves of light. I catch up and hook my fingers to her waist, staying at her pace so she can swim freely as long as she wants to. Giving into her need to be close, she wraps her hands around my shoulders and allows me to take over.

I dive us deeper, her body arching with mine, our tails sliding together in a way that sends my whole body tingling. Ava hugs me closer, her body warming mine, and I finally slow when we're so deep that the moon looks like a blip of light on the surface.

A white shark glides through the water above us, much larger than the two of us, and I touch Ava's chin to get her to look up. As a human-born, I thought Ava would be nervous about being close to a creature many humans fear, but only admiration and awe wash from her to me.

Watching the shark push through the current, she says, "She's magnificent. You sure she won't bother us?"

I shake my head. Sharks are the least of our worries as apex predators, if we had many apart from humans. "You have to be more careful of the playful animals like the sea lions and dolphins. Some whales, too. They think they're guppies when their tails could knock us all the way to Hawaii."

"I'd like to go there someday," she says, her voice echoing through my mind. "Grand Cayman, Tahiti, Jamaica, too. I want to see the ocean from different shores."

I hold her close, imagining what it would be like to travel all the oceans with her. "One day I'd love to take you. We'll practice your long distance swimming. You'll have to be brave enough to try the fish, too. Can't exactly order a pizza down here."

She grimaces, and I laugh. It'll be my sole mission in life to find something she'll eat. I want nothing more than to feed her if she lets me.

I smile and poke her bottom lip. "It's not bad, I promise. It's no dessert, but I'm sure I can find something you like."

Groaning in my mind, she pouts even more. "I'm not ready. Can we start with a sushi restaurant on land?"

I chuckle and kiss her. "You're the only mermaid in the world who was afraid of the ocean and displeased by the meal options."

"I guess that means we can never leave the land," she muses, snuggling to me.

"And we won't." The second the words escape my mind, I hear the soft call of Ava's name. It's then that I realize she's projecting her thoughts to anyone in the sea who is close enough to hear us.

"Carter," a familiar masculine voice calls next. "We're approaching you. Please prepare Ava. We don't want to scare her."

Peering up, I spot the silhouette of a merman. I haven't seen my uncle in over a year as he never strays far from Pearlestria.

Ignoring another plea, this time from my mom, I slide my arms around Ava's waist and jet us in the direction we came from that will take us back to shore. My sudden swimming freaks Ava out so much that she cries out in my mind, her voice surely echoing for all to hear again.

"What's wrong?" she asks me, her voice bouncing around our telepathic channel.

"You don't hear them? They're calling us," I say to her, flicking my tail at my top speed.

From the look on Ava's face, I know she doesn't. Her mind sends her voice out, but either the few members of the royal guard with my mom block Ava from hearing them or she blocks them with her own panic. I was careless to have gone so long without teaching her how to control her thoughts, and it's my failure that'll get us taken to sea if I can't get us back to land in time. If we can make it to the hotel, we can escape. They won't follow us on shore. It would draw too much attention.

"Ava, listen to me," I say, projecting my voice only to her. "I need you to transform when we hit the kelp paddies. I'm going to propel you as far as I can through the waves, and then I need you to run, okay?"

A dozen questions flit into my mind, but none of them were intended for me to hear. She finally manages to ask, "What about you?" She's afraid to leave me. The fear might slow her down if she can't get it under control.

"I'll be right behind you, okay?" I just need to get Ava out of the water. If I do, they won't try to take me. They know well enough how much she needs me, and they wouldn't risk her like that when it is my duty to take care of her.

"Okay." Ava's voice trickles to me much softer, her telepathic channel focusing solely on me.

Flicking my fin, I navigate through the water, weaving and ducking under animals and through the kelp forest to obscure us. While I've been gifted with warrior speed, my ability doesn't compare to those who actively train on the royal guard.

The merpeople race above us, maintaining our speed. Ava's fear pushes me faster than I've ever managed to swim, and I spot the familiar signs of the shallows coming up ahead.

I can do this. I can get Ava to the land where she can run. I have to. If I don't, they'll take her to Pearlestria and force her into a life she'll hate. I will have failed her as her mate. My mom thinks she's helping, but what she's doing could very well destroy Ava. It'll destroy me.

"Don't make this hard on yourself," my uncle says, projecting his voice into my mind. Ava hears his words too, because she stiffens and whimpers in my arms, losing herself to her panic.

I regret not preparing her for this possibility. I was so certain I could make all of this work, and that we could manage on land with no interference. I thought as merpeople living on land, my parents would respect my wishes. I thought they'd choose me and Ava over cruel laws that will surely ruin my future. My mate's heart breaks already, a pain so intense that neither of us might survive.

"We're not going to hurt you," a feminine voice calls, though I can't place it to a face or name. It's been too long since I've been to Pearlestria.

"Be reasonable, Carter," Mom begs, her voice making Ava tremble.

"Mom, please," I send my thoughts solely to her. "You're going to ruin any chance at building a relationship with Ava. Don't do this. Call them off."

"Carter, I can't. You've been summoned by King Attilonious to return to Pearlestria with your mate. If you come now, you won't face any consequences. The king realizes the unconventional start of your coupling to Ava and shows great sympathy. Please, do the right thing, son." Mom's words get under my skin.

"How could you?" I ask, training my gaze on the sea floor as it inclines toward the beach.

"I was counting on you to do the right thing, but your father thought you were too lost in your bond to see what Ava truly needs."

Anger bursts through me at my dad's betrayal. I was certain it would've been my mom to call upon the colonies for help. "That's why he's not here."

"Please, Carter. Don't be upset."

I cut off her telepathic connection and focus on Ava, both our sparks flickering with the adrenaline of fleeing. Moonlight cuts beams of silver across the sand. I loosen my hold on Ava.

"Get ready," I tell her. "The kelp forest is up ahead. You'll only have a minute."

Ava braces herself, her panic exploding at her body faltering to transform. I jet forward through the ropes of kelp, praying to the sea that she can manage. She yells at herself to transform, her thoughts echoing through my mind. All she can think about is failing and how it'll be her fault if they catch us.

With the thought, her body reacts, and she transforms into a human in my arms. The sudden shift in her weight allows me to swim us even faster, her body molding to mine as she holds me tighter. I flick my tail again, adjusting Ava in my arms. Breaching out of the sea, I throw Ava as far as I can to give her a head start. I'm not as fast in my human form, and I need her ahead of me. I can fight against those who will take her, even if it leaves me in the waves. I just need her to get back to the hotel.

Closing my eyes, I transform into a human and swim as fast as I can. Ava kicks through the water, the waves pushing her toward land. She slows down, struggling to find her footing, and I nearly catch up to her already.

"Hurry, Ava!" I yell. "Head toward the hotel. They won't follow if it'll draw attention."

Another wave swells, sending us both to shore. I swipe the saltwater from my face, landing in the surf next to Ava. She screams in surprise, fear picking up the already quick thrums of her spark. Taking her hand, I drag her forward and into the sand. She falls to her knees, her body exhausted from swimming.

I'm not quick enough to grab her. My uncle emerges from the water and locks his hand around her ankle. The terror in her voice cuts through my heart, her panic all-consuming. I tug her wrist, more concerned about getting her away than hurting her, and my uncle automatically lets her go, not taking the chance. It was what I was counting on.

"Ava, run!" I yell.

Someone smashes into me, knocking me off my feet. I collide into the sand and roll a few times at the strength of a trained warrior. Landing on my stomach, I get a mouth full of seawater as the warrior mermaid, who I recognize as April, one of the royal guard's most respected warriors, presses my face in the sand.

"Please, Carter," she says, her musical voice low over the thrum of the waves. "You're going to scare your mate worse than she already is. You need to calm yourself and give her your strength in this transition. Look at her."

April tugs my face from the sand, so I can see Ava thrashing in my uncle's arms. I suppressed her panic so much so that all I could feel was my own anger. And it was wrong of me. She's probably thinking the worst about the merpeople, afraid for her life.

"Please, let me up. I need a moment to talk to her," I say, my voice low, my heart hurting as Ava struggles helplessly against my uncle much too powerful for her to ever best.

He holds her underwater, attempting to force her to change by cutting off the air supply she needs as a human. But Ava's tough. She clings desperately to her humanity, refusing to give into the sea.

"Ava." My voice cracks, coming out too low for my mate to hear.

My mom emerges from the sea to face Ava. Panic ignites in my soul as I realize what she's about to do. Ava spins in my uncle's arms and elbows him in the ribs. The force of her hit allows her to break free of him, but my mom's quick to grab onto Ava's wrist.

"Mom, don't!" I yell. "Please, don't do this."

Ava's eyes flick to mine, the look of complete sorrow and helplessness piercing me right through the soul. And I can't do anything to help her. April holds onto my arm, stopping me from running to Ava.

"Please, you have to let me talk to her," I say.

"I'm sorry, Carter. Not yet."

"I'll convince her to go."

Ava screams and cries, drawing my attention away from April and the same look of sadness crossing everyone's faces. Mom squeezes Ava's hand, digging her nails into her skin to get Ava to open her hand.

"Just let me go," Ava cries, thrashing in my mom's hold.

My mom continues to pry at Ava's hand. "Ava, calm

down before you hurt yourself. I'm not your enemy. I'm saving you."

The second Ava's fingers automatically spread open, April lets go of my arm. "No!" I yell, charging closer to Ava.

But it's too late.

My mom slides Ava's sea stone ring off her finger and steps away. Without her ring, Ava will be forced to transform. The sea will claim her mermaid spark, sinking her under.

Ava wails, scrambling away from my mom and closer to shore. The waves rise around her, lifting her and dropping her on their suddenly rocking current. Her despair crashes over me, stealing my breath away. Arching her back, Ava fights against the triggered transformation, attempting to rush toward me.

But both my uncle and April keep us apart. They know better than to allow me to close the space because I would give Ava the ring off my own finger so that she could return to shore. I'd do anything to see to it that she doesn't drown on the wave of grief consuming her thoughts, sending tears to my own eyes.

"I need to go to her, please," I beg, but April grabs onto me again.

"When she gives in to the sea," she says.

Mom closes the space again to Ava, attempting to comfort her. I open my mouth to tell her to stay away, that she'll only make it worse, but April shakes her head at me.

"She needs her mother," she says like Ava could possibly just accept the ways of the sea and consider my mom to be her mother.

"You're going to be okay, Ava. You'll be happy, I promise," Mom says, touching Ava's shoulder.

Ava scowls without a word, her wild eyes peering around as her determination holds tightly to the land.

My mom tries again with the same determination that Ava possesses. "Stop resisting. It's just making it worse. Let me help you."

"I hate you!" Ava screams.

Mom straightens her back, closing the space completely to Ava to block her line of sight. Ava's fury rushes over me, igniting my own, and I yank myself from April and rush forward. I don't get far as my uncle tackles me and forces me underwater. I transform into a merman and flick my tail, shoving my uncle away.

"Ava, please," my mom pleads again, her voice ringing through the air.

"Just get away! Don't touch me!"

Ava swims away in her mermaid form, cutting around my mom to get away. My uncle abandons me to swim near Ava, keeping close enough to guard her. April and my mom both transform, and I'm forced to follow behind Ava to keep my distance.

Flicking her tail, she surprises my uncle and suddenly

dives, circling back toward shore. I wouldn't put it past her to enter the surf and throw herself onto the sand in her mermaid form, even if she can't transform. If she does and someone sees her, she'll put a human's life in danger. These warriors follow the king's strict laws.

Breaking away from April, I swim and cut Ava off, wrapping my arms around her. I bury my face in the crook of her neck, enveloping her with my strength the best I can to help her fight away the trembles in her body.

"I'm so sorry, Ava," I whisper into her mind, finally meeting her sparkling sad eyes, her anguish burning so hotly through me that I can barely speak to her. "You can't go back."

Her jaw trembles, her pouty bottom lip quivering. "My family. I can't leave them. They'll freak out."

If we weren't underwater, her tears would splash her cheeks. But now? We both drown in her grief at the reality of the situation and how our lives are no longer in our control. Of how I failed her. Her sorrow coils around me, squeezing my chest, and my own misery rises in me. Because I'm not sure Ava will ever be happy again. I'm afraid her love for me will slip through my fingers to get lost on the waves of her heartache.

I squeeze her tighter, swimming us to follow the others before they try to drag us away. "Please, forgive me. I swear we'll figure it all out, okay?"

"But—"

"Please, Aves," I say, begging for her to believe me—to believe in me. "The more you fight, the more trapped you'll be. I have no influence where we're going. You have to try to be strong. We'll get through this."

"I don't know if I can," she whispers, my heart plummeting with hers.

"Please try."

Sinking against me, Ava hides her face in my chest. She remains placid and unmoving—unwilling to swim on her own, and I hate more than anything that I'm the one taking her away from her life on shore. But I will not allow anyone else's arms around her. She needs to feel my strength to know that even though we now journey to Pearlestria and away from the human world, that I'll fight for her. I won't let her lose herself to the sea.

As we near the colony, I inhale a deep breath of the sea, of the magic clinging to every molecule, every grain of sand, every current that'll keep us here and away from shore. I take in the sight of the glittering palace made from pearlescent rocks, the rainbow array of magical gemstones shining beams of color through the colony.

Dozens of merpeople rise from their houses and into the channel, keeping their distances but welcoming me with smiles and waves. Ava keeps her eyes closed, defeat silencing even her thoughts to me.

"Welcome home, son." My dad's voice projects into my mind. He darts up to greet me from the channel, and it takes everything for me not to react. If I react, it'll end badly. I can't risk getting into more trouble or put under more scrutiny than I already am. I ignored the king's laws. I put my mate in jeopardy by allowing her to return home. "The guard has done the honor of gathering what you need to build Ava a proper home here," he adds only for me to hear.

I nod my response, keeping my eyes trained on Ava's beautifully sad features.

Dad gently grasps Ava's shoulder. "Welcome to Pearlestria, Ava. Welcome to your new home."

Slowly lifting her head, Ava peers through thick lashes, her eyes red from her never-ending tears that'll surely make the seas rise. "This is not my home. You dragged me away from my home. This—" She flicks her hand out at the ocean around us. "This is my prison within the sea."

And mine.

But I vow to get Ava back to land. I vow to see to it that we get the life we want.

"Ava," I whisper to her, drawing her attention to me. "We're going to get out of here."

She reaches out and touches my cheek, nodding.

"I vow to you that we'll break free."

 EPILOGUE

MERPEOPLE LIFE

"SMILE ONE MORE TIME," GISELLE says, holding up Ava's phone to snap a picture of me. "Be convincing this time. You look like a shark ate your dinner."

I force myself to grin. "I'm sorry. It's hard to be happy breathing air when..." My voice chokes up, still feeling the sadness radiating from Ava's soul.

My mom insisted I give her a few hours with Ava so that they could bond, and I took the opportunity to leave Pearlestria to come to shore to search for Giselle. I haven't told Ava that I went to shore yesterday at the first chance I could during a hunt outside the colony. Luckily for me, the king didn't take away my sea stone ring. He knows I'd never leave Ava, but he's also aware of the lengths I went through to as-sure she kept her human connections. He doesn't know that

Giselle knows of our existence, but he's agreed to let me attempt to maintain the ruse we've pulled on Ava's parents for the sole purpose to protect my parents' existence on land.

"Ava's strong," Giselle says. "She's going to be fine."

I frown. "I'm not so sure. You don't see her."

Giselle swipes the back of her hand across her cheek. "You know, I might be willing for you to attempt merman matchmaker if it means I could visit her."

I smile at the thought. "You have to work on your commitment issues."

She rolls her eyes. "I'll do anything for my BFF. She's the one person I will commit to."

I chuckle. "I'm not used to this kind of competition. I always thought Ava would be my best friend."

"You mermen," she says. "So grossly romantic. And so you know, Ava can be your best friend. But I'm hers. Got it?"

"Got it, Gi."

"Good." Giselle tugs a bag from her shoulder and digs out a few baggies. "Now, since that's clarified, I have what you asked for."

I go to remove the items from the bags, and Giselle stops me. "You're going to ruin the flavor."

"The merbabes will be disappointed if they think this is a jellyfish," I muse.

"Then you eat it, reuse it, or come to shore and dispose of it properly. It's all I had unless you waited a few days."

I chuckle and shove everything into my waterproof bag. Giselle surprises me with a warm hug, embracing me for a few minutes, dampening my skin with her tears. I stroke my hand along her back until she gets herself under control.

"Same time next week? Apparently you guys are in Oregon now. Maybe heading up to Washington next." She shrugs. "It'll depend on my mood. It's crazy how people will do anything for money. I love getting the postcards from you two," she jokes. Because Giselle has managed to keep our charade on land going, pretending to be Ava. The only thing missing is Ava's phone calls, but Giselle texts Ava's parents as her and sends her pictures of me.

"Same time," I say, nodding.

"Maybe try to sneak Ava away. I don't know how many more blond girls gazing away from the camera her parents will accept."

I hug Giselle again. "I'll try. Thanks for this. I owe you."

"Like I said, I'll do anything for Ava."

I dive off the rock and into the water, and Giselle mounts her surfboard and paddles back to the shallows. I wait to see her safely make it from the water. Dipping under, I transform into a merman and dart along the ocean bottom at my highest speed to race back to Pearlestria, feeling Ava's annoyance grow more intense.

When I reach the shimmering walls of the colony, I swim along the outside and cut over to skip the sand channel that runs along the middle. I head straight home to our small rock house made of the same pearlescent material as the rest of the buildings. It's not as big as the houses for larger pods, and I can barely think of anything to put in it, but I decorated the walls inside with stones of blues and oranges to create a sunset mosaic to remind Ava of the surface.

I could put more effort into our home, but Ava asked me not to. She said if she got comfortable, then she might accept this to be our life, something neither of us wants. We want more. We deserve more than rock houses and a simple life.

Lurking outside the house, I listen to Ava's thoughts to herself about how annoying she finds my mom. Ava never blocks me from her mind, always keeping her telepathic channel open, but she quickly learned to shut the rest of the colony out, something I'm incredibly grateful for.

"If I ignore her long enough, she'll give up," Ava assures herself, making me chuckle.

"They want to celebrate your life," Mom says to Ava, her thoughts projecting as she grows agitated by Ava's lack of response. Ava never talks much, but she definitely goes out of her way to purposely make her dislike of my mom clear. And I don't blame her. My mom's left my dad in San Francisco on a mission to help Ava adapt to a mermaid life. She can't see that she's making it worse, but I don't get a say. It's a tradition that as human-born Ava would have a mermaid to guide her. I can't do it for her as a merman. Stupidest rule ever, but I still try.

"Remember the ceremony I told you about? The one to welcome you? I'd like to start planning it. It's important for Carter too, you know? He has the only mate in the ocean who refuses to make it official. Do you know how sad you're making him by acting like it's the end of the world?"

Ah, shit. I didn't expect my mom to go there just yet, and she puts words in my mouth to try to get Ava to comply. Because I'm happy and thankful Ava still cares for me. That even though I brought her here, she doesn't blame me. She still smiles at me like I'm the best thing she's ever seen, and I'm afraid my mom will ruin it.

"You're being so selfish and—"

"Mom," I snap, drawing her attention to me as I hover in the doorway. "Leave Ava alone, please. You're not helping her any. Why don't you go visit Dad so I can have some privacy with her? You've been smothering us both."

"But—"

"You know we can't run away. Please, just give us some space," I add, now in desperate need of a hug from Ava.

Pursing her lips, Mom exits our house, and says, "Please try to talk some sense into her."

I ignore her, sealing her voice from my thoughts as she disappears from view. Swimming forward, I settle into the sand next to Ava and slide my arms around her to lift her onto my lap, She releases a bubble from her mouth, a wave of happiness suppressing her annoyance toward my mom, and she rests her cheek to my chest and inhales a deep breath of water.

I comb her floating strands of hair from her face. "I'm sorry about my mom, Ava. I know she can be overbearing."

Ava shifts to meet my gaze. "She accused me of destroying your happiness because I'm depressed."

Damn it. I knew my mom would make things worse by trying to guilt Ava. "You know that's not true. I'm unhappy because of what they did to us."

"She thinks I'm embarrassing you."

"Are not. You never could. The only one embarrassing me is her," I assure her, running my hands up and down the length of her shimmering tail.

A few fish from the reef under our window dart in our direction and swim close to Ava, nudging their noses to her arm, enamored by her presence. Fish love mermaids and will congregate if we allow it. I shoo the fish away, scaring them back to the reef. Scaring fish for a good hunt is a merman's specialty. It's one of the ways to show off to our mates how fast we can swim. But Ava still refuses to eat the fish. She won't watch me either.

If I didn't know that we could go for weeks without eating, I'd freak out and beg her to try something. Instead, I waited and asked Giselle to give me something to bring to her. My mom would be furious if she knew. She swears that if Ava gets hungry enough, she will eat, but I can't stand hearing her stomach growl and not feeding her. I can't wait to do so now.

Leaning in, I kiss Ava, sending her all my love and devotion to make sure she doesn't believe a word my mom says about the supposed feelings I have as a merman. I already knew Ava wanted to wait before going through with something serious like a coupling ceremony, and I don't blame her. I love just getting to be with her.

Ava kisses me deeper, more fervently, at the excitement coursing through me. Sliding her tongue into my mouth, she explores my tongue with hers, sending a wave of desire through me. She pushes me back to lie on top of me, and I slide my hands to the back side of her tail, holding her close.

"You taste like home," she says.

I suck her bottom lip between my teeth. "I surfaced."

Ava pulls away, her beautiful features overcome with despair as she thinks about how I got to feel the sun on my skin. She thinks about a dozen things she is sad she took for granted. Horrible grief rises in Ava at my words, surprising me so much so that I scramble to yank the waterproof bag that never leaves my side from my shoulder.

"Wait, wait," I say, desperate to stop her sadness before it sends her spiraling into a place I find hard to pull her from. "I brought you some things."

"You can do that?" she asks, snapping herself out of the misery being trapped in Pearlestria brings her.

I nod. "I had to wait for the chance, but I finally got it

today.”

Unlocking the waterproof bag, I pull out its contents and hold out a baggie of cut up apples Giselle prepared for her. Ava devours them in less than a minute, barely chewing and swallowing. I watch her in silence, smirking at her shoving half of a turkey lettuce wrap into her mouth and how she doesn’t seem to have any qualms with poultry. I guess it’s only fish that are safe from my starving mate.

“I can’t believe you brought these,” she says, not letting even a tiny piece of lettuce escape.

I lean back, smiling, loving every second of her pleasure washing through me. “I couldn’t let you starve, Ava.”

She smirks at me. “You know I would’ve eventually eaten.”

“That’s what my mom said, but what kind of boyfriend would I be if I didn’t try to make you as happy as I possibly could?” I pull out another baggie and hand it to her. “I also picked up the pictures you took from home.”

I expect her to wallow in grief again, but her excitement drenches me in a way I’ve missed so much since our arrival. She jerks her attention from the pictures and to me, her eyes turning into two round saucers that remind me of a clear sky.

“You saw her,” she says, studying my face, talking about Giselle without saying her name.

“She found our bag with your phone on the beach by the room and has been pretending to be you to your parents.

She'll keep the charade up as long as she can."

"So, there's still hope?" she asks in disbelief. "I can go home?"

I tighten my fingers around her, sinking into the hope lighting her spark in quick beats to match mine. "I'm going to do everything I can, but you're going to have to do some things as well."

Her brows pinch together. "Like what?"

"You're going to have to pretend you've come to terms with your mermaid life."

"Is that all? I think I can handle faking it."

"We'll get out of here, Ava. I promise."

Ava hugs me again, throwing her whole body into it so our tails caress together. I snuggle my face against her and shift her on my lap, retrieving one last item to give to her. Ava's eyes widen at the postcard from Giselle, her excitement so intense that I'm not sure our thrashing hearts will recover.

She reads over Giselle's words, her voice trickling into my mind.

Ava,

The sea seems so cruel now that it's taken you. Be strong and fight the current. The waters might be rough now, but they're no match for the girl who survived the waves twice. I love you, Aves. I know we'll see each other again soon. I'll head to sea if I have to. I'll figure out a way. Be safe and don't get into any trouble. I'd like you back with your legs one day, because no one would believe me that my best friend's a mermaid. What would I tell my kids?

Until the sea washes you back to shore, I'll be waiting.

Love,

Gi

Giselle's words resonate with me as they give Ava more hope than ever. She bounces in the sand, staring at the words for another long moment, and then opens the bag to smear the ink and the evidence of her best friend's knowledge of the merpeople secret.

Sliding her fingers through mine, she squeezes my hand. "Thank you. For everything."

I hold her for a long moment, keeping us anchored into the sand as a small current swirls around us from the window cutout. I'm so glad to have given Ava the hope she needs to help me get us both out of here. I'm so thankful for Giselle and the risk she was willing to take to help me with Ava. Because Ava needs more than me and the sea despite what anyone thinks. She needs her family and friends. The land. And I'll give it to her. I know I'm capable of being a warrior. But not for the king. For Ava.

She's the best thing to ever happen to me, and I won't let the sea imprison us forever.

I plan to not only give her the freedom she needs but also to give her the world and life she yearns for. A world as beautiful and incredible as she is. I'll see to it we get the future of our dreams—one of love, hope, promise, and all the romance her heart could ever desire.

To be continued...

Thank you so much for reading *Mermaid Mates*! If you haven't read *Diving Under*, you most definitely should check it out as Carter's story is a retelling of Ava's.

Other Young Adult Series by Ginna Moran

PARANORMAL
Spark of Life Series
Call of the Ocean Series
Destined for Dreams Series
Demon Within Series
Finding Nate Series
Going Ghostly Series
When Souls Collide Series
Demon Watcher Series
The Merman's Spark Series

REVERSE HAREM
The Divine Vampire Heirs Series

CONTEMPORARY
Falling into Fame Series
Life After Lila

ACKNOWLEDGEMENTS

THANK YOU SO MUCH TO Katie Harder-Schauer for her hard work on this book. Also, thank you to my reader group and subscribers for showing such enthusiasm for my mermaids and their mates. Carter got to tell his story because of you. <3

ABOUT GINNA MORAN

GINNA MORAN IS A WRITER from sunny Southern California. She started writing poetry as a teenager in a spiral notebook that she still has tucked away on her desk today. Her love of writing grew after she graduated high school, and she completed her first unpublished manuscript at age eighteen.

When she realized her love of writing was her life's passion, she studied literature at Mira Costa College in Northern San Diego. Besides writing novels, she was senior editor, content manager, and image coordinator for Crescent House Publishing Inc. for four years.

Aside from Ginna's professional life, she enjoys binge watching television shows, playing pretend with her daughter, and cuddling with her dogs. Some of her favorite things include chocolate, anything that glitters, cheesy jokes, and organizing her bookshelf.

Ginna Moran loves to hear from her readers, so visit her online at www.GinnaMoran.com. You can also find her on Facebook, Twitter, and Instagram. To stay up-to-date on new releases, sign up to her newsletter. You'll also gain access to exclusive content on her website.

www.ingramcontent.com/pod-product-compliance
Lightning Source LLC
Chambersburg PA
CBHW061049190726
48286CB00006B/1671